MURDER, SH

I passed Bonelli the note with the young man's name and cell phone number. "He definitely had a wallet at the shop. He paid us a deposit, in cash, to board his cat."

"And you told the desk sergeant there's something funny about the cat?"

I explained what Sarah and I had discovered while bathing Ayesha. Also that a cat of that breed and quality could be worth a lot of money.

"It's still possible that this Rudy was accidentally killed by a hit-and-run driver, and either that person came back to rob him, or someone else did," Bonelli said.

"I thought, because the cat was dyed, that Rudy might have stolen her. Maybe someone followed him, found he didn't have Ayesha anymore, and got angry enough about it to kill him . . ."

Books by Eileen Watkins

THE PERSIAN ALWAYS MEOWS TWICE

THE BENGAL IDENTITY

FERAL ATTRACTION

GONE, KITTY, GONE

CLAW & DISORDER

Published by Kensington Publishing Corporation

The Bengal Identity

EILEEN WATKINS

KENSINGTON BOOKS
www.kensingtonbooks.com

KENSINGTON BOOKS are published by

Kensington Publishing Corp.
119 West 40th Street
New York, NY 10018

All Kensington titles, imprints, and distributed lines are available at special quantity discounts for bulk purchases for sales promotion, premiums, fund-raising, educational, or institutional use. Special book excerpts or customized printings can also be created to fit specific needs. For details, write or phone the office of the Kensington Special Sales Manager: Attn. Special Sales Department. Kensington Publishing Corp, 119 West 40th Street, New York, NY 10018. Phone: 1-800-221-2647.

ISBN-13: 978-1-4967-2650-6
ISBN-10: 1-4967-2650-2
First Kensington Trade Edition: April 2018
First Kensington Mass Market Edition: September 2020

ISBN-13: 978-1-4967-1059-8 (ebook)
ISBN-10: 1-4967-1059-2 (ebook)

10 9 8 7 6 5 4 3 2 1

Printed in the United States of America

For Bela, my funny, feisty, and
faithful buddy for eighteen years.
Named for Lugosi, he lived up to
that legacy by terrorizing the kindly
staffers at the local veterinary hospital.
Here, bits of him live in on Cassie's
satiny black cat Cole . . . and in Ayesha.

Acknowledgments

Once again, I owe much gratitude to the members of my weekly critique group—Elisa Chalem, Susan Moshiashwili, Harry Pollack, Ed Rand, Jeremy Salter, Janice Stucki, and Joanne Weck—as well as to my fellow members of Sisters in Crime Central Jersey, and to my agent, Evan Marshall, and my editor, John Scognamiglio.

Chapter 1

Todd Gillis bounced the keys to my Honda CR-V in his dark-stained palm, as if to remind me that he temporarily held my wheels hostage. "So, Carrie . . ."

"It's Cassie, actually," I corrected him.

"Oh, right. McGarrity?"

"McGlone." Todd seemed too young to have such a poor memory. But I guessed anyone's brain might be affected by this cocktail of exhaust fumes and motor oil, cooking together in the late-July heat of the garage's repair bay. His short, dirty-blond hair rose in a kind of crest above his forehead—with the help of gel, or maybe axle grease? He radiated lechery and BO.

I'd just come by to leave my four-year-old car for its sixty-thousand-mile checkup, and hoped to be on my way soon, but Todd seemed to have other ideas. With several other vehicles also parked in the bay, he'd managed to position himself between me and the glimpse of daylight beyond. There seemed to be no easy escape, unless I wanted to vault over a car hood.

Todd narrowed his eyes now to give me the once-over. "You said this is your first time here? 'Cause you look familiar."

"Maybe you've seen me around town. I have the cat grooming and boarding shop on Wayfair Street." In the next instant, I regretted giving Todd even that much information.

He snapped his fingers. "The bikini car wash last month, out at The Roost. Were you one of those girls?"

That stunned me for a second, before I assured him, "Definitely not!" Jeez, how often had he tried that line, I wondered, and did it ever actually work?

"Aww, don't say that. You're as pretty as any of them." He probably could tell, from the way my eyes frantically searched for an escape route, that he wasn't getting anywhere, and switched his approach. "So you're into cats, huh? Say, didya hear about the killer cat that's loose up on Rattlesnake Ridge?"

All I wanted at this point was to get back to my shop, where I'd left my assistant, Sarah, in charge. So it could only have been temporary insanity that made me take the bait and echo, "Killer cat?"

"Yeah! They say it's big as a mountain lion. Got hold of some old lady's dog, one of those shih tzus." He mispronounced the breed, maybe on purpose, to make it sound vulgar. "Ate it up, right in front of her!"

I didn't find this outlandish tale the least bit funny, and the wide grin that spread across Todd's grimy face reinforced my desire to spend as little time around him as possible.

"That's awful, if it's true," I said. "But someone probably made up that story. We hardly ever get mountain lions in New Jersey, or any other cats that big. Anyway, how soon do you think my car will be—"

"Ha, shows what you know! My dad told me that, back in the seventies, there was a theme park not far from here that had all kinds of wild animals. Jungle World, it was called, and you could ride through. Sometimes the big cats escaped and attacked people and pets. That's one of the reasons it got shut down. They got luxury houses up there now."

This was my first visit to Gillis's Garage, but Todd seemed to think that because we were around the same age—I'm twenty-seven, I figured him to be a little younger—fate had brought us together. If this was his idea of seductive chitchat, it sure wasn't mine. Plus, he was a pretty big guy, and he had edged close enough by now to worry me.

Once again looking for an out, I noticed a rather sinister figure stroll into the repair bay. A lean, middle-aged man with long, graying hair and lots of tattoos stopped in one shadowy corner. He folded his arms across his chest and glared in our direction.

Ironically, it made me almost grateful that I was no longer alone with Todd.

I tried again to cut our conversation short by debunking his local legend. "Well, even if some big cat got loose back in the seventies, it wouldn't still be alive today."

"Maybe not the same cat, but it could have bred with something else, couldn't it? Don't they sometimes cross different cats to get new species?"

"Some breeders do, but certainly not with anything that big," I told him. "Well, as you said before, speaking of cats . . . I've got a bunch back at my shop that need to be groomed and fed, so I'd better get going."

"Sure, sure." He gave me a little more breathing room, but still partly blocked my exit. "Y'know, I don't usually like cats, but I wouldn't mind having one like that. Imagine owning a wildcat—one that could take down a dog!"

His enthusiasm for animal-on-animal combat began to turn my stomach, but I tried to find a nonconfrontational way to discourage him. "Hybrids are very expensive, and I hear they can be hard to handle."

He leaned back against the doorjamb and leered openly at me. "That's okay. After all, I can be pretty hard to handle, too."

Oh, to leap into my trusty CR-V and speed away! Unfortunately, Todd already had pulled it into the repair bay.

Behind us, the guy in the corner with the tattoos cleared his throat. "Hey, Gillis, if you're not too busy putting the moves on your customer, we gotta talk."

His boyish face twisting in annoyance, Todd told me, "I'll let you know when your car's done."

I saw my chance and sidled toward the exit. "You've got my number, right?"

"You bet I do, Cassie!" He winked.

Ugh.

I hurried out the door and across the garage's parking lot. Meanwhile, I could hear the discussion heating up between Todd and his customer.

"Man, how many times I got to bring this van back here before you fix it right?"

"Hey, whadya want from me? That thing's an antique. They don't even make parts for those anymore."

Sounded like Todd had never heard that the customer is always right. I had to give him credit, though, for talking back to a tough dude with flames and skulls crawling down his arms.

I covered the four blocks back to my shop at a brisk clip. I'd thought I lucked out, finding a place to get my car serviced that was within walking distance. Now I wondered if the convenience was worth dodging clumsy advances from Todd Gillis.

With a sense of relief, I neared my own shop, on the ground level of a two-story building that originally served as a single-family home. It was over a hundred years old, and at some point the first floor had been converted for retail use. The last owner had operated a fly-by-night beauty salon and left a mess behind. I'd made a lot of renovations and had given the exterior a coat of cream paint with gray trim.

Now I paused on the sidewalk to admire, once again, my front display window. Large, quirky purple letters spelled out CASSIE'S COMFY CATS, and a smaller font added, FELINE GROOMING AND BOARDING. I'd originally stenciled the lettering myself when I'd opened six months ago. But my first window had to be replaced when a stray bullet went through it during an incident at my shop that spring.

I'd expected running a business in this small, semirural suburb to be pretty uneventful. But in the short time since I'd opened, Cassie's Comfy Cats already had seen more than its share of excitement.

Glancing through the window now, I saw Sarah Wilcox behind the sales counter dealing with a customer. My petite, African-American, sixty-something assistant looked relieved when I stepped through the door.

"Cassie, glad you're back," she said. "I wasn't sure how to handle this."

The young man on the near side of the counter turned to face me. A grayish plaid shirt and faded jeans hung loosely on his thin frame, and his pale, narrow face showed a trace of acne. He needed a shave and a haircut, too. I put his age about the same as mine.

On the sales counter between him and Sarah rested a rectangular, soft-sided black cat carrier. Even the mesh inserts were so dark that I couldn't really make out what was inside.

"You're the owner?" the man said eagerly. "You board cats, right? Can I leave mine here, just for a few days?"

The request wasn't strange, but his manner was. His eyes bugged a little, and his voice had a nervous edge. Still, a customer was a customer.

"No reason why not," I said. "We have room at the moment."

A couple of months ago, we would always have had room. But that spring we'd gotten some unusual publicity, and now our boarding facilities were sometimes filled to capacity. A large room toward the back of the shop featured more than a dozen "condos," each the size of a broom closet and with three different levels for litter pans, food and water dishes, and lounging.

"May I see your cat?" I asked. "Can you take him out?"

"Her." He unzipped the mesh door of the carrier.

Its occupant stepped out with a confident, fluid stride. She was a big, athletic-looking shorthair with a dark brown coat. Her long legs and slightly large ears hinted at some exotic genes.

A murmur from Sarah told me she also was impressed.

"Quite an animal," I said, while the cat allowed me to stroke her back. "What's her name?"

He hesitated. "Ayesha. Y'know, like the queen in *She?*"

I don't think he expected me to understand this reference, but I actually had seen the nineteen-sixties fantasy-adventure movie. One of my college boyfriends had a thing for Ursula Andress. My bad luck—a mere brunette, I also couldn't compete in terms of my chest or cheekbones with Andress the Goddess.

"That's certainly regal," I said. "What breed is she?"

"No idea. I got her from a shelter as a kitten."

Ayesha, who had been scanning the counter with her brilliant golden eyes, suddenly pounced on a pile of our brochures, scattering them to the floor. Sarah caught her before she could jump down after them. The blond man helped get her under control.

"Has she had all her shots? Do you have any recent vet records?" I asked him. "She certainly looks healthy, but I have to be careful about bringing in any cats that might be carrying contagious diseases."

"Sorry. I don't."

Which raised another question. "Is she spayed?"

When he shook his head, I prepared to turn him down. I'd never yet had to refuse a customer, but my boarding area is pretty close quarters. A cat with FIV or another contagious disease, or a female in heat, could cause serious problems. "I'm very sorry, but we have rules. . . ."

The guy looked on the edge of tears. "Please, I'm desperate! My . . . my house burned down last night. I can't go back there, and I have to find someplace else to live that will let me keep Ayesha. I just need a couple of days!"

I worried that it might take him more than a couple of days to find new quarters. Still, I sympathized. I have three cats of my own, and couldn't imagine what I'd do if all of us were suddenly homeless. "You don't have any friends or relatives . . . ?"

"Not around here. I came from out of state, and I can't go back. Please, this is an emergency. I'll come get her as soon as I can."

I thought of the extra-large condo that my handyman, Nick Janos, had recently built on a wall opposite the others. I'd asked for it just in case we ever had to quarantine a boarder.

"All right," I told the blond guy. "Maybe I can keep her kind of isolated."

"That's great!"

He paid a week's board in advance, cash, and wrote down his name—Rudy Pierson—and a cell phone number. With his help, Sarah urged the lively Ayesha back into her carrier. Though a standard size, it almost seemed too small for her.

"Does she need any kind of special diet or handling?" I asked.

Rudy requested an all-natural food that I figured I'd have to get from the big pet-supply store on the highway. "She's well-trained, but she needs a lot of exercise." He glanced through the wood and mesh screen that separated our playroom from the front sales counter. "I can see you've got a big space with cat trees and wall shelves. She'll like that."

I nodded. "We let the boarders out there every day, in shifts."

"Terrific! Oh, and she'll walk on a leash. Y'know, with a harness."

"Really?" Sarah peered into the carrier.

"Anyway, thanks so much," Rudy said, on his way out. "You guys are lifesavers!" From the doorway, he cast a sad, backward glance at the black carrier, as if he feared he might never see his pet again.

"What a shame," said Sarah, after he'd left. "I wonder where the house fire was? I didn't hear anything about it on the local news."

"He said he's from out of state, so maybe you wouldn't have. I also wonder, though, how he heard about my place?"

"You're on the Web. If he's got a smartphone, he might have found you that way."

"Yeah, maybe." I shrugged off the small mystery. "Well, let's get Miss Ayesha settled. I'm going to put her in that big condo away from the others. Let's just hope she doesn't go into heat while she's here, or even our neutered male boarders might freak out."

Sarah put a pan with fresh litter at the bottom of the quarantine condo, while I filled one dish with water and another with high-quality dry food. Her Highness would just have to make do until I could track down some of the fare Rudy had recommended.

If it's a natural brand, Dawn even might carry it at Nature's Way. That would be convenient. I dropped by my friend's health food store frequently, just to visit.

I toted the black carrier back to the condo area, where a few of the other boarders looked up or meowed in interest. Meanwhile, the lean cat's weight surprised me. When I unzipped the bag and lifted her out, I noticed again how muscular she was. Before putting her in her new quarters, though, I hesitated. Although Ayesha had short, sleek fur, in some areas it looked matted.

I usually groom boarders at a discount, anyway.

Given Rudy's circumstances, I'd throw in the service for free.

"I want to deal with her coat first," I told Sarah. "It's kind of sticky or something."

My assistant followed me into the grooming studio. "Maybe from the house fire?"

"Could be. From the smoke or some other kind of fumes in the air." I set the carrier on my stainless steel grooming table, let the new boarder out, and gave her fur a sniff. "Definitely has an odd, perfumey smell."

Though lively, restless, and strong, Ayesha didn't fight the grooming process. Sarah was able to hold her by the scruff while I started working with a slicker brush. The cat's coat had a slightly stiff texture, and it took a bit of effort to pass the brush through.

"What breed do you think she is?" Sarah asked. "She's an unusual color—such an even, dark brown."

"There is a Havana Brown breed," I told her. "I've seen them in pictures, but never in person. And Burmese are brown. But those are valuable purebreds. Rudy said he got her as a kitten from a shelter."

I switched to a comb, which seemed to glide through the hair more easily, but then noticed something weird.

Most cats have at least two kinds of fur—the silky or smooth guard hairs on top and a fluffier undercoat. The colors of the two can sometimes be different. Ayesha didn't have much of an undercoat, but her guard hairs changed color close to her skin. It wasn't the kind of "tipping" that occurs in some cats' fur, though. I'd never seen anything like this before.

I ruffled her hair back in several places and always found the same thing. In some areas, the dark brown color went a little deeper. In others, like her belly, the light, golden shade showed up more. But it didn't follow any typical, natural pattern.

When I paused, perplexed, Sarah asked me what was wrong.

"Forget grooming," I said. "This cat needs a bath."

"O-o-okay." She sounded confused. "Think she got into something oily in the fire?"

"Let's just say, whatever she's got on her coat might not be good for her, and I don't want her licking it off."

We put Ayesha in the big bathing sink, filled it partway with warm water, and squirted shampoo over her. Again, she was a surprisingly good sport, as if she'd been bathed before. Wearing thin latex gloves, I massaged the soap deep into her coat and scrubbed gently with my hands. Sarah held the sprayer close to the cat's skin to rinse her without upsetting her too much.

Dark brown begin to swirl into the shallow bath water.

"What on earth?" Sarah gasped.

"There's a reason we couldn't tell what breed she was," I guessed out loud. "And maybe a reason why Rudy claimed he didn't know. She's been dyed."

In spite of our efforts, only a little of the stuff washed out. Finally we gave up and towel-dried the cat. But not before we could just make out a faint pattern of leopard spots over her whole body.

"That's so bizarre!" my assistant said, with a shake of her head. "Why would anyone dye such a beautiful coat?"

"Maybe to hide the fact that she's worth thousands?" I flashed back on Rudy's anxious and secretive behavior. "I'm betting Ayesha is a purebred show cat. And possibly stolen."

Chapter 2

While we put Ayesha in our drying cage, with a stationary blower turned toward her to finish the job, Sarah began to see my point. "She does act like she's used to this kind of treatment, doesn't she? You really think that guy stole her from someone?"

"Well, he probably didn't get her from a shelter as a kitten—not a dark brown one, anyway," I pointed out. "I'll bet the story about the house fire was a lie, too. And if she's a purebred, she might not have been spayed because someone wanted to breed her."

Sarah peeled off her vinyl gloves and dropped them in the trash can. "But if Rudy stole her, why park her here?"

"Good question. Maybe somebody's on his trail and closing in." I planted my hands on my hips and studied our mystery cat, who seemed to be rather enjoying her blow-dry. "The question is, what should I do about it? If anything?"

"You could tell the police. Your pal, Detective Bonelli."

I could. During the excitement that spring, I'd developed a professional friendship with Angela Bonelli, detective with the Chadwick P.D. I wondered, though, whether this was a serious enough issue for her to bother with. So far, I had absolutely no proof that Rudy Pierson—if that was his real name—had committed any crime.

"I'd hate to sic the cops on him if it turns out that there's some innocent explanation," I told my assistant. "After all, it's not even as if he was abusing the cat."

"No." Sarah cocked her head over Ayesha, who stretched out like a sphinx, eyes blissfully closed, in the drying cage. "She looks like she's in great shape."

Deciding I should give Pierson a chance to explain himself, I pulled out my cell phone.

I got a generic recording, not even in his own voice. Was he using some kind of disposable phone? I left a message to say that, in cleaning up the cat, we'd discovered something odd and I was curious about it.

"Probably a good thing not to tell him too much in the message," Sarah said, after I'd hung up.

"Yeah, I don't want to spook him," I said. "In the meantime, I guess Her Highness will be staying here for a few days, if not longer. Let's go ahead and put her in the isolation condo, and then I'll call Dawn."

Dawn Tischler had unintentionally influenced me to open my business in Chadwick. We'd become friends in high school, as perhaps the only two students who really enjoyed our art history class; we also discovered a mutual interest in reading mysteries. Dawn's enthusiasm for cooking far exceeded mine, though, and she aspired to be a nutritionist. Although we went off to different colleges and pursued different career paths, we'd stayed loosely in touch.

When we'd reconnected a couple of years ago, it felt as if no time had passed. By then, Dawn was running a successful health food store in Chadwick. I'd visited her here a few times, noticed the town was affordable but also on the upswing, and got the idea to start my own shop. I'd even found a storefront about four blocks from hers. That wasn't as unusual as it sounded, since the retail district of Chadwick was only about a mile long. The downtown consisted of ten blocks to the north of the highway ramp and six blocks to the south. Like Dawn, I'd gotten a bargain by finding a vacancy just off the main drag, Center Street.

I called her now and, as I'd hoped, she did have a case of the mystery cat's special food in stock.

"Super," I told her. "I'll be over in just a minute."

Sarah's normally mocha complexion blanched a little when she heard I was going out. "It's just that . . . if that guy did steal the cat, and she's really worth thousands . . . Well, from your message, he might guess that we found out about the dye job. He *could* come back here really angry."

I kicked myself, mentally, for not having considered that. "I don't think you have to worry. At least now we've got the alarm system, remember? If you think you're in trouble, just hit the panic button under the sales counter and it'll bring the cops."

"That's right, I almost forgot." Sarah felt beneath the counter for the button and smiled in relief.

Even so, I promised her, "I won't be gone long."

Nature's Way occupied a Victorian structure, originally the town feed store, a block from Center Street, Chadwick's main drag. Dawn Tischler had painted the outside in two shades of soft green—lighter for the body, darker for the fancy trim—which helped draw attention. I entered to the familiar jangle of bells above the front door and Dawn's voice calling out sharply, "Tigger, rug!"

Her six-month-old kitten must have been used to the command by now. He halted in his dash toward me and doubled back to the braided rug in front of the store's old cast-iron stove. There, he sat obediently until Dawn fed him a cat treat. By that time, I had closed the front door, so he couldn't escape.

"I can't believe I ever doubted you," she told me, "when you said I could stop Tigger from running out by clicker-training him. Now I don't even need the clicker anymore."

"I see that. You deserve credit, too, though. Not everybody can get the hang of that training or do it consistently."

Tigger had adopted Dawn a few months ago by taking up residence in her storeroom—she never did figure out how he'd gotten in. She'd made an honest attempt to find out if he belonged to anyone, then took him to the vet for the standard shots and neutering. She'd also managed to break him of his bad habit of racing for the shop's front door every time it opened. She'd had to stash many of her products behind glass, though—small bottles of essential oil, stone pendants on shiny chains—because the little tabby still needed some outlet for his playful predatory instincts.

Having behaved long enough, he romped over to me now and pretended to attack the laces on my sneaker.

"You're a goofball!" I managed to give him a quick squeeze before he bounded off again.

Dawn had dressed for the hot day in her typical elegant-hippie fashion, which suited her statuesque height and figure. Her terra-cotta tank top almost matched her wavy, shoulder-length hair and coordinated with the print of her long Indian cotton skirt. She made me feel blah in my khaki shorts and sleeveless polo. But then, she had only one cat to shed on her, while I had more than a dozen.

"I've got your food right here." Dawn crossed to the big oak display cabinet, one of many weathered pieces that helped give character to her rustic store. "Wild Life, right?" She glanced at the label on one can. "'Grain-free, all organic meat.' Sounds ideal, but I gotta say, I've had this case on the shelf for a month. Most customers look at the price sticker and put it right back."

I almost did the same. "Usually, when an owner requests a special food, they provide it or reimburse me. With this guy, though, I don't know if I can count on that."

She picked up on my tone. "What's the problem?"

I explained about the edgy young man who'd left me only his name and cell number, and the feline who seemed to be traveling incognito.

"Wow, that really is strange," she agreed. "You think somebody was trying to disguise the markings? But don't a lot of cats have similar coats?"

"They do, but hers is really unusual—rings, all over, like on a leopard. I think they're called rosettes. Only a few types of cats have those markings, so by hiding them he's also hiding her breed." I plucked a can of Wild Life from its case and read the label. " 'Especially recommended for exotics such as Bengals, Ocicats and Savannahs.' There you go! I think Ayesha is one of those. And if she's an unspayed female, she could be worth a lot of money."

"I've never even heard of any of those breeds, so I'll take your word for it." Dawn let out a yelp as her kitten snagged the hem of her long skirt with his claws. "This guy's a mutt off the street, and he's wild enough for me."

I smiled at the kitten's attempts to get a rise out of my friend. "I shouldn't stay too long. Sarah's nervous about being in the shop on her own, just in case there is something weird going on."

"Before you leave, I have to show you something." Dawn unfurled a new table runner that she'd had designed for the upcoming Chadwick Day sidewalk sale. Of sturdy nylon, most of it was plain white and would lie across the middle of a display table, where any products she put on top would anchor it. The front part would hang down and show the name of her shop and the logo—two green leaves sprouting from one stem and framing a golden sun.

"Looks sharp!" I said. "The printer did a nice job."

"I used Alpha Printing, right here in town, and he gave me a good price. You should get one for your shop, Cassie. You took a table for the sale, too, didn't you?"

"I did, but . . . You know me, always playing catch-up where marketing is concerned. I do have one of those pop-up canopies, though. My folks used it sometimes, while my dad was alive and we had a house, for backyard parties."

"Well, that's a start. Put out your brochures, and some of the cat trees and carriers that you sell . . ."

I nodded. "I should step it up a notch this time, though. My display at Small Business Sunday this spring was pretty lame." Silently, I wondered if any of my own three cats would be willing to hold still for a live grooming demonstration. I didn't relish losing one of them in the crowd if he or she made a sudden bolt for freedom.

The bells over Dawn's front door jangled again, and a tentative young woman stepped in. She wore a gauzy top with belled sleeves over cutoff jeans that bared sunburned legs. Shagged brown hair that was blonder at the ends framed her oval face, and her features and movements were sharp and birdlike.

When Dawn's kitten raced toward the visitor, she knew enough to shut the front door quickly. "Who's this?" She laughed, stooping to greet the tabby.

He screeched to a stop a few inches from her, then hopped sideways with his tail puffed, inviting her to chase him.

"That's Tigger, our resident lunatic." Dawn held out her hand. "I'll bet you're Teri."

"You guessed right. Easy to find this place—I love the green building!"

"Thanks." Dawn smiled. "It took a little effort to get permission from the Chamber of Commerce, but eventually they came around."

"We've got your order." Teri pulled out a checklist and ran down the quantities of squash, green beans, cucumbers, eggplant, tomatoes, and other summer vegetables that Dawn apparently had bought for the fresh produce section of her store.

"All sounds right to me," Dawn said. "Can I have a look before you unload?"

"Sure." Teri glanced toward a fit-looking man of about thirty, with short bangs and a beard, who also had come in the front door. "That okay, Rick?"

"No problem. Can I pull the truck around to the back?"

"Perfect," said Dawn. "I'll be out in a minute."

After the two vendors went back outside, Dawn explained to me that she'd been disappointed lately with the produce from her usual supplier, so she was trying out a local, organic farm. "Teri came by last week with a brochure, so I figured, what the heck," she told me. "Can you wait here till I come back, Cassie? I won't be long."

I nodded, and Dawn headed out to check out the truckload of produce. Meanwhile, I phoned

Sarah. She told me all was well, and for good or ill, Rudy had not been back to the shop.

"Our new boarder is raising a racket, though," my assistant added. "She's got some lungs. He should've called her Beyoncé!"

I laughed. "When I get back, we'll figure out some way to keep her occupied."

While I had the phone out, I went online and checked a couple of cat breed Web sites. I concentrated on the exotic breeds and tried to determine what Ayesha might be. First I checked out the Savannah, a cross between a domestic cat and a type of African wildcat called a serval. But big and long-legged as Rudy's cat was, she didn't match the cheetah-like proportions of a Savannah, which also could weigh up to twenty-five pounds. After a little more research, I was convinced Ayesha had to be either an Ocicat—really just a domestic cat with wild markings—or a Bengal, a true hybrid developed from domestic stock and Asian leopard cats.

I'd know better after I could see more of her real coat . . . and her temperament.

The produce delivery must have passed Dawn's inspection, because she let Teri and Rick unload the crates of vegetables into her store and settled up with them. After they'd gone, she offered me first pick before she arranged everything on the tiered shelves of her produce display.

"Maybe another time," I said. "I've got the case of cat food, and that may be all I can carry."

"Come back with your car," she suggested.

"It's in the shop, getting its sixty-thousand-mile checkup. Say, have you ever had work done at Gillis's Garage?"

"Just a brake job once. Why?"

I described the juvenile come-ons from Todd that had made me squirm, including his creepy fascination with vicious animals.

Dawn groaned. "He actually asked you if you did a bikini car wash? Gross! Tell him you have a boyfriend."

"He'd probably try to convince me that he could do more for me than any other guy." I looked down at my boring, casual clothes and ran a hand through my shoulder-length brown hair, limp from the heat. "I got myself *so* glammed up today, too, with no makeup and my bangs needing a trim. Guess I was just asking for it."

"That's right, you shameless hussy." My friend grinned. "Maybe Todd likes a challenge."

"I don't care what he likes. Hey, jerk, just check my car and fix anything that needs it. That's all I ask."

Shaking her head in amusement, Dawn walked me toward the door. "When I went there I dealt with an older man, maybe his father. Bob, I think his name was—nice enough. Somehow, I must have escaped Todd's attention. Maybe I'm just not his type."

"I get the sense that anything female would be his type." Remembering the exotic boarder waiting for me back at the shop, I had an unnerving thought. "In fact, I'd better keep Ayesha under wraps. Todd was going on about how great it would be to own a wildcat."

* * *

Back at my shop, Sarah welcomed me by crossing her eyes and pressing her hands to her ears. Even from the customer's side of the front sales counter, I could hear the reason. Someone back in the condo area was making the most unearthly noise, a full-throated yowl that trailed off into a low, guttural warble.

"Beyoncé?" I guessed.

"Who else?" Sarah nodded toward the case of food I carried. "Maybe she'll calm down when she gets her filet mignon."

"I don't have that, but I do have quite an assortment." Breaking the plastic wrap stretched over the cans, I read a few labels. "There's beef, all right, and trout . . . duck . . . venison . . ."

An extra-loud caterwaul suggested that our royal guest had heard me.

"We'd better hurry," Sarah suggested, "before she starts snacking on one of her neighbors."

"Oh, I doubt that'll happen." Nick Janos, my handyman, had built the closet-sized cat condos with sturdy mesh doors to take some abuse and still keep the boarders secure.

I chose a can of the beef dinner and went back to feed Ayesha myself. At least when she saw me, her mournful tone took on a happier lilt. She stood with her hind legs on the second level of the condo, where the food and water were kept, and stretched nearly to the top of the door, with her front claws hooked into the mesh. Her pose clearly displayed the half-camouflaged rosettes on her lighter belly.

"*Yowrwrr!*" she demanded.

She already had scoured her ceramic bowl clean

of all the dry food Sarah gave her, but I guess as a big girl with a high metabolism, she felt entitled to more.

"Okay, okay. Keep your spots on." I cracked the condo door open just enough to grab the empty bowl—didn't need our newcomer running loose right now—spooned out the new food, and popped the dish back in. Ayesha dove into it as if she'd been starved for weeks, although her excellent body weight didn't show any evidence of that.

Sarah joined me, and we both contemplated our mystery boarder in silence for a minute.

"The thing is," I said, "whether or not Rudy stole her from somewhere, he took good care of her. I had the sense, when he was talking to us, that he really was attached to her."

"So did I," Sarah agreed. "Maybe he took her from someone who was abusing her?"

"That's possible. Though she doesn't look abused, and she's very confident and trusting with us."

"No collar. Think she has a microchip?"

I snapped my fingers and congratulated my assistant on this idea, which I'd stupidly overlooked. I reached into the condo while Ayesha was chowing down and probed the area around her nape and shoulders with my fingers. The cat stopped eating and flinched when I touched a rough patch about an inch long.

"She's got something here," I told Sarah. "If it's an implant, the vet did a heck of a sloppy job. Looks like the wound's still healing."

"Maybe Dr. Coccia could check it."

I pondered this. Ordinarily, I wouldn't take it upon myself to bring a boarder's cat to the vet unless it became seriously hurt or sick. But this might be a special case.

Glancing at the clock, I noted, "It's almost five now . . . he'll be closing. I'll call tomorrow and see if he can fit us in. Unless Rudy gets back to me before that, with a darn good explanation for this dye job."

"Maybe it's Ayesha who's on the run from the cops," Sarah fantasized while we started to close up the shop. "Rudy just felt sorry for her and helped her escape."

"There's an idea. What's the charge?"

Another loud, wavering yowl told us that Her Highness had already finished her second supper.

Sarah winced. "Disturbing the peace."

"That must be it." I laughed, tossing a damp towel into the hamper. "She's a cat on the lam!"

Chapter 3

After dinner that night I checked in with my mother, who lives in an apartment in Morristown, about forty-five minutes from Chadwick. She works as a paralegal for a big law firm with offices in the same town. Mom had actually taken a couple of days off this week, rare for her, for a nasty root canal procedure. I'd offered to come by, but she had a retired neighbor helping her out and sounded as if she was already recovering nicely.

In truth, running my own business—especially one where I was responsible for other people's pets—made it hard to get away on short notice. I don't like to leave Sarah alone at the helm too often, either, since I technically am only paying her to assist me.

Now I lounged with the phone on my beige-slip-covered sofa in the apartment above my shop, with my own three cats picturesquely arranged in various spots around the living room. "How are you feeling?" I asked Mom.

"Not so bad today," she told me, her voice still just a bit slurred. "Mainly, my jaw aches being forced open for so long. Naturally, it had to be the very last molar."

I could sympathize, having inherited my mother's small jaw. It challenged every dental professional who worked on either of us.

While my calico Matisse kneaded my sweatpants, Mom asked me what was new. I considered my answer carefully. Better not to mention the new boarder that appeared to be dyed and might have been stolen. My mother is a major worrywart, and the least hint of something being awry can get her going, especially where I'm concerned. So I just said things at the shop were great and tried to steer the focus back to her dental work and recovery.

Not quickly enough, though.

"And how are things going with Mark?" she asked. "You haven't mentioned him lately."

"Oh, everything's fine with him, too. He's just been very busy, pulling some long hours."

Three months earlier, I had started dating Dr. Mark Coccia, a veterinarian with a clinic just six blocks away. We'd started off like a house on fire, thrown together by all the craziness in my life that spring. Lately, though, he seemed to have less free time, and when we did go out, he sometimes acted like his mind was elsewhere. Call me an optimist, but it seemed more like he had professional worries rather than a problem with me.

I wasn't going to tell Mom about any of that, either.

"Huh!" she said now. "I know human doctors have emergencies, but I wouldn't expect that problem with a vet."

"It's the same in many ways. He'll have a full day booked but need to squeeze some more patients in for emergencies. If there's an animal recovering at the clinic, and it develops a problem near the end of the day, he'll have to stay and cope with it." Matisse, jealous that I was paying attention to someone besides her, began rubbing her face against my phone. I gently deposited her on the floor before continuing. "Plus, Mark's in practice with Dr. Reed, and they alternate working Saturdays and staying late one weeknight."

Though all of this was completely true, even to myself I sounded as if I were making excuses for Mark's preoccupation. I expected Mom to pounce on this, but her pain medicine must have had a calming effect—she completely let it slide.

"Anyway," I added, "I'll probably be seeing him tomorrow." I didn't have an appointment yet, but I felt sure the case of the camouflaged cat would intrigue Mark.

"That's good." I heard Mom yawn. It was only ten o'clock, but she'd always been an early-to-bed, early-to-rise type. Even when not on pain medication.

"I'll let you get some rest," I said. "Feel better."

"Oh, I am already. I'll probably go back to work tomorrow. But thanks for calling, dear."

Clicking off, I took stock of my feline companions. Having been evicted from my lap, Matisse now sat among the windowsill plants and gazed out at the twilight. Her dark-gray and rust patches marched like stepping-stones down her white back, and her tail occasionally switched when something aroused her hunting instinct. The window air conditioner must not have been cool enough for sleek black Cole, because he stretched in a backward arc on the sofa next to me, airing his belly fur. Mango, an orange tabby, caught the chilly air flow more directly by perching on a narrow shelf, one of a series that I'd mounted on the living room wall. Besides letting the cats survey their domain from on high, they also provide an escape route during skirmishes.

All three could be considered rescues, although only Cole came from an actual shelter. I'd accepted Matisse to help a friend deal with her cat's unexpected and unwanted litter, and I'd found Mango scavenging in a restaurant Dumpster. Fortunately, they all got along pretty well and did their part to keep this single career woman from feeling lonely. Most of the time.

Following my conversation with Mom, I found myself missing Mark tonight even more than before. Well, no reason I couldn't call his cell to see if he had an opening in his schedule tomorrow. I could fill him in ahead of time on what little I knew about Ayesha. Maybe I could even steer him onto the topic of why we hadn't seen as much of each other lately.

My call, though, went to voice mail. I briefly explained about the mystery cat and asked him to let me know in the morning if I could bring her over to the clinic.

I snapped on the TV to catch the local news before bed. Even tonight's newscaster reminded me a little of Mark, with his straight dark hair and high cheekbones, though he lacked the vet's striking blue eyes.

The evening's news was fairly mundane. A crew had been brought in to remediate asbestos discovered at the old high school, hopefully before classes resumed next month. The mayor promised that this year's Chadwick Day celebration would be bigger and better than ever. (It was the first one I'd be experiencing, so I wouldn't know the difference.) The body of a man, apparently hit by a car, had been found out on rural Morton Road, with no ID. (Some lowlife probably came across the dead man and took his wallet, I thought—despicable!)

Nothing about a house fire, though, or a stolen exotic cat. I pressed off on the remote and decided to turn in early. Maybe tomorrow Dr. Coccia could help me come up with some clues as to Ayesha's true identity.

"Isn't that the damndest thing!" Mark ruffled the brown cat's fur against the grain, pretty much the way I had, and saw the uneven dye job.

"Sarah and I already gave her a good washing, which is the only reason you make out the spots at all," I told him.

"Wonder what kind of dye they used." He scratched the side of Ayesha's face. She leaned into his touch, purring, and I envied her. "I think there is a kind that's nontoxic hair dye for animals, but the average person probably wouldn't know about it."

"Who would? Maybe somebody involved in showing cats?'

He shrugged. "Maybe. Anyone could order it online, though, if he was really concerned about not poisoning the cat."

Mark also checked Ayesha's eyes and mouth. She only raised one paw in a mild protest, with claws sheathed. "I don't see any sign of the stuff making her sick," he said. "I'd have to draw blood to be sure . . . but I can't do that without the owner's permission. I'd need to shave a spot on her neck, so he'd know."

Yes, probably not a great idea to tip Rudy off that I'd brought her to a vet. "She's got a fresh scar between her shoulder blades. Can you check whether she has a chip? That should give us some information about who really owns her."

Mark fetched his pet scanner and passed it over the area a couple of times. "No reading." He examined the healing wound and frowned. "That was a nasty gash. Could be that somebody took her chip *out,* and not exactly with surgical skill."

I found it hard to imagine that Rudy would treat the cat so callously. Maybe someone else did, and he'd rescued Ayesha from that person?

"I'm thinking she's valuable," I said. "Hard to tell with the dyed coat, but what breed would you say—"

"Bengal, definitely, with those rosettes. I worked on a couple when I was in Philly, and she's got the perfect body type. She's an adult, maybe three years old. Looks like she's got a champion coat pattern, too, underneath all this brown. If she's an

F1 or F2—close to the Asian leopard cat strain—she could be worth four, maybe five figures."

Even more than I imagined. "Might really be worth it to steal her, then!"

Mark straightened and looked me in the eye with concern. "And now you've got her in your shop. If this Rudy guy did take her and thinks you've discovered his game, he might not be too happy when he comes back."

Though I heard the warning, I couldn't resist an evil grin. "Hey, why do you think I brought her over *here?*"

A tight laugh from Mark. "Oh, now she's my problem, eh? No thanks—I have more than enough on my plate right now."

That gave me the opening I needed. While he gently guided Ayesha back into her carrier, I asked, "What's wrong, Mark? I know something's been going on with you lately."

He zipped up the carrier and sighed. "It's just been crazy around here. One thing after another. People I've been working with for years, that I thought I could trust . . . I don't like to talk about it, though, until I have proof."

"You can always talk to me," I told him quietly, even though the door to the examining room was shut. "I wouldn't tell anyone else. I just don't like to see your work issues coming between us."

Mark slipped the stethoscope from around his neck and studied me for a second, his handsome face sober. "You're right. That has been happening, hasn't it? I'm sorry." He pulled me into his arms for a quick hug. "Why don't we have dinner tomorrow night? Ironclad, no cancellations for any reason. Then I'll fill you in, as best I can."

It was what I'd been hoping to hear, and I smiled. "Ironclad? I like the sound of that. Now I'd better let you get to your other patients, and take Ayesha back in case Rudy comes looking for her."

"Be careful, Cassie. Seriously. The kind of trouble you had a couple of months ago . . . you don't want to go through that again."

"Well, I do have an alarm system now," I reminded him. "But thanks for worrying. Give me a call and we'll firm up tomorrow night."

"You got it."

En route back to my shop, Her Highness let it be known that she'd been cooped up too long in the cramped carrier. Not by yowling as much as by clawing at the nylon mesh panel until I worried that she might actually tear through it. The minute I stepped in the door, I told Sarah, "We've got to let this wild child loose in the playroom!"

She chuckled. "No problem. Just let me put Mrs. Lowenstein's Burmese away."

A few minutes later, I released Ayesha from her portable prison into the cat-safe area, which was outfitted with all types and sizes of carpeted tunnels and towers, as well as many floating wall shelves built by my faithful handyman, Nick. Our newcomer quickly took in her surroundings, then launched herself from the tile floor straight onto a shelf about five feet from the ground. She leaped effortlessly from there to the next shelf, another two feet up, and paused to survey her human underlings with a haughty air.

"Wow," said Sarah. "She really does move like a panther, doesn't she?"

"Mark has pronounced her a Bengal, probably with a good dose of Asian leopard cat," I said. "At least she doesn't seem at all aggressive, though we shouldn't take too much for granted. She's going to need a lot of time in this space and a lot of interactive play. We can split that—you take maybe half an hour a day, and I'll do the same."

"She's shaping up as a pretty labor-intensive boarder," my assistant observed. "Think we'll ever see that guy Rudy again?"

"I have no idea. But on the upside, we do have a heck of a mystery to solve." I told her what Mark had said about the cat's wound—that someone probably had cut out her microchip.

"Oh, man." Sarah shook her head of short, graying curls. "Cassie, I can see that working for you, I'll never be bored."

"I'll take that as a compliment. Speaking of excitement . . ." I picked up a fishing pole toy with a bunch of feathers at the end of a long string. "I'm going to try to tire this wild animal out."

Of course, it ended up more the other way around. As soon as I started wiggling those feathers, Ayesha homed in on them like they were her next meal. I tried to keep ahead of her, but it wasn't easy—she was *fast.* When I dragged them over the wall shelves, as high as I could reach, she happily gave chase and always nailed her prey in seconds. Starting to flag, I stood still for a while and just flipped the string to bounce the feathers high in the air. Ayesha shot straight up to catch them, executing some Olympic gymnastic moves in the process.

When she finally started breathing hard, I let her have the toy. The athletic cat, so gentle with people, grabbed the tightly bound bunch of feathers in triumph and began ripping at them with her teeth. I'd hate to be any bird she caught, though at least she'd probably kill me quickly.

I turned to find Sarah watching me with crossed arms and a bemused smile.

"Glad you found that entertaining," I said, "because you're doing the afternoon session. I'm beat."

"Rudy said she walks on a leash, too."

I sniffed. "If we ever do that, it'll be indoors. I wouldn't want to try to catch this lady if she ever got away."

Having stripped most of the feathers from her toy, Ayesha stalked up to me now, sat at my feet, and let out one of her distinctive warbles.

"I suppose now we want to be fed again." I called over my shoulder to Sarah, "What flavors do we have left? Any water buffalo?"

My assistant chuckled. "None of that, but will the venison do?"

"Close enough."

With Ayesha back in her condo, dining once more, I sat at the sales counter and revived myself with a cold Diet Coke. I returned a call from one of our best customers, Cindy Reynolds, who brought in her Maine Coon cat about once a month to be tidied up. Luckily Bear, who weighed over twenty pounds and had the coat of a miniature yak, knew the grooming drill by now and rarely gave me or Sarah any trouble. But Cindy knew he still took a lot of time to groom and paid us accordingly. She made an appointment for the following week.

After that, I opened my laptop computer and tried to create a design for a table runner similar to the one Dawn had ordered from the local printer. If I got something to him this week, maybe he could still have it ready in time for Chadwick Day. Experimenting with different fonts, I tried to come up with whimsical purple lettering similar to what was on my front window.

And maybe a cartoon of a fluffy cat?

For the next half hour, I attempted to draw one. But despite the fact that I'd minored in art in college, I wasn't happy with any of my efforts. As recently as ten years ago, I'd been painting, drawing, and using a computer to create my own artworks. Had I lost my chops, as musicians say, that quickly? Lately, I'd been channeling all my artistic talent into sculpting the coats of various felines. Still, you'd think if I could draw anything decently, it would be a cat!

Maybe I was being too hard on myself, but I wanted a more slick, professional-looking image. I looked at a few online sites that offered graphics for royalty fees, but came away frustrated. Nothing there was exactly what I'd had in mind, either. *If only I could get someone to draw it for me. . . .*

Keith, of course! Dawn's longtime boyfriend was a graphic artist who also did caricatures on the side. If I was going to pay for an image, I might as well give him the work and get just what I wanted. He should be able to create something for me, if he wasn't too busy. I shot him a quick e-mail to ask, and gave him an idea of what I was looking for.

Sarah, meanwhile, had been leaning on the sales counter and checking messages on her cell phone. I knew her two grown children e-mailed and texted her regularly to let her know what was going on in their lives. I could tell she also was catching up with the local news, because she made a "Tsk!" sound and added, "Imagine all the kids who've gone through the town's high school over the years and were exposed to that asbestos."

Sarah had taught high school herself, though not in Chadwick, and her son Jay still did, so I could understand why such a scenario troubled her. "Well, they say it's not dangerous unless it's disturbed. They're just removing it now because they want to renovate—"

I heard Sarah catch her breath, and she turned her phone toward me. "Cassie, look!"

Leaning nearer, I saw what appeared to be a police sketch of Rudy Pierson with wide, staring eyes and a slack-jawed face. The headline beneath stated:

STILL NO ID ON VICTIM OF DEADLY HIT-AND-RUN

Chapter 4

This wasn't my first visit to the Chadwick Police Station, but it was my first time in an interrogation room. Sitting alone Wednesday morning, at a metal table in the stark, white-cinderblock space, put me on edge. Even though I certainly wasn't suspected of any crime.

I relaxed a bit when Detective Angela Bonelli entered and took the chair opposite mine. It helped that she'd brought coffee for both of us and actually remembered that I took milk and sweetener.

I tasted it and smiled. Hazelnut, probably from the little red Keurig unit she kept in her office.

Bonelli wore her virtual uniform of a navy pantsuit with a tailored blouse—pale yellow today. Her dark, chin-length bob needed a touch-up, the gray roots starting to show. Her large, soulful features always had a slightly world-weary appearance, offset by her dry sense of humor.

"Cassie," she said with a smile, "it's been a while."

"Couldn't stay away," I joked nervously. "How are Lou and the boys?"

"Busy, like me. Lou's had plenty of construction work this summer, and the kids are always at their baseball or soccer games. Helps them burn off energy, though." She set a manila file folder on the table between us, as a sign of getting down to business. "So, you think you can identify our dead man?"

"From the sketch I saw online, he looks like a customer who left a cat with me yesterday."

Bonelli opened the folder to reveal the original forensic photo, printed out in color at eight-by-ten. I flinched. Unlike the sketch in the paper, it showed Rudy's actual, dead face. He looked battered, maybe from being dragged across the road.

"That's him. He's even wearing the same plaid shirt as when he came to my shop. Here's the information he left with us." I passed Bonelli the note with the young man's name and cell phone number. "He definitely had a wallet at the shop. He paid us a deposit, in cash, to board his cat."

"And you told our desk sergeant that there's something funny about the cat?"

I explained what Sarah and I had discovered while bathing Ayesha and what Mark had turned up during his examination. Also that a cat of that breed and quality could be worth a lot of money.

Bonelli jutted her lower lip thoughtfully as she took all this in. "It's still possible that this Rudy was accidentally killed by a hit-and-run driver, and either that person came back to rob him or someone else did," she said. "We had reports this summer about fights out at The Roost, a roadhouse that's big with local hunters. He might have just gotten on the wrong side of a really mean drunk."

"I also wonder if there was anything to his house fire story," I said.

"We'll look into that. And we'll try to locate any relatives he might have had and question them."

I shifted in my straight metal chair to ease a cramp in my hip; Bonelli's guest seating left something to be desired. "I thought, because the cat was dyed, that Rudy might have stolen her. Maybe someone followed him, found he didn't have Ayesha anymore, and got angry enough about it to kill him."

"If he knew his killer, maybe the wallet was taken to hide Rudy's identity. Makes it harder to track down his associates." Pulling out a pen, the detective scribbled a note on the file in front of her. "I'll check with some of the other PDs around here to see if anyone has reported a stolen cat."

"The killer could still be hunting for Ayesha," I pointed out. "Maybe Rudy even admitted to someone, before he died, that he left her at my place."

Bonelli shot me a worried look in the same vein as Mark's. "Let's hope he didn't. For the present, we won't reveal any of these details regarding the cat to the press. But wouldn't you rather turn her over to an animal shelter, where there would be more security?"

I considered this for only a second. I'd already experienced problems with someone trying to break into my shop that spring, motivating me to install the new security system. But keep Ayesha caged at a shelter? That could be a miserable experience for everyone involved.

"This is a special kind of cat," I explained. "Very high-energy, very vocal. I think she'd go crazy in a place like that. Probably drive her handlers and the other animals crazy, too. We've got better facilities to give her the attention and exercise she needs."

Bonelli relented with a nod. "Then we'll leave her at your place for the time being. If we find out that she's stolen, though, or if anyone bothers you, we may have to move her. No sense putting yourself in danger over an animal that isn't even yours."

I was walking back to my shop, preoccupied with questions about the dead Rudy Pierson and the mysterious Ayesha, when a driver hailed me from the curb.

"Hey, hot legs, want a lift?"

Startled, I stopped and looked around. I'd been street-hassled a few times in cities, but never since I'd come to Chadwick. Couldn't I even wear shorts on a sweltering summer day without having some jerk embarrass me?

Even more bizarre, the car creeping along beside me looked like—was!—my own silver-blue Honda. My stomach clenched as I saw Todd Gillis smirking from behind the wheel. "Thought I'd return it to you," he said. "C'mon, get in."

I really, really didn't want to. But it was a broiling, humid July day—a New Jersey specialty. I figured Todd couldn't pull anything on me in broad daylight on the way back to my shop, especially not if he wanted to get paid for his labors. Stepping into the car, I thanked Honda for placing a substantial console between the front passenger and the driver. Unfortunately, I still sat close enough to Todd to smell him.

After we started rolling again, he asked me, "Not so bad, huh?" Gloating, as if this were a mini-date.

I ignored the subtext. "Yes, the car seems fine. How did it check out? Any major problems?"

"Nope. I changed the oil and the filters, rotated the tires, replaced your front brake pads and one of your belts. Everything else was pretty much okay."

I let out a breath; that didn't sound too expensive. "Yeah, it's been a good car. I bought it used, but even so, no big repairs so far."

Todd creased his nose with an air of disdain. "It's not the ride for you, though, Cassie."

"Huh? Why not?"

"It's a soccer mom car!" he sneered. "You need something sexier."

"I need something reliable, with good cargo space," I shot back, refusing to play this game. "I cart around grooming supplies, cases of cat food, extra-large bags of kitty litter, and cats in carriers. . . . This is my street, make a right."

Todd looked annoyed that we had arrived so soon. "C'mon. If somebody gave you, like, fifty thou to spend on a new car, wouldn't you want something with more horsepower, more pizzazz?"

I considered the hypothetical offer. "Actually, if that ever happened, I probably *would* upgrade. Let's see . . . I could get a van with all the bells and whistles, so I could go wherever I wanted. Trick it out with a fold-down table, a hair dryer, a bathtub with a sprayer . . ."

When Todd got a wild gleam in his eye, I knew he'd spun off into his own fantasy. "Now you're talking!"

"My name on the outside in purple, of course. And it would be completely lined in fur. . . ." I waited until his greasy cowlick was standing completely at attention before I added, "At least, it would be after I finished grooming my customers' cats. Yeah, I probably could do a *lot* more business with a vehicle like that."

He scowled at me. "Maybe you deserve a boring car."

"I absolutely do. This is my place. . . . Just pull up in front."

We stepped onto the sidewalk, where Todd noticed the purple lettering on the shop's front window. Making the connection to my fantasy van, he sniffed in distaste. With a sullen air, he pulled out his paperwork and accompanied me inside to settle up.

I spread the bill flat on the front sales counter and read the total. Man, if this was what Gillis's Garage charged for routine maintenance, I hoped I never had a big repair job. I borrowed a ballpoint from Todd—metallic gold, of course—to write a check.

Meanwhile, Sarah wandered in from the playroom with Ayesha. "Look, Cassie. She really does walk on a leash!"

We keep lightweight nylon harnesses on hand

for any cats that are especially hard to groom. My assistant had managed to strap one onto Ayesha and threaded some twine through the ring on the back, for a leash about four feet long. Although the big, elegant, brown feline seemed to be leading Sarah, instead of the other way around, she appeared perfectly happy to explore the area behind the sales counter for a minute. Then she paused and looked up, her brilliant golden eyes tracking the shiny ballpoint pen just as I handed it back to Todd.

In one fluid move, Ayesha leaped onto the counter and batted the pen from his fingers to the floor. She jumped down after it and began knocking it around like a soccer ball, until Sarah managed to rein her in.

"Sorry!" My assistant handed the ballpoint back to Todd. "Hope she didn't scratch it."

He accepted the pen back without ever taking his eyes off Ayesha, who now sat calmly at Sarah's feet. "Wow. What kind of cat is that?"

Uh-oh. The good news was, he'd probably given up all hope of scoring with me. The bad news: He might have spotted something else he felt driven to possess.

"Just one of our boarders," I told him. "We think she's a Havana Brown. Y'know, one of those prissy, purebred show cats."

Catching my glance, Sarah hustled Ayesha back to the playroom, to Todd's disappointment.

"Doesn't act like a show cat," he said. "She acts wild! The way she grabbed that thing, right out of my hand—"

"She's just frustrated with being cooped up. Sarah was giving her some play time." I tore off my check and passed it to him with a tight smile.

He folded it and stuck it in the breast pocket of his work shirt. "Thanks, Cassie." With a wink he added, "See you again soon."

"Could be awhile," I warned him cheerfully. "Like I said, it's a really reliable car."

"Bo-ring," was Todd's last declaration as he let himself out.

Sarah returned to the front counter, minus Her Highness. "Did I mess up?"

"Don't be silly, you couldn't have known. But it so happens that Todd Gillis has a fixation about owning a 'wild' cat." I peered out the front window to make sure he'd continued down the block, toward his garage. "The last thing I need is for him to spread any rumors that we've got one. At least until they catch whoever murdered Rudy."

Over dinner that night, I repeated Todd's story about the "killer cat" to Mark.

"That's partly true," he said. "Some big cat did attack a woman's dog up on Rattlesnake Ridge. It didn't *eat* the dog—your garage guy exaggerated that—but the shih tzu did die afterward from the attack. I actually know the vet who tried to save it."

We sat in a booth at Chad's, an old diner not far from Chadwick's original train station that had been refurbished in fifties style. It had become a favorite of ours for quick, inexpensive dinners. Since the day had been so hot, we both opted for light meals—a large Caesar salad for me, skewered chunks of fish over a curried rice for Mark.

Even on a weeknight like this, the hip diner was pretty full. Still, our booth, upholstered in retro turquoise vinyl, gave Mark and me a fair amount of privacy. That could only be a good thing, I thought, since we were discussing the grisly rumor Todd had passed along to me.

"Wow, that's scary." I speared a forkful of dark romaine leaves lightly coated with Caesar dressing. "Did the vet have any idea what kind of animal it was? Todd heard it was a mountain lion."

Mark gave a polite snort. "I strongly doubt that, around here. Most likely, it was just a large bobcat. That's still strange, though, because they usually aren't vicious and avoid humans. This one attacked the dog in its yard. Even after the owner came out and started screaming and hitting it with a broom, it took a while to give up and run away. Maybe it was rabid, but of course, the only way to know would be to kill it and test for that."

"Is anyone looking for it?"

"Animal control has been, but without much luck. If it had attacked a person, I suppose they might ask the local hunters to help trap it, maybe even offer a reward. From what I hear, some guys are taking it upon themselves, anyway. Guess there's not much for them to hunt in the summer."

I remembered something I'd read. "Isn't killing a bobcat illegal in New Jersey?"

Mark nodded. "If this *is* a bobcat, anybody who shot it would be in trouble with the law. But if it's the 'killer cat' from the news, he'd probably also be a big man to his buddies."

I took a sip of my iced tea before voicing my darkest concern. "Mark, it couldn't have been Ayesha, could it?"

He stopped a square morsel of cod halfway to his mouth. "No . . . what makes you say that?"

"Well, I gather this happened about a week back. Rudy showed up at my place a couple of days ago with a disguised cat that he wanted to keep safe. Maybe he knew she killed the dog and was afraid animal control would catch her and put her to sleep."

Mark seemed to consider this idea, but only for a second. "That cat? She's tame. She had no problem with me examining her, and you said she even was fine with being bathed. I know she's large, but from what I heard, the animal that attacked the dog was even bigger. And it had kind of a ruff, more like a bobcat."

I trusted Mark's judgment, because he had plenty of experience with both domestic and feral animals, in both urban and rural locations. He'd grown up just outside Philadelphia—which accounted for the way he still sometimes shortened his *a*'s and dropped his *r*'s—and he'd gotten his DVM degree at the U of Penn. But afterward he had spent a few years with a larger veterinary hospital in South Jersey, where he'd doctored his share of farm livestock. I knew he'd decided to start his own clinic in Chadwick because it seemed like an underserved area and the small-town atmosphere appealed to him.

If Mark didn't believe Ayesha could be responsible for the violent attacks, I could breathe easier. I couldn't picture her being so aggressive, either. It was just the timing of Rudy's appearance at my shop, so soon after the wildcat's attack, that had worried me.

"Weird coincidence, though," Mark admitted, "that the guy who brought you the cat was found dead. I can see why you'd wonder. . . ."

"If one thing might be connected to the other? Yeah, I do."

I had finished as much as I could of my salad, and I sensed Mark might be about to warn me against keeping Ayesha at my shop. Hoping to avoid this, I excused myself to freshen up in the restroom.

I followed the black-and-white checkered floor past my fellow diners, who sat at the counter on one side and in more of the turquoise booths along the other. Conversations were slightly raised to be heard over the fifties and sixties music playing in the background. One man's harsh voice caught my attention, even before I reached his booth, because of its agitated tone.

"Look, admit it. You got in over your head, so you need my help. We can't keep this situation quiet much longer. If we don't do something soon, the cops are gonna come sniffin' around. Is that what you want?"

The speaker paused briefly, as if listening to a response, while I passed his booth. I recognized him as the same scary, tattooed guy who had been arguing with Todd at the garage.

"Trust me," the guy said into a cell phone. "I know people who can get the job done. Nice an' quick, off the radar." His voice sank lower, and as I walked on toward the ladies' room, I only heard him mutter a last phrase: ". . . damned animals!"

I had no idea whom he might be talking to, or about what, but I carried away the impression that he must be one stressed-out guy. The few snippets I'd heard gave me chills. He was involved in something he didn't want the cops to know about, maybe something criminal. He and someone else wanted to "get the job done . . . nice an' quick, off the radar." And did that last line refer to actual animals, or just vicious people?

In the restroom, I built up a dread of walking past the long-haired man on my way back. Fortunately, by the time I emerged, he already stood by the cashier, facing away from me and paying his bill. Before I had to pass him again, he stalked out of the diner, slapping the door open with his palm and letting it slam behind him.

I began to wonder again what his problem was, then told myself to forget it.

Nothing to do with you.

When I slid back into the booth across from Mark, I saw the waitress had removed our dishes. He greeted me with a warm smile, but a slight darkness under his eyes hinted that he hadn't been sleeping so well. That reminded me.

"You were going to tell me about the problems you've been having at your clinic," I said. "Your staffers have been screwing up?"

He ran a hand through his dark hair, which was shaggier than usual, as if he'd missed a couple of trims. "It's so hard to understand. Either I misjudged all these people when I hired them, or they're all getting burned out and cutting corners."

Mark ticked off the issues that had developed over the past month or so: A normally reliable, middle-aged receptionist frequently coming in late and/or leaving early. A young but formerly meticulous male vet tech slacking off on safety procedures. Another vet tech handling sick and injured animals too roughly. There had even been reports of his partner in the clinic, Dr. Margaret Reed, saying brusque and callous things to some clients who expressed concern about their animals.

"I know it sounds paranoid, but I almost feel like they're all conspiring to undermine me—or the clinic," Mark added. "But that doesn't make much sense. And it's not as if they're flaunting these things in my face. In fact, I wouldn't even know about some of the incidents if they hadn't been pointed out to me."

That piqued my curiosity. "You mean, the staffers are ratting on each other, too?"

He colored a bit. "I wouldn't call it that. . . . The receptionists have just noticed some things. Jennifer Hood, who's newest on the desk, has picked up on a lot of it. At first, she innocently commented to me that some procedure was different from the last clinic where she worked, or that she guessed the hours were flexible for some of the staff. That's when I first realized people were shirking their responsibilities."

I remembered Jennifer from my recent visit. Not only had I never seen her behind the desk before, but I could hardly miss her porcelain complexion, full lips, and long dark hair styled in loose, spiral waves.

"I thanked her for tipping me off," Mark continued, "and after that I made sure to double-check certain things, too. Still, I'm busy with the customers and patients most of the time. It's the staffers who work alongside one another who are in the best position to notice these mistakes."

"People like Jennifer."

He nodded. "She's only twenty-two, but really sharp. And very gung-ho. She'll come in early to get the front desk set up for the day, or stay late if there's some kind of urgent situation. The other receptionists usually want to get home to their families, which is understandable, but it's good to have someone who's willing to go the extra mile."

So, little Jennifer is probably single. I'd never thought of myself as the jealous type, but I started to worry about how "gung-ho" this new girl might be. And how far she might be willing to go to win Mark's admiration and make herself indispensable to him.

For the moment, I kept these suspicions to myself. Would I even be having them, I wondered, if Jennifer weren't beautiful?

We moved on to coffee and discussed the design for my Chadwick Day booth. Mark's clinic had taken part during its first few years in town, but recently, no one there could spare the time to staff a table.

"I can display a stack of your brochures," I offered.

"Would you? Then I won't feel so guilty about not taking part at all."

"What're friends for?" I teased.

"Well, I hope we're a little more than that." Taking advantage of the turquoise booth's extra privacy, he reached across the table to cover my hand with his.

Of course, at that very minute, his cell phone had to ring. With a wry frown, he answered the call.

"Un-huh . . . Mr. Stevens's dog, the Yorkie? Yeah, I operated on him this afternoon. There's a problem with his stitches?" Mark listened for a beat, then blew out a breath in frustration. "No, no, I'll have to come back in and fix it. Who checked him before you came on?"

From Mark's words and tone, I knew even before he hung up that our date would be cut short.

"Sorry, Cass, but we've got a minor crisis. A Yorkie that's recovering from surgery got out of his cone collar somehow and ripped out his stitches. I've gotta go back and redo them." He pulled out his wallet and reached for the check.

I intercepted it first. "Let me pick up the check this time."

"You sure?"

"Of course. The first time we went out, you paid and told me, 'You can get the next one.' That was three months ago, so it's about time I took my turn."

Mark accepted that explanation with a smile and a nod.

A few minutes later, we were in his cobalt blue RAV4, headed down the main drag of town, Center Street. It was only a short hop to my place, after which he could continue on to his clinic.

I made it sound offhanded when I asked, "Who called you about the emergency, Jennifer?"

"Huh? Oh, no, I'm sure she's long gone by now. It was Sam, the tech who's on night observation."

We rode in silence for a minute while I glanced at the CDs stockpiled on his console. Mainstream rock and jazz. I knew Mark had taken some lessons in jazz guitar as a hobby, and he'd played for me once. He wasn't half bad.

"Keeping up with your guitar these days?" I asked.

Not the upbeat change of subject that I'd intended, because he frowned. "Nah, I've really let that slide. Just another fun thing that I don't seem to have time for anymore."

Mark pulled up in front of my shop, not even turning off the engine. I knew he was in a hurry to deal with the dog that had pulled out its stitches. Still, before I could slide out of the car, he planted a serious kiss on my lips. "We'll do something Saturday, okay?"

"Ironclad?"

"Double-triple ironclad."

As he pulled away, I wondered if our relationship would always be like this. As I'd told Mom, it was almost as bad as being married to a "human" doctor.

Maybe I would be better off with a garage mechanic. Though, God help me, not Todd Gillis!

Chapter 5

At home that evening, I opened my laptop to find that Keith Garrett, Dawn's significant other, had already sent me a few cute sketches of long-haired cats for my table runner.

His note asked, *How are these? I tried to give them some Jersey attitude.*

I laughed, because he'd definitely done that, and it was just the touch the online illustrations had been missing. They were all fluffy and sassy, but after a few minutes, I picked one Persian that looked particularly well-groomed and vain. I downloaded the image and copied it into a file beneath the name of my shop. The fancy purple font set it off perfectly.

You work fast! I e-mailed back to Keith. *They're all great, but No. 3 is purrrfect! Send me your invoice, and I'll drop off a check with Dawn tomorrow.*

About five minutes later, his very reasonable bill

arrived, accompanied by the message, *Glad to be of service, Cassie. All my clients should make up their minds as fast as you.*

Keith probably would have done the illustration as a favor, but I knew he struggled to make ends meet as a freelancer. I printed out the invoice, shut off my computer, and gave all my own cats a bit more food for the night. After I got into bed and turned out the light, though, I realized that I heard yowling. It sounded faint and far-off, but only because it was traveling through the solid walls and second floor of my turn-of-the-century shop.

Ayesha—damn. I hope she doesn't keep the other boarders up all night.

Then I wondered why that should concern me. Did they have jobs to go to?

They're cats. So, they'll sleep during the day.

The next morning, when Sarah and I fed all the boarders and cleaned out their cages, I found that in addition to using her litter box, Ayesha had started "spraying" the upper wall of her condo. This was unusual for a female, but the fact that she wasn't spayed and was a wild hybrid probably explained it. Along with the fact that she hated being so closely confined and was ready to jump out of her artificially colored hide.

Sarah and I gave her another bath that morning with a strong shampoo, and more of the brown faded from her coat. Now we could clearly see the rosette pattern all over. I suspected, though, that after one or two more washes, her coveted golden background hue might finally resurface. I'd been reading up on Bengals and now knew what to look for.

With Chadwick Day a little more than a week off, I knew I should get the design for my table runner to the printer, so I set off with my laptop under my arm. Alpha Printing was a good six-block hike, slightly uphill, but I could pass Dawn's on the way back and drop off the check for Keith.

As far as I knew, Dawn and Keith had been dating exclusively for about three years, but had never moved in together, much less discussed marriage. She once joked to me that her very conservative Jewish mother couldn't accept the idea of Dawn being involved with an agnostic Irishman. Still, I doubted that would stop someone as strong-minded as Dawn from following her heart. Most likely, she and Keith were just free spirits, perfectly comfortable with a looser arrangement.

One of the things I loved about downtown Chadwick was my ability to get plenty of exercise running errands, instead of making time to go to a boring gym. At the print shop, I showed my concept for the table runner to the owner, Dave Gross—a rotund guy with a comb-over that fooled no one and a good-natured grin. He also thought Keith's design was clever and promised he could have the runner done for me "at least by Friday," meaning the day before the street fair. Cutting it close, but what could I expect after I'd put off the project until the last minute? I thanked him and moved on to Dawn's.

When I handed her the check for Keith, she laughed. "He's going to faint. None of his clients ever pay him this promptly! He did a corporate ad campaign last spring, for big bucks. They gave him a small down payment, but he's still waiting for the rest."

"Must be tough, being a freelancer. At least if my clients don't pay, I can hold their pets for ransom." I thought of Ayesha, and a Persian I'd boarded recently named Harpo. "Of course, when the owners go and die on me, then I'm stuck with their cats."

Tigger wandered up to us, as if summoned by the word *cat.* Dawn scooped him into her arms and sat on a low bench near the oak display counter, her eggplant-colored boho skirt pooling around her ankles. "So that hit-and-run victim really was your guy? What the heck is up with that?"

"Darned if I know." I gave her the rundown on what I'd been able to deduce so far, with the help of Bonelli and Mark. "Todd, from the garage, told me about some big cat killing a woman's dog up on Rattlesnake Ridge. Mark said that was actually true, and for a while I thought it might have been Ayesha—that Rudy was trying to hide her from animal control. But Mark knows a little more of the story and said that was probably a bobcat, maybe rabid. They haven't caught it yet, though."

Dawn's amber-brown eyes widened. "Really? Gee, Rick and Teri's farm is up by Rattlesnake Ridge."

I snubbed my nose. "Sounds like a delightful area."

"It's beautiful, in spite of the name. Wild, though. Dense woods, caves leading to some old iron mines. Keith and I have hiked up there a couple of times . . . but you do have to watch out for rattlesnakes. I wonder if Teri and Rick had any trouble with the bobcat."

"Just don't offer to go there to pick up any produce," I advised, with an edgy laugh. "Make them keep bringing it to you!"

"On that subject . . ." Dawn put her kitten down and led me over to her tiered display of fresh fruits and vegetables. "I see you've got your laptop along today, but can you take at least some of this stuff home with you?"

"Oh, I think so. I've built up my muscles, wrestling with all those cats." I picked out a nice head of escarole and a medium-sized zucchini. Maybe I'd save some for Mark—he'd probably put them to better use than I could. As I also plucked a couple of prime Jersey tomatoes from the display, I uncovered a skinny green leaf with serrated edges. "Uh, Dawn, I'm not much of a gardener, but . . . is this a tomato leaf?"

She peeked over my shoulder and chuckled. "Hmm . . . maybe not."

"What do you think it's doing, mixed in with the produce?"

My friend still grinned. "Actually, there's a logical explanation. Some people do grow tomatoes and pot together. The plants need the same conditions, and from a distance it can be hard to tell them apart."

"So they're less likely to get busted," I realized. "And you know this because?"

"C'mon, Cassie. I run a health food store. Some of my best customers, and friends, are neo-hippies."

"Looks like one of your suppliers may be, too." I turned the leaf in my fingers, examining it. "Sloppy of them, to let the evidence get mixed in with their delivery."

Dawn lost her smile and snatched the leaf from me. "What are you, a narc? I think you've been spending too much time down at the police station with your detective friend. Jeez, it's not that big a deal. Weed is even legal in New Jersey now, for treating some medical conditions."

"Teri and Rick didn't look sick to me," I pointed out.

"Don't you dare tell Bonelli and get them busted. They have the best produce around!" She popped open a clamshell container of raspberries. "Here, taste one of these."

I did, and had to admit it beat the supermarket kind by a mile. Bright pinky-red, juicy, and sweet, with just a hint of tartness.

"Well?" Dawn prompted me.

I considered that she *was* giving me all this produce for free, even throwing in the raspberries. Though that might have qualified as a bribe, I relented. "Okay. I guess whatever happens on Rattlesnake Ridge can stay on Rattlesnake Ridge."

By the end of the week, Ayesha started settling in at the shop, though occasionally her vocalizations still rattled some of our customers, who could hear her all the way out by the sales counter. I went to a big-box pet store on the highway and bought her a more secure mesh harness, designed for a small dog, and a real leash we could use to walk her. My Ayesha-related expenses kept mounting, but I clung to the faint hope that someday her real owner would reimburse me.

Now, on a nice day, Sarah would take Ayesha for a short spin around the parking lot in back. The Bengal generally behaved, though she did show an intense attraction to the neighborhood birds and sometimes resisted coming back inside.

Saturday morning, while Sarah was exercising Ayesha in the playroom, a new customer came in. He brought two non-pedigreed and unrelated cats that he needed to board while his family relocated from Newark, Delaware. He worked for a pharmaceutical company with its headquarters not far from Chadwick, and enthused about how convenient the commute would be and what a nice house they'd been able to get for their money in our town. I hoped he'd spread the word that Chadwick was a happening place, though I wouldn't want it to boom too much and lose its nostalgic charm.

Luckily, he had called ahead, so I did have a condo free, but only one. I settled his two cats together and hoped that, with three levels, they wouldn't object to sharing the space.

I was on my way back to the front counter when Sarah called out from the playroom, "Cassie, come quick!" Afraid the high-strung Bengal might have hurt herself, I hustled back there.

But Sarah was laughing. She held one of the colorful fishing poles with a stuffed mouse at the end of the string. Ayesha gripped the toy rodent in her mouth and pulled the string taut, crouching low and growling like a puppy.

"She plays tug-of-war!" Sarah declared. "Did you ever see a cat do that?"

"Can't say as I have." I worried for Sarah's safety when she approached Ayesha, but she only had to stroke the spotted head and the cat let her take the toy away. "She's a character, all right!"

Later that afternoon, Detective Bonelli called to say she had not been able to find a Rudy Pierson who fit the age and description of the dead man, and suspected it was an alias.

"We got a call from the Days Inn out on the highway about a guest who disappeared, leaving his bill unpaid," she said. "The desk clerk saw Pierson's photo on the news and ID'd him as their missing guest. We sent an officer over to check the room. It had a duffle with a few clothes, a bag of dry cat food, a litter pan in the corner, and some black stains left in the bathtub."

"That must be where he dyed the cat," I jumped in. Since bathing Ayesha, I had done a little research on nontoxic dyes for pets. According to the online reviews, they didn't always produce the color you expected. Maybe Rudy had hoped to dye her black and settled for a dark brown?

Bonelli went on. "There was also some kind of map drawn on a piece of paper, with landmarks. Looks as if it might be a trail through woods, but we can't tell where it is. No guarantee it was even a location in New Jersey."

"So whether or not there really was a house fire somewhere, Rudy must have holed up at the motel long enough to decide what to do with the cat," I guessed. "Maybe he was headed for this place in the woods when he got hit by the car."

"That could be. Doesn't tell us, though, whether or not the cat is stolen."

I sat down on a low, blue-carpeted cave in the playroom to think this over. "What if we go with the possibility that she is? Mark seems pretty sure that she's a Bengal, and I agree. We could contact Bengal breeders in both states and ask if they've had any thefts."

"We?" Bonelli asked, her tone wry.

"I'd be happy to help. I can start out just by searching under 'Bengal cat lost, northeast US.' But I also subscribe to a couple of cat magazines that run ads by breeders. The top ones probably will have Web sites, too."

"Are you going to take a picture of the cat you've got and ask them to identify her? Because any breeder could easily lie and say she was stolen from them. If she's worth that much money . . ."

"You're right, of course. And even a photo wouldn't give them a true idea of her appearance right now. Her spots are still kind of muted by the dye."

The telephone fell silent for a beat while we both considered our strategy.

"If it was a dog," said Bonelli, who was more of a canine enthusiast, "you could ask them what tricks they've taught her or what commands she'll obey."

I smiled. Few cats obey any commands, and Ayesha was more strong-willed than most. But . . . "Great idea! She's been trained to walk on a leash. And Sarah just found out today that she plays tug-of-war."

"The cat?"

"Yep. Those are things only her real owner would be likely to know."

I heard fresh enthusiasm in the detective's voice. "Okay, let's try that approach. Make a list of any breeders that you can find, and we'll figure out how we're going to handle this—whether to place an ad or reach out to them individually."

"I'll get right on it, chief!"

That was something of a fib. First, Sarah and I had to return a Burmese boarder to Ruth Lowenstein, an elegant brunette Realtor with a local firm. While she settled her bill, we chatted about The Reserve, a new condo development just outside of town that was selling out quickly. As I watched Ruth leave with her lovely, quiet pet, I told myself he'd probably sleep a lot better now, without Ayesha singing rock opera all night long.

The first break I got, I searched Bengal catteries on my cell phone. I found only a few each in New Jersey and Pennsylvania, but those were licensed breeders with Web sites. Probably, there were small, unlicensed places that might still run ads in cat magazines and online.

Lord, they could even be advertising on sites like Craigslist! How in the world are we going to reach out to everyone who might have lost a female Bengal cat?

I made a list of all the legitimate-looking breeders with their contact information and checked the classified sections of some recent magazines for more. For the heck of it, I included places in New York State, too. I ended up with roughly a dozen breeders who offered Bengals, either exclusively or along with one or two other types.

"Cassie, you about ready to close up?" Sarah asked me.

Surprised, I checked the time on my phone. Ten of five already! "Oops, you're right. Let's feed 'em all and then you can get going."

Just shows how involved I'd gotten in this mystery, that I'd let the time get away from me. Even though it was Saturday night, and I actually had a date with Mark—at his apartment! Time to get upstairs, shower, and pretty myself up.

I'd been half expecting a last-minute cancellation due to another emergency at the clinic. But so far, my luck was holding.

Chapter 6

Mark lived in a 1980s condo complex in the next town over. I'd visited only once so far, because working in Chadwick, he found it easier to come to my place. Also, I had all of the cats to tend to, while he did not have any pets, so far.

His building, one of several, made a stab at traditional architecture, combining pale gray vinyl siding with vertical shafts of fieldstone. Mark had purchased his second-floor unit about two and a half years ago, when he'd set up his practice in Chadwick. It came with no garage, but two parking spaces, so I pulled in next to his blue RAV4. I had to speak through an intercom for him to buzz me up. Then I climbed a flight of stairs with a small landing halfway, toting a bag of salad greens from Nature's Way and my bottle of Chianti.

He was cooking dinner tonight, he'd said, to make up for our lack of time together lately. More often, we'd either gone out, picked up Chinese, or ordered a pizza. I'd made dinner for us once, but it wasn't fancy—I'd broiled a couple of salmon filets, nuked a packaged rice mix, and heated up some frozen vegetables. I expected about the same from Mark tonight, thought maybe with more of an Italian flavor.

Now I stood outside the teal green lacquered door of his unit, and the aroma from within raised my expectations.

He opened the door wearing jeans and a dark red T-shirt that I always liked on him. At the clinic Mark usually wore scrubs, which came in either dusty blue or dusty green. It was often a pleasant shock to see him in his own clothes, especially the shirts—usually in deep, rich colors that played up his olive skin, nearly black hair, and sapphire-blue eyes.

He greeted me with a warm kiss that immediately improved my state of mind.

"As per your recommendation." I handed over the wine. "And the greens are courtesy of Dawn."

"Terrific," Mark said, taking the bag from me. "I'll add them to the mix."

Sniffing the air, I wandered into his small but efficient kitchen, which was still outfitted with the original Reagan-era oak cabinets. "If that dinner tastes as good as it smells, you may get stuck with all the cooking from now on."

He shrugged modestly. "It's a fairly easy recipe. Linguini with chicken, spinach, and Parmesan. Only the second time I've tried it, but so far, so good."

He lifted the lid of a large pan to check on some bite-sized pieces of chicken that were browning.

On the next burner, linguine and spinach simmered together in a pot. I felt like the ultimate liberated woman, having a man cook dinner for me.

"All that can sit for a minute while we have some wine," he said.

I followed him into the living room, which also suited my comfort level. Mark had left the walls a standard off-white, but otherwise had furnished the space nicely. A navy blue sofa formed a right angle with a modern, chamois-colored recliner on a blue and brown rug with a modern tribal design. A cubist-style print of a jazz combo hung over the sofa. The side and coffee tables and the TV cabinet were all dark-stained wood. Everything looked easy to care for and in contemporary good taste.

Wineglass in hand, I took a seat on the sofa and nudged aside a couple of the throw pillows—in coordinating patterns of tan, navy, and red. They reminded me that Mark had decorated this place with help from his last girlfriend, a travel photographer named Diane. They hadn't quite been living together, but I knew she'd spent a lot of time here. I suspected that a small photo on a side table, showing Mark and three friends by a waterfall in some exotic setting, also represented Diane's work. They'd broken up because she'd cheated on him, but I could never be sure how much of a torch he still carried for her. I knew he'd started dating me on the rebound.

As Mark sat beside me and slipped his arm around my shoulders, I observed, "Ah, just the two of us! Lately, that doesn't happen very often."

"I know. We're usually at the clinic or your shop or a restaurant . . . someplace out in public."

"Why do you think that is? Are we still taking it slow?"

He sipped his wine before answering. "Fair question. If we are, I guess it wouldn't be surprising. We've both just come out of some intense situations, with exes who treated us pretty badly. I guess it takes time to get past stuff like that."

I supposed so, too. It had taken some time for me even to tell Mark about my scary experiences with my last boyfriend. Andy had been one of the reasons I'd moved to semirural Chadwick in the first place, and he'd kept trying to lure me back—albeit in a creepy way—for months afterward. Mark, closing in on thirty, had been ready to propose to Diane when she'd told him she wanted to see other guys; in fact, she already had started doing so.

Leaning against him now, I searched for a lighter topic. "Well, at least it's just the two of us until you make up your mind about a pet. Any progress along that line?"

"Haven't had much time to think about it lately," he admitted. "Condo rules say I can have a cat that stays indoors or a small dog that's kept on a leash."

A bulb lit up in my head. "How about a cat that walks on a leash? Ayesha's trained to do that."

"Whoa! I'm not sure I want to bring that Bengal into a one-bedroom condo."

I laughed. "You probably don't. Anyway, she'd get you evicted. She howls like a banshee, she marks outside the box, and she'd probably climb and destroy your window blinds. Seriously, if we don't find her real owner, I'm not sure who'll take her."

"A breeder." Mark sounded confident. "They're

used to that kind of stuff, and she looks like a very high-class animal."

"Speaking of high-class . . ." I made a show of sniffing the air. "That gourmet meal of yours smells as if it's reached perfection."

He smiled and stood up. "Yeah, I'm hungry, too. Shall we bring our wine to the table and try the salad?"

I matched the formality of his invitation. "But of course!"

In a large, Tuscan-patterned bowl, Mark tossed all of the greens together with a vinaigrette dressing, then meted out our portions on salad plates. The escarole and red leaf lettuce that I contributed were as fresh and flavorful as all of the other produce Dawn had provided to me that week. While we ate, I told Mark a little more about the organic farm that she was trying out as a new supplier, omitting any mention of the renegade leaf I'd found among the tomatoes.

Finally, we tucked into the chicken, linguini, and wilted spinach, which Mark had topped with minced garlic, grated Parmesan cheese, salt and pepper, and a little olive oil. He wielded all of those ingredients like a pro, and predictably, the result was delicious.

"Did you get this recipe from your mom?" I asked Mark as we ate.

"Ha, and I thought you were a feminist! So happens, my dad is an excellent cook. He put himself through medical school by working part-time at a restaurant."

So far in our relationship, Mark hadn't talked very much about his family. His parents had divorced a few years back, and his mother still lived outside of Philadelphia, while his orthopedic surgeon father now was on staff at a hospital in San Francisco. I knew Mark also had a sister with an advertising firm in Manhattan and a brother who had just graduated from U of Penn and was job-hunting. As yet, I'd never met any of them, but since they were so widely separated from each other, I didn't give too much weight to that.

This was the first I'd heard, though, about his father's culinary experience. "No kidding! That's so lucky, because . . . well, you've had my cooking."

Mark smiled kindly. "It's not so bad. Just a little basic."

As I'd feared, the meal set a new standard to which I might have to aspire. Mark confided that the secret was using fresh linguine, which he'd found at a reasonable price at his local Italian deli.

We went on to discuss light stuff, such as the upcoming Chadwick Day celebration and my attempts to prepare for it.

"Our clinic had a table out in the park the first couple of years," he told me. "It definitely helped make people aware of us and the services we offer. Now we're so busy that I don't really think we need the promotion. And the way things have been going, I don't really like to take my eye off the ball for that long."

I sensed we were getting down to the main topic of the evening—why he didn't have more time for me these days—and tried to draw him out. "You told me a little about the problems with your staff, but what exactly is going on?"

"Don't I wish I knew! First, I found out that

Elena, who's been our office manager since we opened, has been sneaking in maybe fifteen minutes late some days and leaving early on other days. When I questioned her, she denied it, and the one time I saw her head out early, she claimed she was just going to get something from her car."

"Hmm. And you only saw her do that once?"

"Yes, but Jennifer had been noticing it for a while and even asked me if Elena worked part-time. Another day, Jen was putting away some files and saw one of our vet techs handling a cat very roughly, even though it had a broken leg. And she said last week, when Dr. Reed told a client his dog had been diagnosed with lymphoma, she acted very cold and brusque about it, even though the man seemed on the verge of tears."

I laid my fork cross my empty plate, patted my lips with a napkin, then spoke in a neutral tone. "Sounds like a troubling pattern, all right."

"Also, you remember the situation with that terrier the other night, when I had to cut our date short? I'd put one of those Elizabethan collars on him—those cones that keep an animal from licking or biting himself. I know I fastened it securely, but somehow he got out of it. By the time I got back to the clinic, he'd ripped half of the stitches out of his side, so I had to sedate him, disinfect the area, and stitch him up again."

I winced. "That's pretty serious."

"The last person to look in on him was a tech named Jim Brunner, who's always been on top of things before. When I questioned him, he swore he even opened the cage to check the collar." Mark took another swallow of his wine before continuing. "I told Jim he must've accidentally loosened it, and to be more careful from now on. He said he always was careful, and I should take his word for it. He sounded so annoyed that I backed off, because I thought he might quit on me. But damn, that Yorkie didn't open the collar by himself!"

I commiserated as best I could. "Well, I guess no matter how careful you are, sometimes things just go wrong."

"I've always thought I had the best team in the world! It wouldn't be a shock if one or two of them lost focus or started to burn out, but I can't believe so many are falling down on the job." Mark noticed I was done with my pasta, stood up, and took our plates to the kitchen. "Got room for dessert? I bought cannoli."

"I'll make room," I assured him. "You really went with the whole Italian theme tonight, huh?"

He laughed. "Thought it might be fun."

As he passed my chair on the way to the kitchen, I grabbed him playfully around the waist. "Maybe for Christmas, I'll buy you an apron. A tailored, manly one, of course."

Struggling to balance the empty dishes, he looked down at me with a mock frown. "Sounds like I'd better put the coffee on."

I released him with a giggle, something I don't utter very often. "Are you implying I've had too much wine?"

Truly, I didn't have much of a capacity for booze. *I probably should take it easy if I'm going to drive home tonight. Or am I? It's Saturday, and neither of us has to work tomorrow. . . .* Calculating vixen that I was, I'd made sure to leave extra dry food and water for all the cats.

We took time to enjoy our dessert, and Mark waited until we were sipping our coffees to ask, "So, Cassie. You were a psychology major in college, and you read all those murder mysteries. What do you think is going on?"

"With the folks in your office?" I proceeded with caution. "If I were you, I'd look for the common link among all these incidents."

"There are a few, I guess. These people all have worked for me for at least a year, and all their mistakes seem to come from inattention, carelessness, or just a bad attitude."

"There's one more. Correct me if I'm wrong, but you found out about all of these mistakes from Jennifer?"

"Yeah, but . . . that's just because she's new and keeps her eyes open. She's more likely to notice anything not being done like she was taught to do it. Probably, also, she isn't as inclined to give somebody a pass because he's a friend or has worked there a long time."

"You said Elena and Jim both denied doing anything wrong. Did you confront any of the others, and did they admit to their mistakes?"

Mark wrinkled his brow. "I didn't want to question Dr. Reed—she's my senior and has more experience than I do. Sam, the tech who made an error on a prescription, said he didn't remember doing it but admitted he might have been distracted. The guy Jennifer saw roughing up the cat insisted he'd never do a thing like that. He demanded to know who accused him, but of course, I wouldn't tell him."

"So you really have no proof. You're just taking Jennifer's word for all of it."

"But why would she lie? It's not even as if it's just one person that she doesn't like and wants to get into trouble. If she's making all these stories up, she'd have to be psycho, and I can't believe that."

Even very smart guys, like Mark, could be naïve about women, I thought. "Not necessarily. She could have a very clear goal: to get your attention."

"My attention?" he echoed, in a skeptical voice.

"You said she comes in earlier than the others and stays later. That would give her time to alter a prescription or tamper with other things. And by reporting negative stories about the rest of the staff, she sets herself up as the only one you can really trust."

To my relief, Mark seemed to consider this. "But even if that were true, why would she do that? Does she think she'll get a promotion, more money, or—"

"Maybe she thinks she'll get *you*. In case I haven't mentioned it lately, you're pretty hot."

He actually blushed. "Ah, c'mon. She's got to be aware that I'm dating you. We've been low-key about it, but everybody at the clinic knows."

"Don't you see? That's why she isn't coming right out and putting the moves on you. She may not be psycho, but she could be . . . devious."

Mark didn't like hearing this, I could tell. Not that he wasn't flattered, but I was chipping away at his image of sweet, wholesome Jennifer, who only wanted to help him maintain high standards at the clinic. “No, I’m sure you’re wrong. She’s not like that.”

“Then just ask yourself one thing. Would you find my theory more credible if she were middle-aged and homely, instead of twenty-two and gorgeous?”

He flung a hand into the air. “Oh, now we’re getting to the bottom of this. You’re just upset because she happens to be attractive. I never would have expected this of you, Cassie! To accuse the poor girl of—”

Muffled music interrupted our argument—the sauntering guitar intro of “Stray Cat Strut.” It drifted from a coat stand by the front door, where I’d hung my purse. I would have ignored it, but Mark waved me away, as if he welcomed the break. “Go on, answer it.”

I crossed to the stand, pulled out the phone, and checked the caller ID. Home’n’Safe, the security firm that had sold me the alarm system for my shop.

What the heck?

No reason why they’d call me at almost nine o’clock at night. Unless . . .

Chapter 7

"You're receiving this call because a breach has been detected in your system and the alarm triggered," a well-modulated female voice informed me. "We're checking to see if you are on the premises and might have set it off by mistake."

"No, I'm at a friend's," I told her, heart thudding high in my throat. "There shouldn't be anyone in the shop or the house."

"Then we'll report it to your local police department," the woman said. "The motion detectors haven't registered any movement inside the building, so if it was an intruder, the alarm may have scared him away. You'll want to wait until the police investigate, though, before you go inside."

"Yes, I certainly will. Thank you."

I hung up to see Mark listening from the dining room doorway, one eyebrow raised in a question. I relayed the news to him.

"Not again?" he moaned. "Didn't you go through

enough of that crap this spring? I thought the new alarm was supposed to solve the problem."

"It might have—they don't think anyone got in. I've got better locks now, and that alarm is ear-splitting. The cats are probably going crazy, though. Not to mention Mrs. Kryznansky, next door." My elderly neighbor had put up with enough disturbances last spring, I thought; her patience had to run out sometime. Automatically, I hooked the purse strap over my shoulder.

Mark took notice with a disappointed frown. "Yeah, I guess you've gotta go check it out. I'll come with you."

I hesitated, maybe because we'd just been arguing. "You don't have to. The police will get there before I do. There shouldn't be any danger."

He grabbed his car keys from a wall hook near the front door. "C'mon. You take your car, I'll follow."

"We've both been hitting the Chianti," I pointed out, as we took the stairs down one flight.

"We'll drive slowly. Let the cops check the place out before we show up."

At least, separate cars meant we had to postpone our argument over Jennifer for the time being. We arrived at my place in tandem and parked at the curb, because there was a Chadwick PD patrol car in my rear parking lot, its lights rotating. The shop alarm had been shut off, though, which told me the cops already had been inside.

In the lot we met up with Officer Bassey, whom I'd gotten to know during my adventures that spring. I introduced him to Mark.

"What's happening?" I asked.

"We found signs of tampering around one of the windows. Pry marks—maybe from a screwdriver." Bassey, broad-shouldered, deep-voiced, and dark-skinned, pointed to a window that opened onto the boarder's area. "The vibration must have been enough to set off your sensor."

At that point, Dawn burst out the back door, looking frazzled. Her long, sage-green, gauzy garment could have been a bath-robe, but passed muster for bohemian street wear. I'd forgotten that, under directions from the security company, I'd left an emergency key with her in case I was away when the police needed to enter. A younger, blond cop, whom I recognized as Officer Steve Jacoby, came out the door a few steps behind her.

"Everything looks okay inside," Dawn assured me. "All the cats are fine, though I'm sure they're glad I turned that alarm off."

Bassey told me, "You should have a look around yourself, Ms. McGlone, to make sure nothing's been disturbed."

Inside, I found Ayesha leading a chorus of caterwauls, like a rock diva and her backup singers. I gave them all an extra meal, which helped quiet everybody down.

Mark, meanwhile, checked every corner of the shop. "Too bad you don't have security cameras with video. They might give you an idea of who tried to break in."

"Those cost a lot," I told him. "This alarm system was pricey enough, but at least it did the job—it chased the guy away."

"This time. What if he rethinks his approach and tries again?"

Maybe I was already developing a hangover, or maybe I was tired from my six-day workweek. But just then, I didn't need Mark coming up with dire scenarios. "Why are you purposely trying to scare me?"

"Wouldn't think I needed to try, after what happened a few months ago." He reconsidered and gave me a one-arm hug. "I'm sorry, Cassie, I don't mean to be so negative. But think about it—why would someone try to break in here? Compared to some of the other stores in town, you don't sell expensive things or keep a lot of cash around. Unlike my clinic, you don't even have drugs on the premises."

I stared at him. "So, what are you saying?"

"The burglar tried to break into your boarding area. The only thing you have in your shop that might be valuable enough for someone to steal is . . ." He jerked his head toward the hallway, where Ayesha let out another plaintive trill, right on schedule.

"Well, great. What am I supposed to do about that? Turn her over to a public shelter, where she'll be shut up in a small cage and go nuts? If she acts up there, the workers might not know how to handle her. And if no one ever claimed her . . ."

I paused when I heard a saxophone faintly playing melodic jazz. Mark and I had been dating long enough for me to know that "Take Five," by Dave Brubeck, was his ring tone for personal calls, as opposed to the generic tone he used for work contacts.

He took a step away from me and frowned. "Who can that be, at this hour?"

As he pulled out the phone and glanced at the screen, I smirked. "Probably Jennifer. Maybe she's dug up some new dirt on somebody and can't wait to tell you."

Okay, it was a cheap shot, but I didn't think it would make him as mad as it did.

Just as Dawn walked in from the back, Mark jammed his phone back into his jeans pocket and glowered at me.

"Y'know what? You got the cops here to protect you, and Dawn . . . you seem to be in good hands. So I'll just head back to my place, Cassie. We'll talk tomorrow."

"Mark, I'm sorry. . . ."

But he was already out the front door. A second later, I heard the RAV4 pull away.

"What was all that about?" Dawn asked.

I groaned. "Too much stress, I think. And too much Chianti."

So that night, instead of me staying over at Mark's place, Dawn spent the night at my place. I called him to apologize for my smart remark, which obviously had touched a nerve, but he didn't pick up or call back. I figured he needed time to cool off, and in a way, I did, too.

"Why is he so touchy about this Jennifer, anyway?" I asked Dawn, as we lounged around sipping her panacea for frayed nerves, chamomile tea. (I'd already learned that Chianti wasn't the answer.) "Maybe he does have some interest in her, after all."

"Not necessarily. But you *were* sort of questioning his judgment, weren't you? He believes she's loyal and trustworthy, and you implied that she's a sneak who's tattling on other people to impress him." With my calico Matisse dozing in her lap, my friend took a sip of her brew. "Not that I think you're wrong."

"Aha, so you see it, too? I mean, what newbie just a few months on the job takes it upon herself to call the boss's attention to the mistakes of people who've been there a long time? I would see *that* as questioning his judgment."

"If she worked in some high-powered environment, I'd think she was super ambitious and angling for a promotion," Dawn reasoned. "But in a clinic—without a veterinary license—how far can she hope to go?"

I wondered. "Possibly the office manager's job, but I doubt that pays very much more than Jennifer's. And you'd think she could at least work a year and pay her dues before going after that."

"So she's either a pain-in-the-butt Goody Two-Shoes by nature, or . . ."

"Or she's trying to impress Mark in particular, right?" I reached one arm along the back of the sofa to stroke Cole's satiny black head. "I just wish I could make him see it without coming off as the big, bad witch who's picking on poor, innocent Jennifer. That's just playing into her hands."

"Mark's a bright guy. His ego may be a little bruised right now, but if Jennifer really is up to no good, he'll catch on sooner or later. You planted the suspicion—now let him find out for himself."

"He's probably thinking real well of me right now while he's alone cleaning up after that nice dinner he made for us." I finished my tea and gazed for a minute at the leaves in the bottom of the ceramic mug, wishing I could gain some insight from them. "Dawn, do you think I'm subconsciously pushing him away? For just a minute downstairs, when he lost his temper, I felt afraid he was going to hit me. Of course, he never even came close to that—he walked away instead. But after what I went through with Andy . . . do you think I'm scared to get involved again?"

She mulled this. "If you're a little gun-shy, who could blame you? On the other hand, Mark's the one who's been working such long hours that he hasn't been free to see you lately. And on the subject of Jennifer, it sounds like he asked your opinion and then got angry when you gave it. Maybe you're both afraid to really commit."

I sighed. Even though I'd majored in psychology in college, all this analysis was making my head hurt. Or maybe it was the wine ebbing from my system. "I can't worry about it anymore right now. I need a good night's sleep, and tomorrow I need to figure out if someone tried to break in here to steal Ayesha."

"How do you plan to do that?"

"Contact Bengal breeders, I guess, and ask if they lost a cat. There's only a handful of reputable, licensed ones in the New Jersey–New York–Pennsylvania area. That might not help if she was taken from some unlicensed, backyard breeder, but I have to try."

Mango, to my left, stretched out a front leg and yawned extravagantly. Dawn and I both laughed.

"You're right," she told the cat. "Enough yammering. Time to hit the hay."

I went to get Dawn a bed pillow and a throw blanket. When I came back to the living room she was studying one of my framed artworks, from school, that hung over the sofa. Self-consciously surrealistic, it depicted a submerged room with a woman and a few pieces of formal furniture floating suspended, though the draperies still hung straight and the window showed a sunny sky beyond.

"I've always liked this one," Dawn said. "Is it computer-generated?"

"Yeah, back when the programs were a little more primitive." I set down the pillow and shooed Mango off the sofa.

"Y'know, that new gallery downtown, Eye of the Beholder, has got a surrealism show on right now. I stopped in for a few minutes the other day, and the stuff is pretty wild. You should check it out."

"No kidding? That's kind of daring for Chadwick. Maybe I will drop by."

Finally, Dawn sank, clearly exhausted, onto the sofa. We speculated over which of my cats would snuggle up with her, since I didn't allow them in my bedroom while I slept.

"At least neither of us has to be up early tomorrow," Dawn said.

"We may not *have* to," I warned her, "but Ayesha could have other ideas. Don't be surprised if you hear the call of the wild from downstairs around sunrise. She makes a very effective alarm clock."

* * *

At least we had no more break-in attempts during the night, and even Her Highness didn't disturb us until nearly seven. Dawn had seen the Bengal only briefly, behind the mesh door of her condo, the evening before. After breakfast, I brought Ayesha out and played with her awhile, for my friend's entertainment.

"She's lively, all right," Dawn agreed. "I can see why you don't want her cooped up at a shelter."

"It'd be a disaster," I said. "Even here, she's ripped the screen on her condo door in a few places by climbing on it. I'll have to call Nick to stop by and fix it."

My friend wrinkled her long, elegant nose. "Her apartment is smelling a little riper than the others, too."

"Tell me about it. When she gets frustrated, she sometimes sprays outside her litter box. Imagine how that would go over with the staff at a busy shelter. Combined with her appetite for destruction, they could see her as a major problem. No one would want to adopt her, and it wouldn't end well."

"Just as long as she doesn't turn into a major problem for *you*," Dawn cautioned. I knew she was referring to more than just a damaged or smelly cat condo.

Could the previous night's break-in attempt mean that someone was still out to steal the Bengal?

After Dawn left, I released another of our boarders, a beautiful fawn-colored Abyssinian named Latte, into the playroom. Though it was Sunday, and Sarah was off, the cats still needed to be fed, watered, and exercised. While sleek Latte explored the high shelves, I made some handwritten notes on what to do for Chadwick Day.

Maybe I'd also have the printer make me a sign, ASK THE CAT LADY, and answer people's feline-related questions. Sarah and I had discussed doing a live grooming demonstration for just an hour or two. She'd volunteered to bring Harpo, her cream Persian. Another cat who'd ended up at my shop after his owner died, Harpo had the ideal temperament to stay calm even with hordes of strangers milling around him. Chadwick Day would be the first weekend in August. . . . I hoped with his abundant coat, Harpo could bear up okay in the heat. If he showed any signs of distress, though, we could always hustle him back into the air-conditioning.

As I pictured Sarah helping me during the outdoor event, I realized that would leave no one to watch the shop. I supposed I could close it up for those two hours, or even the whole day. But if someone had their eye on the place, looking to break in, that might give them the perfect opportunity. And maybe next time, as Mark had said, they'd find a way to defeat the alarm.

Dawn will be tending her own table on the street, and Keith will have his own display, too. If Mark doesn't take part in Chadwick Day, it will be because he's busy at the clinic. Wish I could find someone trustworthy to at least staff the shop's front counter that day.

Maybe Jennifer would like to pick up a few extra bucks? She sounds like such an expert on everything!

By noon Mark still hadn't returned my call from

last night. I was too proud to phone him again. I'd made the first move and said I was sorry—now the ball was in his court. I still felt bad, though, that I had ruined our plans for a romantic evening, first with my burglar alarm going off and then with my jealous barb.

I put Latte away and went upstairs for lunch. Made a tuna sandwich, waving away three furry beggars, and opened my laptop while I ate. No e-mails from Mark, either.

With a little free time, I decided to get out of the apartment and the shop. Do something to take my mind off Mark, work, Rudy's murder, and the stolen cat.

That gallery show Dawn told me about? What's the name of the place again?

I found it online, Eye of the Beholder. And as I suspected, it was open on Sunday to take advantage of random tourists. I headed out into the hot, sunny afternoon.

Only a few doors down from two of my favorite Chadwick establishments, Cottone's Bakery and Towne Antiques, the gallery featured a large display window on Center Street. A sign on an easel there advertised the current show as NEW SURREALISTS, and two artworks on view drew me in immediately. One acrylic painting showed a man walking across a calm ocean, by night, using the circles of light from his flashlight as stepping-stones; treacherous-looking sea creatures lurked beneath the surface. The other piece, a sculpture, consisted of an old Kodak camera mounted on eight black-and-red tarantula legs with the title, *Smile!* It made my skin crawl at the same time as I laughed out loud.

I stepped inside, savoring both the air-conditioning and the churchlike quiet I usually experienced in a gallery or museum. Probably converted from some other type of store, the space preserved the original oak floors, refinished dark, and the tin ceilings, updated with white paint and track lighting. The center of the main exhibition space featured movable panels that I guessed could be adapted for different types of shows. I glimpsed a woman whom I took to be the owner seated at a small desk in a side alcove.

Serene as the setting was, the artworks were designed to shake up your everyday perceptions. In one computer-generated print, the yolk of a cracked egg hovered in midair and gave off a brilliant glow like a setting sun. In a colorful pen drawing, a woman's face, composed of multicolored butterflies, started to disintegrate as they flew away. A foot-tall ceramic sculpture called *Willow* resembled a tree with a pair of fused human legs and a limbless torso for the trunk, topped by a cascade of silky hair. *Layers,* a large color photograph, showed a nude woman from the back with a long zipper opening down her spine; it revealed yet another zipper underneath.

I'd been browsing for a few minutes when the owner approached me with a smile and introduced herself as Nidra Balin. Elegant in a sleeved turquoise tunic and black leggings, her dark hair in a sleek knot, she asked if this was my first visit to the gallery.

"Yes, although I've been curious about it for a while." I told her about my own business in town. "A friend of mine—Dawn, from Nature's Way—told me about your surrealism show, and I had to check it out."

"Ah, yes, Dawn was in the other day." Nidra's smile widened. "You like surrealism? So do I, but I realize it isn't the most popular style. It takes a special kind of person to appreciate it."

"That's why I was so intrigued that your gallery took the chance. How has the show been received?"

"Pretty well. I have to say, our last exhibit of modern impressionist landscapes was the most popular by far. We sold quite a few of those paintings, and I don't expect we'll match that this time around. But people do enjoy discussing these works. They'll come in with family members or friends and argue about what a piece means."

We strolled around for a minute, and she told me a little about the various artists, most new on the scene and just making their reputations.

"Here's one you should enjoy." She stopped in front of a framed silk-screened print maybe two and a half feet tall by twenty inches wide. It featured a woman in a short slip standing in front of a full-length mirror, but seen only from the back. Her reflection was a spotted leopard that sat erect and stared back with hypnotic green eyes.

"I've seen that look from my cats," I joked. "Whenever supper is late."

Nidra smiled and asked me a few of the usual questions about how I came to groom and board cats for a living. After explaining a little about that, I noted that many of the pet groomers I'd met had some kind of artistic leaning or background. I admitted that I'd studied art in college and dabbled in surrealism myself.

"Did you!" she said. "You'll have to show me some of your work."

Embarrassed, I waved a hand. "No, really, it was just student stuff. Nothing gallery-worthy. But I have to say, this makes me realize how far I've gotten away from my school days. I'm so rusty now! Yesterday I was trying to draw a cat cartoon for Chadwick Day, and I felt like a complete beginner."

Nidra tilted her head sympathetically. "It's true—any skill, just like a muscle, needs to be exercised to keep it in shape. Obviously you enjoy your job, and it takes a lot of your time, but maybe you still can fit in a little drawing or painting now and then?"

"I guess I should try." I hadn't even realized how low I felt until that insight brightened my spirits. With a laugh, I told her, "And maybe you should practice psychology on the side!"

"I do find it fascinating," she admitted. "That's probably why I like surrealism."

Nidra's phone rang then, and she went back to her desk to deal with a business matter. Meanwhile, I pondered some of the things we'd discussed. I did feel I'd landed in the right line of work, which gave me the chance to help animals and their owners with their problems. Interesting, though, how I continued to be drawn to the mysterious, and even dangerous, in art and even in the human mind. *Maybe that's why I get a rush out of helping to solve murders?*

I returned to the silk screen of the woman who saw her secret mirror reflection as a proud, alert leopard. This time I also checked the small sticker on the wall nearby, which gave the name of the artist and the title of the work: *Alter Ego.*

A different interpretation, for sure, of the Cat Lady.

On my walk home, I checked my messages. Mom reported that she'd gone back to work with no more problems from her tooth. She still managed to find something to stress about, though.

"Did you know about this? Hope it's not close to you!" And she included a link to an article from the county newspaper:

VICIOUS CAT STRIKES AGAIN—MAULS TODDLER IN BACKYARD

The story reported another attack, the day before, in the vicinity of Rattlesnake Ridge. A young mother had been gardening while her four-year-old wandered around the yard eating an ice-cream cone. While the woman's back was turned, the child spotted a "big kitty" at the edge of the yard and tried to lure it with the ice cream. When he got close to the cat, it lashed out at him, and he screamed. His mother grabbed the garden hose and doused the animal until it ran off. The boy seemed only to be scratched, not bitten, but he'd receive a series of uncomfortable rabies shots anyway, just to be safe.

The young mother described the animal as about twice as big as a domestic cat, tawny with small black spots and a slight ruff around the face. The article noted that this description also fit the creature that had recently mauled the small dog.

Animal control had consulted with Scott Naughton, director of the county SPCA, to determine why the wildcat might be attacking people and pets and how to catch it.

"From the description, this doesn't sound like either a pure bobcat or a domestic cat," Naughton was quoted as saying. "Both witnesses—in the case of the dog and the boy—said it had a normal, long tail. Bobcats have short tails, and they're also usually nocturnal and too timid to approach humans. Of course, this one might have rabies, or it might have had contact in the past with people who fed it, so that it's lost its natural fear."

Naughton speculated the new predator might be a cross between a bobcat and a large domestic type. "That rarely occurs in nature, but it's possible someone created such a hybrid on purpose. Sadly, that's not illegal, though in my opinion, it's highly irresponsible." He offered his expertise and services to help capture the animal before it did any more harm.

Sounds like Todd Gillis's dream pet! If I thought he knew anything about crossbreeding animals, I'd have suspected him of creating this nasty hybrid.

Otherwise, though, the news story lifted a weight from my mind. The animal had struck again while Ayesha was confined at my shop, and it looked different from her. At least I didn't have to worry that she'd been the one terrorizing Rattlesnake Ridge!

Let animal control and the SPCA worry about who bred the "killer cat." I need to find out where Ayesha came from.

And just in case whoever ran over Rudy is still hunting for her, I'd better do it fast!

Chapter 8

Next, I did a general search online for anyone in the northeast who might be missing an exotic cat. Found one article about a Savannah stolen the previous month in upstate New York, but he already had been located and returned to the breeder. No recent Bengal losses or thefts had made the news.

Over the rest of the afternoon, I made a list of e-mail addresses of all the licensed Bengal breeders I could find in the tri-state area, then composed a generic message:

Did you recently lose a female cat, or have one stolen from you? I am a professional cat boarder in New Jersey. Someone left a Bengal with me under questionable circumstances and has not returned to claim her. I am not seeking any reward money, just to return her to her rightful owner. Please reply to this e-mail only if you can prove the cat belongs to you.

I addressed the e-mail to myself, with blind carbon copies going to all the breeders, and hit send.

I still wasn't sure how I intended to make someone prove Ayesha had come from their particular cattery, but her behavioral quirks should help. Also, after a couple more baths, her real coat should show up in all its splendor, and maybe I'd find something distinctive in its pattern to identify her. In the ad, I did not include the name that Rudy had called her, because it was unusual; if a breeder could come up with *Ayesha,* that would be a definite point in his favor. And I made it clear I wasn't seeking a reward, so they'd be less likely to think that maybe I'd helped to steal her.

At least contacting the big, legit breeders was a start. If none of them worked out, I could begin responding to classified ads from what might be less reputable sources.

Tomorrow, Monday, I'd check with both the local shelter and animal control to tell them about Ayesha. Those might be the first places someone from nearby would think to go if they had lost an animal. I could explain to both agencies that I was fostering the cat for the time being, in cooperation with the Chadwick PD, because they suspected she might be evidence in a crime.

Tired from my detective work, I was trying to decide whether to exercise another boarder, watch a bit of TV, surf the Web, or just read, when my cell phone sang out. I hoped it would be Mark, but saw an unfamiliar number and the name Gillis Garage on my screen.

Oh, no! Is Todd going to start calling me now? It shouldn't be anything about my car or my bill. This is Sunday—the garage shouldn't even be open.

I didn't answer, but after the caller recorded a message, I played it out of curiosity. Heard the gravelly voice of a mature man who probably smoked too much.

"Hello, is this Miss McGlone? It's Bob Gillis from the garage. This might sound strange to ask, but . . . have you seen my son Todd?"

I called the man back. Apparently, Todd lived with his parents in town, and they hadn't seen him since the previous afternoon.

"His cell phone's not working, but he's terrible about letting the battery run down," Gillis said. "We've been worried that maybe he had a car accident, but the cops say there haven't been any reported. I can tell they think he's gone off with some other guys, drinking or whatever. But I know Todd wouldn't take off like this, not without even calling us to check in."

"I can see why you'd be worried," I said, "but why did you think I'd know where Todd was?"

Bob's embarrassment came through over the line. "Maybe I jumped to conclusions. Todd said he returned your car to you the other day, and the two of you got to talking. He said you were . . . um . . . attractive, so I thought maybe you and he hit it off."

Lord, does he think Todd spent the night at my place? Well, maybe his parents were eager to believe that some woman had finally shown an interest in him. "He did return my car and drop me off at my shop, but after I paid my bill, he left. That was Friday, and I haven't seen him since."

"Oh." Gillis let out a huff of frustration. "Well, then, sorry to bother you. His mom and I already called all his friends that we could think of, and then I remembered that he mentioned you."

Annoying as I found Todd, I couldn't help sympathizing with his father. "When did you last see him?"

"Yesterday morning. He said he was going for a drive, but he'd be back in the afternoon. He's got a red '02 Camaro he's always tinkering with, and he likes to open it up on the back roads. His mother always worries that he's going to get in a wreck, out in the middle of nowhere."

"He didn't give you any idea where he was headed?"

"Naw, he was playing it mysterious. His birthday is next week, and he said he might get himself 'a real nice present' this year. I thought maybe he went to look at another flashy car. . . . He was reading the classifieds yesterday morning, in the *Courier,* but if he answered an ad, I don't know which it was."

Now Bob had *me* worried about his son. Could the ad have been some kind of trap—had Todd gone expecting to look at a car, and gotten beaten up and robbed? Or did he test-drive an unsafe vehicle and crash?

"I wish I could help you," I told Gillis, sincerely. "Guess all you can do is ask the cops to be on the lookout for his Camaro, since that should be easy to spot. After forty-eight hours, they can do a missing persons search. But I hope Todd gets in touch with you before then."

"Thanks, Miss McGlone. I can see why he likes you—you're a good person."

As I switched off my phone, I felt rotten about ever making fun of Todd, if only because his dad seemed to be a nice guy.

At least, I felt bad until I remembered Todd's interest in Ayesha. Was it possible that *he* had tried to break to into my shop the night before?

It might fit with the idea of getting himself a "real nice" birthday gift. He didn't ask what it would cost to buy her, and I told him she was a boarder. Would he actually go to the extreme of trying to steal her?

I didn't really know enough about Todd to pass judgment on that.

For dinner, I broiled half a chicken breast, nuked a potato, and tossed a simple salad with the leftover greens from Dawn. Meanwhile, I reflected on my lack of cooking skills—or was it just patience?—compared to Mark. I felt bad again about the way our Saturday night had ended, but reminded myself it was up to him now to get back to me. I'd been through one relationship where I'd been made to feel that everything was my fault, and wasn't about to fall into that trap again.

Although I'd told Mark the story of my abusive ex, I'd refused to divulge the guy's name. Always a chance that, being the intense type, Mark might obsess over it or even decide to look him up and get in a fight with him. That painful chapter had closed and should stay that way.

As I ate, I tried to start reading a new psychological thriller I'd gotten from the library. It was too dark for my present state of mind, though, and after dinner, I tuned in to one of those quaint British murder mysteries on PBS instead. My pets vied for couch space next to me, with Mango winning out this time.

Dawn called to make sure there had been no more disturbances at Cassie's Comfy Cats since she left. I reported that, for now, the intruder seemed to have learned his or her lesson.

"I would think so," she said, "with the window locks, the loud alarm, and the Chadwick cops showing up so quickly. All of that should discourage anyone."

"And if anybody tries to break in while I'm actually here, I can just slash them to ribbons with my razor-sharp tongue," I added, in chagrin.

Dawn's throaty laugh told me she got the grim joke. "I trust that you and Mark patched things up?"

"I left him a phone message. He hasn't called back."

"Ouch. Maybe he's still licking his wounds." She paused. "Veterinarian joke unintended."

"Yeah, Mark and the Yorkie." I felt the need to change the subject. "Dawn, maybe you can give me some advice. I figured I had everything lined up for Chadwick Day, but now I'm having second thoughts. Sarah is supposed to bring Harpo so the two of us can use him for a grooming demonstration, but that means leaving the shop empty for at least a couple of hours."

"Is that a problem? How much business would you be doing, anyway? The publicity you'll get from the demo should more than make up for it."

"That's what I thought, too. But now I'm worried that the person who tried to break in yesterday might give it another shot."

"I dunno. This will be the middle of the day. And why would he go to the trouble, when there are probably easier places to break into? Unless . . ."

"Yeah, unless there's a reason he picked my place. What if he's after Ayesha?"

Silence as Dawn pondered my problem. "Maybe you could leave Sarah in the shop and do the demo by yourself? Harpo's easy to handle."

"It may come to that," I agreed. "Sarah's not exactly a threatening figure, but just having the front counter staffed ought to make any cat-napper think twice."

That night, though, I dreamed about the long-haired, tattooed man I'd seen at the Gillis garage and in the diner. He had tied up and gagged Sarah and was stealing Ayesha. The Bengal had morphed into a full-sized leopard with a jewel-studded collar, but she let him walk her out of my shop on a leash. They made their getaway in a red Camaro with Ayesha sitting proudly in the passenger seat, as tall as the man.

Not especially violent, the dream was an almost comical mash-up of my real-life worries and the artwork I'd admired in the gallery. Still, I woke around three a.m. with a sense of dread.

Eventually, I settled back to sleep, but with the superstitious feeling that maybe I ought to skip Chadwick Day altogether.

* * *

The next morning, I was getting the shop ready for Sarah's arrival when I heard a scuffle and a scream from the rear parking lot. Hurrying out, I found my sixtyish helper sprawled on the gravel, her flowered easy-care tunic askew above her blue knit slacks, and her gray curls mussed.

"Are you all right?" I wondered if she had tripped somehow. "What happened?"

Sarah actually muttered a mild four-letter word, very much out of character, as I tried to help her to her feet. When she put weight on her left leg, though, she gasped in pain.

"Uh-oh," I said. "Don't try to stand, then. Just sit down on the steps." I helped her over to them.

She caught her breath and finally answered my second question. "Some punk just now ran past me and knocked me down."

"Back here in the parking lot?"

"I think he was trying to grab my purse, but I hung onto it." She clutched the large brown satchel against her lap. "When I screamed, he ran away."

"That's awful!" It was the first purse-snatching attempt I'd heard of since I'd moved to Chadwick. My adopted town doesn't have much random crime—mostly domestic disputes and the occasional fistfight at one of the backwoods bars.

"Lucky I got a low center of gravity." The little woman threw me a crooked smile, then rubbed her leg. "But I do think I did something to my ankle."

I considered closing up and driving her to the emergency room, until I realized this was more than just an injury—it was a crime. "I'll call the cops."

"Oh, please. It wasn't that big of a—"

"That guy didn't get your purse, so he's liable to pick on somebody else. Besides, after the police question you, they'll get you to a hospital to have your ankle checked. You won't sit around all day in Emergency."

Gamely, Sarah tried again to put weight on the foot but sank back down on the step in defeat. "Maybe that wouldn't be such a bad idea."

If young, square-jawed Officer Jacoby was getting tired of answering calls to Cassie's Comfy Cats, at least he didn't show it. He questioned Sarah patiently about the would-be purse-snatcher, though she couldn't tell him much.

"I'd just got out of my car and started for the back door when I heard somebody walking fast behind me," she said. "Making noise, y'know, on the gravel. That got my attention, because nobody should be back here except me, Cassie, and maybe a customer."

"He came in from the street?" Jacoby asked.

She shook her head. "Must've come through those trees, where the houses back up to the lot. Before I could even look around, he slammed into me from behind, and I went down. I figured he might come back for my purse, so I screamed my head off, and he ran back the same way he came."

"Did you get a look at him?"

"Only from the back. Not too tall, slim, wearing

sweatpants and a hoodie. Both dark—navy blue, I think. From that angle, the hood blocked his face completely."

At least that description didn't sound like Todd Gillis, I thought.

"Might've been just a kid," Jacoby said. "Kind of a lamebrained move, anyway, to knock you down and not expect you to scream."

"At nine in the morning, too," Sarah noted. "There could've been witnesses. Another minute and Cassie might have come to the door to let me in."

"Wish I had," I told her. "That might have scared him off sooner, and I might have seen his face."

A minute later, EMTs arrived, and one examined Sarah's ankle. He diagnosed it as just a bad sprain, but thought she should get an X-ray to be sure, so the ambulance would transport her to the nearest medical center.

"Call me if you need to be picked up later," I told her as she was leaving.

"That's okay, honey. First I'll try my son, Jay. He's just tutoring for the summer, so he should be able to take time off. If you don't mind, though, I'll leave my car here until we see if I'm able to drive."

Watching the ambulance pull away, I faced another day of caring for the boarders and the human customers all by myself. I'd lost more than just an extra pair of hands, though, because Sarah had become a friend. I worried that, at her age, even a badly sprained ankle might not heal so quickly.

And of course, it was unnerving to think a mugger had attacked her right in our small parking lot, even if he hadn't succeeded in grabbing her bag. It almost sounded like he'd been lurking in the cover of trees, waiting for a victim to show up. Fifteen minutes earlier, he could have struck me. I'd like to think I'd have been faster to react than Sarah, but maybe not.

I also wondered if this incident had any connection with the foiled break-in of Saturday night. They both looked like robbery attempts, but other than that, I couldn't see what they might have in common.

After lunch I turned out two long-haired "tuxedo" cats, Heckle and Jeckle, in the playroom. They were brothers and belonged to an elderly man who had named them after two cartoon blackbirds from a 1960s TV show. When I looked it up online, I could better appreciate his sense of humor. Their owner had opted to spend July in Maine rather than New Jersey, for which I couldn't blame him, though his cats probably could. They got the most out of our playroom, though, chasing each other up the shelves and through the tunnels, with an occasional brother-versus-brother wrestling match. Their markings were so similar that I could barely tell Heckle from Jeckle.

To keep an eye on them, I pulled a chair into the space and checked messages on my phone. Two of the licensed breeders I'd e-mailed already had responded. One in New York said tersely that she was not missing any of her cats. A second also claimed all of his stock was accounted for, but warned me that if the cat had been dropped off at my shop under suspicious circumstances, there might be an unlicensed, backyard operation involved.

Especially with a cat as valuable as a Bengal, there are a lot of unscrupulous people out there trying to make a quick buck, he said. *I hope you will make sure that this animal ends up in a reputable place.* He may have been suggesting that he'd be willing to take Ayesha, but to his credit, he didn't come right out and say so. He concluded, *You might want to check with these people as to whether any breeders have reported stolen cats,* and he gave a link to a Bengal rescue group for the northeastern US.

I thanked him—this was a resource I wouldn't have thought of. Going to the site, I clicked on the Contact Us button and sent the rescue group a variation on my original query.

While still online, I found a text from Mark. He finally apologized for his abrupt exit on Saturday night and his radio silence since then. "We've had a couple of emergencies at the clinic," he said. "Had to work Sunday, came home exhausted and sacked out immediately. Things were more under control today, though. How are you? No more break-ins, I hope?"

I texted him back about Sarah's mishap in the parking lot and her possible sprained ankle, figuring that would make him feel just guilty enough. He answered immediately to express condolences about Sarah, and asked if I was okay holding down the shop alone.

"No sign of any more trouble since then, and I've only got a few hours to go," I said. "I've locked the back door, and if any bad guys come in the front, I can always punch the panic button." As I said this, I had a flash of the muscled-up, tattooed guy from my nightmare looming in my doorway.

A few seconds went by before Mark wrote back, "I should be out of here on time today. I'll drop by before you close, okay?"

"That would be nice," I told him.

I put Heckle and Jeckle away in their shared condo. When I checked on Ayesha, I noticed she'd actually left some food in her dish, which was unheard of. She rubbed her cheek compulsively against her frayed condo door and meowed pathetically at me. From the smell of things, she'd also sprayed outside the box again.

I cracked the door open and scratched her under the chin. "What's wrong, princess? Didn't get to play with Sarah today, did you? I'll let you out for a while before I close up." Give me a chance to scrub out the condo, too, I thought.

Hours had passed, I realized, since my assistant had gone off in the ambulance. I was just about to call her when I had a knock on my front door. Bonelli strolled in.

"Hi," I greeted her. "To what do I owe this honor?"

"Your assistant got mugged this morning."

Of course, she would know about that. "Yes, unfortunately."

"Sarah all right?"

"She went off in the ambulance around ten, and I haven't heard from her since. I was just going to try her cell. But she said her son might be picking her up."

We sat on stools behind the front counter, and she accepted my offer of a bottled water. Though I'm sure it looked like a casual visit, I worried what passersby might think if they looked through my window and recognized the police detective.

Bonelli twisted off the top of her bottle. "That's our second trip to your place in three days."

"Pretty soon I'll be over my quota for the week, eh?"

"The chief is starting to ask questions." She took a long swallow of the water. "Is this latest attack mere coincidence?"

"Sarah seemed to think it was just an attempt to grab her purse. Maybe a kid looking for drug money."

"When she's able, she should come down to the station and make a report."

"I think Jacoby already told her to, but I'll remind her."

Bonelli started to say something else, but a wailing from the condo area almost drowned her out. She squinted in annoyance. "Is that cat okay? Do they always carry on like that?"

I realized I'd almost tuned out the din. "That's our royal boarder. She's a glutton for attention."

"I can see what you mean about not putting her in a shelter. That noise would get on their nerves, all right."

My own fur bristled. "Dogs can bark for hours at nothing. I find that more annoying."

The canine-loving detective smiled. "Fair enough. Anyway, your royal boarder is the other reason I stopped by. Since she might be evidence in our hit-and-run, I thought I should see her for myself."

I figured if Bonelli was put off by the yowling, she'd really be grossed out by the stinky condo, so I brought Ayesha out front in her harness. I showed the detective where the rosettes had begun to show through the cat's dyed coat, and the scar where someone might have removed her microchip. We speculated again about what Rudy's plans might have been when he'd left her with me.

Because the Bengal seemed so restless, I let her jump to the floor, then gave her a stuffed mouse to wrestle with while Bonelli and I kept on talking.

"Y'know, I was wondering if Todd Gillis tried to break into my shop Saturday night." I explained about his fascination with Ayesha. "Might be a stretch, but he is kind of strange."

"That would be strange, all right," Bonelli said. "Our guys didn't find any fingerprints on the windowsill, just the pry marks. So whoever made the attempt had the sense to wear gloves . . . in late July."

"Bob Gillis told you, I guess, that Todd has gone missing."

She nodded. "He called us Sunday. He's worried that Todd might have wrecked his car somewhere, but we haven't had any reports of serious crashes."

"No bar fights he might have been involved in?" I asked. "Or hunting accidents?"

"Nothing reported. Always possible, of course, that something happened and was kept quiet. We're taking it seriously, though."

Bonelli stood and tossed her empty water bottle into my recycling can. I thanked her for stopping by.

"We'll keep checking for leads on Sarah's attacker," she told me. "When you hear from her, let me know how she is. And meanwhile, Cassie . . . be careful, okay?"

"I always am, but thanks."

As the detective left, Ayesha darted after her. If the Bengal hadn't still been wearing her harness and I hadn't been holding the leash, she might have gotten out the front door.

"Lady, what is *with* you today?" I grabbed her favorite fishing pole toy and tried to lure her up onto the playroom shelves the way Sarah did. But Ayesha wasn't in the mood. She rubbed against my legs and every piece of cat furniture she passed. All the while she meowed pathetically and incessantly, like a smoke alarm with a dying battery. Then she flattened her belly on the floor and lifted her rear end, in an unmistakable message.

Oh, crap. I'd seen that routine before, when I first got Matisse, so I should've recognized the signs sooner. I'd gotten off easy so far, but my luck couldn't hold out forever.

Mark picked that moment to walk through the

front door. I welcomed him by yelling hysterically, "Close it! Close it!"

He followed my voice into the playroom. "I did. What now?"

"Grrreat news." I nodded toward my feline friend, who coyly rolled onto her back. "Ayesha's in heat."

Chapter 9

With his hands on his hips and a slow shake of his head, Mark observed the Bengal's lovelorn behavior. "She certainly is."

I started to wail, myself. "What am I going to do? She was noisy enough before. Now she'll get all the other boarders stirred up."

"Well, you're in luck, aren't you?" he announced, as Ayesha went back to furring everything in the playroom.

"Oh, really? I almost had a break-in on Saturday, Sarah was mugged this morning, and now I've got this complication. How am I in luck?"

"Because I'm here." Mark waited with a grin to see if I would take this declaration for arrogance.

But I could tell he was teasing. "You mean, because I don't have to be as frustrated as Ayesha? Or . . . ahhh, because you're a vet!"

"Exactly." He picked up the spotted siren—in every sense—to stop her from obsessively rolling against his sneaker. "I can give her, and all the rest of your gang, some relief."

"We can't spay her," I warned. "If it turns out she was stolen from a reputable breeder, they'd be furious if we did that. They might even sue me."

"I don't need to. Breeders sometimes want to stop a female cat's cycle when she's going to a show. I can just give her a shot." Putting the cat down, he talked over her trilling. "The effects won't last very long, but it should keep her calmer until you can find her owner. It'll probably stop the spraying, too."

"You're right, I am lucky to have you." I crossed to Mark to give him a hug and a kiss. "I hate to ask, but . . . how soon could you do this?"

He checked his watch. "It's only about five-thirty. We'll bring her over to the clinic now. Sam will already have started his night shift, and at any rate, it's a quick procedure."

A few minutes later, Mark drove us to the clinic, Ayesha still meowing from her carrier in the back-seat. I dared to ask him, "I guess this means you accept my apology?"

"About Saturday? Please, I should be the one apologizing. I'm sorry I stalked out like that."

"Sometimes when I try to be funny, I go too far," I admitted.

He glanced at me sideways, a glint in his eye. "Yeah, sometimes you do, but I should be used to that by now. We were both tired and stressed. Let's forget it."

Notably, neither of us even mentioned the name of Jennifer Hood.

Mark changed the subject. "Actually, I've been

doing a little sleuthing myself about your mystery. I asked a few other vets in the area if they've heard any reports about exotic cats that went missing or might have been stolen. I talked to a couple in this area, and also some that I trained with at Penn."

"Great idea," I said. "And had they?"

"Nothing specific and nothing too recent. One did say, though, that he'd heard of purebred cats being 'flipped'—stolen and resold to new owners—as pets or for breeding. Of course, they're sold without papers or medical records, so anyone who buys a valuable cat under those circumstances has got to know it's a shady deal. The cases he heard of were in other parts of the country, though, not New Jersey."

I gave this some thought. "I may need to widen my search beyond New Jersey. No telling where Rudy got this cat from or how far he traveled with her."

By now it was about five forty-five. This was not one of the clinic's late nights, and we found only two cars in the lot. One was an older model, navy blue Toyota sedan, the other a cute little white Chevy Sonic. I figured the first probably belonged to Sam, who had night observation duty. As Mark stepped out of his vehicle and reached in the back for Ayesha, he did not speculate aloud about whose the other car might be.

I had my suspicions, though, and they were confirmed when we spotted Jennifer behind the reception desk. She looked pleasantly surprised to see Mark, not so pleasantly surprised to see me.

"Oh, you're back!" she greeted him. "Nothing wrong, I hope."

"Nope, just a little emergency with one of the cats from Cassie's shop. Have you two met?"

"Not formally." She seemed to force a sweet, dimpled smile and extended her hand. Even this late in the day, her makeup looked freshly applied.

Mark introduced us, then asked Jennifer, "A little late for you to be hanging around, isn't it?"

"I'm just wrapping up. I was straightening some old files and lost track of time. But if you need me to stay until you're done . . ."

"No, that's not necessary. No billing for this job, it's just a favor." He headed into one of the examining rooms with the cat, leaving the door ajar.

I hung by the reception desk a minute longer. Jennifer had a manila folder open in front of her, with forms that someone had filled out by hand. I noticed a fluorescent green Post-it note stuck to the upper left corner of the top one.

"I guess the paperwork never ends in a place like this," I said.

"Never! And there's such a backlog. I can't imagine why the last receptionist never purged all these dead files. That's the right name for most of them, too, because either the owners moved away or the patients are deceased."

"Isn't a lot of your information computerized these days?" I asked.

"Most of it is, but the owners fill out printed forms that we keep on file. Besides, there are insurance forms, invoices for medications and all that. Some still come in by fax!" She rolled her eyes toward heaven, as if this were the equivalent of pony express. "Elena, the office manager, usually logs the important stuff into our computers.

She's been here longer and is more familiar with the system."

I was surprised to hear Jennifer admit that anyone at the clinic might be more competent than her. "Well, it's good of you to stay late to sort things out."

"I try to keep things running smoothly for the doctors, because they work so hard. Especially Mark." Flashing another dimple, she added, "He's so dedicated, it's really inspiring."

Before I could think of a reply for that, the source of Jennifer's inspiration stuck his head out the door of the exam room. "Cassie, want to come help me with this crazy lady?"

"Sure." I'd almost gotten to the doorway, then remembered I'd left my shoulder bag on one of the waiting room benches. As I passed the reception desk again and bent down for my purse, I saw Jennifer peel the bright green Post-it from the handwritten form. She studied it for a second, crumpled it, and threw it in the trash. Then she rose, crossed to the pale gray, lateral file cabinets behind her, pulled out a drawer, and tucked the folder neatly away. Even her medical scrubs—bright blue stretch pants and tunic patterned with cartoon animals—seemed tailored to show off her curves.

Bet she can cook, too!

Shaking off these jealous observations, I joined Mark in the exam room and closed the door behind me. Ayesha wasn't exactly giving him trouble, but she compulsively rubbed her head against his arm, her carrier, and the edge of the metal table.

He chuckled in frustration. "Hold this sex kitten still for a minute, would you? Just long enough for me to give her the injection."

I did so. I worried that the Bengal might turn on him when she felt the needle, but she barely noticed. When I stroked her head afterward, she turned all of her crazed affection onto me.

Mark smoothed the fur on Ayesha's back. "Her spots are really showing up now, aren't they?"

I nodded. "Every time we wash her, a little more of that brown goes down the drain. I can't wait to see what she looks like when it's all gone."

He put away the syringe and the bottle of medication. "That shot should quiet her down pretty soon, and it'll last at least a few weeks. With any luck, you'll find her a new home by then—either with a breeder who doesn't mind her going into heat, or someone who just wants a pet and will let us spay her. I wouldn't want to give her this stuff too often, because it can have side effects down the road."

"I do know of one person who'd probably love to own her," I admitted, "but I'm not sure he'd take good care of her. Todd, from the Gillis garage. Remember, the guy who told me about the wildcat killing the dog?"

"Oh, right. And said it ate the dog?" Mark made a disgusted face.

"Yeah, he seemed to think that was exciting. Or maybe he was just trying to impress me." I let that register for a second before adding, "I wasn't impressed."

"I'm sure you weren't." Mark guided the Bengal, already a bit more subdued, back into her soft-sided carrier.

"Anyway, when he returned my car, he came into the shop for a minute and saw Sarah walking Ayesha." I explained how the cat had fascinated Todd. "Today I was wondering if he was the one who tried to break in on Saturday. It would be a loony thing to do, but he's a very immature guy. Maybe he'd see it as an adventure."

"You should mention that to the cops."

"I did, earlier today—Bonelli came by the shop," I said. "But now Todd seems to be missing. According to his father, Todd went for a drive yesterday and never came back. Before he left, he said something about getting himself a birthday present."

We left the exam room, Mark toting the cat in her carrier. "He might have gotten into some kind of trouble. How old is he?"

"Early to mid twenties."

We went out through the reception area, and I was almost surprised to see that Jennifer had finally left. Short, stocky Sam appeared in the hall, and we said our good-nights to him.

Mark didn't lose the thread of our conversation, though. On our way to the parking lot, he asked me, "Does Todd hunt?"

"Don't know, but it wouldn't surprise me," I said.

"Like I told you the other night, some hunters have being going up on the ridge trying to bag the wildcat. Maybe Todd got the same idea. Thought he'd get his name in the papers and be a hero. Sound like something he might do?"

"From what little I know of him, yeah, it does. Jeez, maybe he had a hunting accident."

Mark narrowed his eyes at me. "You sure you don't like this guy?"

I laughed. "I absolutely don't, but his parents are worried, and I feel sorry for them. Besides, I wouldn't want to see anybody I knew get hurt or killed for such a stupid reason."

We loaded Ayesha into the backseat of the RAV4. She had grown quiet and actually seemed to be dozing.

"I think she needs a cigarette," I joked.

"You'll see. By tomorrow, she'll be a changed woman—demure and ladylike."

Sliding into the passenger seat, I had an evil thought. *Maybe Jennifer could use a shot of that stuff!*

But I sure knew better than to say it out loud. Mark and I might still have a chance at that romantic night together, and I wasn't going to sabotage it with any more witty remarks.

We finally did cash the rain check for our ill-fated Saturday night date, and I tried my best to drive any fantasies about the brunette bombshell receptionist from Mark's mind. He certainly acted reluctant to leave me as he headed off for work the next morning. I wondered smugly if Jennifer would notice him arriving in the same clothes he'd worn the day before.

I went down to the shop still feeling lazy and dreamy, and was opening up a few minutes late when Sarah appeared at the front door. Wearing an ankle brace and using crutches, she nevertheless hopped over the threshold with a grin.

"My gosh, I wasn't expecting you back yet," I said as I let her in.

"Got Jay to drop me off on his way to work," she told me. "Why sit home, doing nothing, when I can at least come here and accomplish something? I felt bad about leaving you on your own. The doctor said I should be able to drive my car home tonight, too."

"Well, I'm certainly glad to have you here. You can staff the counter, but I'll do all the heavy lifting until you're fully recovered."

Sarah said she felt comfortable enough on her usual stool, but I brought over one of the low, carpeted cat tunnels to support her injured foot. I also got her a cup of coffee, amused by the idea that I was assisting my assistant.

"You'll be glad to know that your mugging is on Detective Bonelli's radar," I said, "though she admits the perp will be hard to finger, with so little to go on."

"I know," Sarah lamented. "I wish I'd gotten a look at his face, but I'm sure he arranged things so I wouldn't. He had that hoodie pulled all the way forward."

"Sounds like he planned it well, the jerk. I'm sure he was frustrated that, in spite of it all, he didn't get your bag." I poured myself coffee, too. "In other crime news, it's occurred to me that maybe it was Todd Gillis who had the brilliant idea to break in here to steal Ayesha, setting off the alarm. But I can't question him about it, because now his father says Todd has gone missing."

"See why I couldn't stay home? I'd miss all the action! This shop has more drama going on than any talk show or soap opera." Sarah sipped her coffee. "And how is my girl, Ayesha?"

"Oh, that's another news bulletin." I recounted the Bengal's lovesick behavior of the previous evening and Mark's speedy solution. "You'll notice it's a little quieter around here today, and her condo also stayed cleaner overnight."

"That's good. Though I wouldn't want to see her lose all her spunk."

"Don't think there's much danger of that." I perched on the other stool, with a full view of my assistant's ankle brace, and raised a more sober subject. "I may have to forget putting out a table for Chadwick Day. Under normal circumstances, it would be tough enough to do a grooming demo and keep the store staffed at the same time. But now that you're hurt . . ."

She waved a dismissive hand. "I could be back on my feet by then."

"Sarah, it's less than a week away. You probably need more time than that to recover. And even if I could groom Harpo by myself, I wouldn't want to leave you alone in the shop. Not after we've had an attempted break-in plus an attempted mugging. If someone is targeting this place, for whatever reason, you'd be a sitting duck . . . no offense."

"None taken." She turned thoughtful. "Seems a shame for you to miss out on the street fair, though. Maybe you could find someone else to help you?"

I shrugged. "Dawn and Keith will both be holding down their own tables, and Mark will be at the clinic."

Our brainstorming session was cut short by a summons from my phone. *Bonelli again. At this rate, she might as well put me on the force.*

"Everything quiet over there?" she asked.

"Just fine so far. And Sarah's back, although on crutches. Can't keep a good woman down."

"Is she? That's good news. So maybe you can come down to the station for a while. Say, around one o'clock?"

"I should be able to." I played it cautious. "What's up?"

"I'm meeting with someone else at that time, Scott Naughton of the county SPCA," Bonelli said. "You two might want to compare notes, since you've got something in common: You're both investigating crimes that involve big, spotted cats."

Chapter 10

The traditional brick and limestone façade of the Chadwick Police Station always felt at odds, to me, with its sleekly modern and efficient interior. At least the light maple office furniture and plentiful ceiling lights dispelled any sense of an ominous jailhouse. That might not work so well for intimidating criminals, but as an innocent visitor, I appreciated the lack of menace.

I arrived a little before one, hoping to have a few minutes to talk to Bonelli alone before Naughton joined us. Her office had a glass wall along the main corridor. I guess this let her keep track of what was going on outside and also let passersby see whether or not she was busy. I knocked on the door anyway before going in.

A console table to one side held a Keurig coffee maker, which I knew had been a joint Mother's Day gift from her two boys, and today Bonelli offered me a cup of almond toffee. Because the station was well air-conditioned, I accepted. I sat in one of the two straight-backed metal chairs provided for visitors and faced the detective across her Formica-topped computer desk.

I told her, "I remembered something else that might be relevant to Todd Gillis's disappearance. The day I took my car to the garage, he got into an argument with a customer. I didn't think much of it then. The guy was complaining that his van still wasn't fixed, and Todd was saying it was just old."

Bonelli stifled a laugh. "Not so hot at customer relations, eh?"

"Exactly—it was only making the guy madder. But this customer was a real character, too." I described the tattooed man with the three-day shadow and long, graying hair. "He looked pretty rough. Like a biker, maybe."

"Get the license number of his van?"

"No," I admitted. "I didn't even see it—it must have been parked somewhere out in the lot. Anyway, at the time I never imagined that might be important."

Bonelli opened her legal-sized, vinyl-covered notepad and jotted. "I'll call Gillis, see if he knows who the guy was."

"Something else," I said. "Did Bob tell you that Todd was reading the classified ads in the *Chadwick Courier* the morning before he took off?"

"No, he didn't." The detective made another note.

"I read the *Courier* online now, but I've also seen the paper. From what I remember, there's only one page of classifieds. If we could get a copy of that edition, maybe something would jump out at us."

Bonelli considered that. "You can find all the ads that run in the county papers through the main Web site."

"Okay . . . but that won't help us pinpoint what Todd saw in the actual newspaper, *that* morning."

She bent her head to acknowledge this. "It's published Wednesday, Friday, and Sunday, right? So on Saturday, he probably was looking at the Friday paper. We may still have it with our recycling." Using the old-fashioned, multiline phone on her desk, Bonelli asked a clerk to check for the issue. Then she paused to listen and responded, "Oh, good. Send him on in."

Right on time, Chief Inspector Naughton appeared in the office doorway. He stood about six foot two, with a lean but athletic build. Probably in his late thirties or early forties, to judge by his slightly receding sandy hair. Square, clean-cut jaw, brown eyes with a determined squint. He wore tan chino-type pants and a black polo shirt with an SPCA badge embroidered above the heart.

Bonelli introduced me, and we shook hands. As Naughton took the seat beside me, I noticed that the back of his neck was sunburned and the tan on his arms stopped just below his short sleeves. He'd gotten that color from working long hours outdoors, I thought, not lying on a beach.

He said, "Angela told me about how much you went through this spring—taking in that cat after his owner was killed and trying to keep him out of the wrong hands. I was impressed. Not many people would go to so much trouble."

I felt my cheeks warm. "Thanks. I just stepped up because no one else was very concerned about him. Anyway, he's in a good home now—my assistant adopted him."

"I also told Scott about the cat that was dropped off at your place last week, with the dyed coat," Bonelli said.

I gave Naughton the full details on that, and also related what I'd been told about valuable cats being flipped for resale. "Our local veterinarian, who was doing some checking for me, heard that from another vet."

"Unfortunately, it's true," he said. "Dyeing a spotted cat is a new one on me, but exotics are often stolen and resold by people trying to make a fast buck. A reputable breeder would question where they came from, but someone with a backyard operation might not."

"That must be awful for the people whose cats disappear, and who have no way to trace what happened to them," I said.

"And an unlicensed breeder isn't the worst place to end up. Lately, feral cats and wild hybrids are in demand by urban dog-fighting rings, as bait animals to train the dogs. The gangs that run these fights will pay pretty high prices, because they think those cats make better fighters. Not that any of them would be a match for a pit bull."

The scenario shocked and sickened me. "That's horrible! Maybe Ayesha is lucky this guy never came back for her."

On the one hand, Rudy had seemed so protective of the Bengal that I couldn't picture him handing her over to a cruel and violent fate. On the other, the sort of person who would buy a cat for such a purpose might also have no scruples about running a man down and leaving his unidentified body on a lonely road.

"I heard he was found dead," Naughton said. "Of course, investigating how he was killed is Angela's area, but she and I are pooling resources. I've suspected for a while that someone in this area is breeding hybrids. My investigators have spotted blind ads in hunting and fishing magazines for wild pets. We tried answering one and leaving a message, to set up a sting, but so far they haven't responded. My personal theory is, the cat that mauled the dog and the child might have escaped from that type of breeder."

"Because it had no fear of humans and was hunting during the day?" I asked.

"Exactly!" He seemed to eye me with even greater respect. "You know your wildcats, too."

The praise made me self-conscious again. "I just remembered what you told the *Courier* reporter. You also pointed out that it had a longer tail than the typical bobcat."

"See, this is why I brought you two together," Bonelli injected, with a restrained smile. "Sounds like there just might be a link between Cassie's mystery cat, the breeder the SPCA is looking for, and maybe also the wildcat."

"It'd help if I could find out if Ayesha really was stolen, and from whom," I said. "I've reached out to about ten licensed catteries, but so far only two got back to me, and neither was missing a cat."

"There are quite a few national groups online that run ads for lost or stolen pets," Naughton told me, "though it might be tough to search through them all. But you can try National Bengal Rescue. They have regional chapters. For example, if the cat was stolen from New York or Pennsylvania, and the owner notified the national group, it would show up on their Web site under that region."

I committed this information to memory. "Good idea, thanks."

A slightly overweight young woman in a print blouse and gray slacks knocked on the doorjamb. "Detective, here's the newspaper you asked for."

"Oh, good timing, Maggie, thanks." Bonelli took the Friday *Courier* from her, hesitated, and handed it to me. "Want to do the honors?"

Meanwhile, she offered Naughton his choice of coffees from the Keurig pods, and he chose the House Blend.

While it brewed, I searched through the newspaper. It wasn't too thick, so I found the classified ads with little trouble. The items for sale were broken into categories, but it was hard to know what to look for. First I checked "Autos," in case something along that line had lured Todd away from home, but none were offered for sale, only "Wanted to Buy." After that, I went immediately to "Pets and Livestock." Someone was trying to sell a "dead broke" (quiet and reliable) trail horse. There also were ads for puppies of all kinds. I sincerely hoped none of those would be bought as bait for urban dog-fighting rings.

Then I saw it: "Like to walk on the wild side? Our half-breed cats will blow your mind—they look and act like the real thing! Crosses you won't see anywhere else."

And there was a phone number.

"Got it!" I crowed, and showed the ad to Bonelli. "I'll bet anything this is why Todd took off that day without telling his folks where he was going."

Naughton, already on his feet to get his coffee, read over Bonelli's shoulder. "That's it, the same ad we've been watching."

"You called the number?" I asked.

"Left a message and never heard back. Whether they managed to trace the call to our organization, and that scared 'em off, I can't be sure."

"Let me try." I pulled out my cell phone. "Mine's a private line, so they shouldn't suspect anything."

Naughton agreed to this, but spent a minute coaching me on what to say and not to say to the breeder. "We don't want them to suspect a sting."

Once I felt confident, I dialed. Got a familiar three-tone signal, followed by a recorded message.

"No longer in service," I told Bonelli and Naughton as I hung up.

Bonelli frowned. "Burner phone. They either dumped it or deleted the number. Yeah, *that's* a legit operation."

Naughton shared her opinion, and told me, "If your friend did go off to answer that ad, who knows what the hell he got himself into!"

* * *

Walking back to my shop, I checked my phone again and found a message from my mother. "Just wanted to know how things are going," she said.

Good Lord. It had been less than a week since we'd last talked, and maybe half a dozen crises had come and gone in the meantime. I'd have to review which ones I could tell her about, which ones I had to downplay, and which I dared not mention at all. No press secretary for a corrupt politician works harder than me when I spin the news that I release to my mother.

Sarah still sat at the front counter with her left foot elevated. I told her, "Guess what? Mom wants to know what's new in my life. How much do you think I can tell her before she has a meltdown and insists I give up the shop and move in with her?"

My assistant, a mother of grown children herself, answered with a deep chuckle. "You might have to do some editing. Guess you'll want to play down my little accident."

"Among other things," I agreed.

I multitasked by turning a Siamese named Mia loose in the playroom and keeping an eye on her while I returned the call. With some privacy, I gave my mother a sanitized version of the past week's events, minus the melodrama: We had an exotic new boarder, a Bengal female who was very vocal and high-energy. I'd had dinner with Mark at his place, and he'd asked my advice on some problems he'd been having with his staff. Sarah had sprained her ankle in my parking lot; no, no, she wasn't threatening to sue me, but now I wasn't sure if I could take part in Chadwick Day, because Sarah would have to staff the shop all by herself.

"Oh, that's a shame," Mom said. "When is the event, this Saturday?"

"Yeah. Not much chance that she'll be fully recovered by then."

A pause. "Maybe I could come out and help you. If it's just a matter of keeping an eye on things . . . or waiting on customers . . ."

The idea had never crossed my mind. When I was growing up and collecting pets, it had been mostly my father who shared my enthusiasm. Mom usually complained about the fur shed on the carpets and furniture, the birds that occasionally flapped around the ceiling, and the lizards that escaped to skitter up the walls. She had a stoic side and hated to show fear. At times, though, she'd seemed to have even more of an aversion to cats than to the cold-blooded creepy-crawlies.

Also, what if Mom was on duty when the person who'd tried to break in made another attempt? Granted, if that had been Todd, maybe I had nothing much to worry about, now that he'd vanished. But if it had been someone else . . .

"Thanks for offering, Mom, but I'd hate to put you out. I mean, you work hard all week long. And you just had that root canal. . . ."

She laughed. "My tooth is fine—it only hurt the day after. Besides, we haven't seen each other in a while. This will give us a chance to catch up."

Oh, dear. A chance for her to find out that Ayesha's owner was probably murdered, that someone tried to burgle my store, that Sarah was knocked down by a potential mugger, and last but not least, that Mark's receptionist was trying to steal him away from me. All things she was much better off not knowing.

"Tell you what," Mom said. "Why don't I pop up Thursday night, and you can show me what needs to be done? Then I can arrive on Saturday ready to go."

She sounded so willing that I couldn't refuse without hurting her feelings. "Okay, if you don't mind. We'll just . . . see how it goes."

I hung up with mixed feelings. Having put in many years as a paralegal with a Morristown law firm, my mother was nothing if not responsible. If she was willing to hold down the store, at least I wouldn't have to worry about her not taking the job seriously. More likely she would overachieve somehow, maybe rearranging all the boarder cats alphabetically by name.

I put the Siamese away and straightened the grooming studio. Saw an empty shampoo bottle in the recycling bin. We'd really been burning through that stuff by washing Ayesha every few days. *I ought to run and get some,* I thought, *along with more of our regular food.*

"Will you be okay here for another half hour or so?" I asked Sarah. "I should make a trip to the Pet-Mart out on the highway."

"Anyone scheduled to drop off or pick up a cat?"

"None 'til tomorrow," I told her. "And I'll make it quick."

* * *

I could have picked a better time than four o'clock to head for a highway mall. Rush hour was already starting, to judge by the traffic. Well, maybe I could wrap up my errand and still get back to downtown Chadwick before it got too crazy.

Of course, this was wishful thinking, because it's hard for me to get in and out of any pet supply store quickly. This one has a bank of cages right inside the front entrance with cats for adoption, and I could never pass by without visiting and commiserating. The kittens were always adorable, but my heart went out even more to the ones several years old, curled up tightly in the back corners as if they'd lost hope. Notes on their cages often explained that the cat had been surrendered after an elderly owner died or moved to a nursing home. I knew the playful, outgoing kittens would have no trouble finding new homes, but the mature cats might spend what was left of their lives in a noisy shelter, with minimal attention from overworked staffers. After being someone's cherished pet, that had to be a tough comedown.

I always fought the urge to take an older cat home with me. My small apartment was pretty much maxed out with my three pets, all rescues of one kind or another themselves. Also, they had established a delicate balance of power among them that could easily be upset by the addition of a newcomer.

Trying to stay on mission, I grabbed a shopping cart and headed for the grooming supplies. Along the way, I passed other distractions, such as aisles of colorful toys, cat furniture, and feeding and training gadgets. I resolved to be strong, remembering I'd already left Sarah alone for a couple of hours today. I stocked up on shampoo, then swung over to the cat food section to pick up a couple of bags of dry kibble. I also searched for the special food Ayesha required, but didn't see any in stock.

While standing in line to check out, I spied a cat magazine I didn't subscribe to; it included classifieds in the back, so I stuck that in my cart, as well. Might be time to expand the search for Ayesha's owner beyond just the Bengal breeders in our area.

I used my member's card and a coupon to get a nice discount on my haul, paid up, and steered my cart toward glass front doors that parted automatically. Pausing on the sidewalk to remember where in the huge lot I'd left my car, I noticed a matte black commercial-sized van in the loading area, a few yards away. Actually, the chief thing that caught my eye was the tattooed man who stood by the van's open rear doors.

The same one I'd seen arguing with Todd at the garage and talking in an agitated tone on his cell phone in the diner. I'd built him up as such a threatening figure in my mind that it stopped my heart for a second to see him unexpectedly again.

This afternoon he was doing something else intriguing. He had filled several shopping carts with empty pet carriers that he was loading into the back of the van. I counted maybe two dozen carriers, a few large, most medium to small. All were the store's cheapest model—hard-sided, in light gray plastic with a wire grill door.

Sometimes I do shoot off my mouth without

thinking, but in this case, I actually considered my strategy. My instincts told me I shouldn't let the opportunity pass without trying to find out what this guy was up to. Yeah, he looked a little rough, but it was daylight, with people all around. Besides, I didn't intend to accuse him of anything.

I steered my cart close to his van, as if headed for a car in that direction. In a naïve, cheery tone, I called out, "Wow, you must have a lot of animals!"

The stranger's head whipped around, as if he'd been hoping no one would notice what he was doing. Today he wore his hair tied back in a bushy tail that hung between his shoulder blades, and his weathered face showed heavy stubble. As the muscles in his arms worked, the ink designs moved with a life of their own—assorted skulls, flames, snakes, and sexy women flexed in a twining, sinister dance.

Interrupted by my question, he shot me a warning glare. "Not *me,*" he snapped. "Just relocating 'em. For . . . a friend." Then he emphatically turned back toward the shopping carts and grabbed two more carriers by the handles. He tossed them easily onto the pile, which almost reached the top of the van's cargo space.

Guess he's not one for casual conversation. So it shouldn't be a total loss, I glanced at his license plate. It was so dirty, I could only read a few letters—*N, O,* and a *Y* or *V,* plus the last number, *2.*

As I continued toward my car, I wondered if I was being overly suspicious. But really, who buys two dozen pet carriers, except someone breeding and/or selling animals? I stashed my own supplies in the hatch of my CR-V, slid in behind the wheel, and pondered some more. Then I pulled out my cell and dialed Bonelli.

Luckily, I caught her at her desk. I told her what I'd seen and gave her the partial plate information for the van.

"I realize this isn't exactly criminal behavior," I added. "I'm sure he must have paid for all those carriers, or they'd never have let him out of the store. But I thought you'd want to know, just in case he's tied in somehow with that mysterious breeding operation. He said he was 'relocating' animals for 'a friend.' That could mean the breeders have gotten spooked and are pulling up stakes."

"Mm. It's possible, from what Naughton said, that they figured out the SPCA is investigating them," Bonelli agreed.

"Plus, this was the same tattooed guy I saw last week at Gillis's Garage, arguing with Todd. Considering Todd is still missing—"

"Another good reason to check the guy out," she agreed. "Speaking of vehicles, Cassie, I have news for you, too. We got a call about a car that was abandoned at a roadhouse not too far from where that hit-and-run took place. It might—or might not—have been used to run down the guy who gave you that Bengal."

Chapter 11

That sounded like a lucky break, but . . . "'Might or might not'?" I asked Bonelli. "What do you mean?"

"According to the VIN number, it's registered to a Peter Reardon of Harrisburg, Pennsylvania."

That deflated me a bit. "Then there could be no connection."

"There still could be. Sounds enough like 'Rudy Pierson' to have been an alias. The fingerprints on the steering wheel are a match with the dead man's. Our forensics guys found a tuft of brown cat hair in the backseat and an unopened bag of litter in the trunk. But most interestingly, they found traces of blood on the tires, the same type as the dead guy's."

My breath caught. "Oh, my God. He was run over with his own car?"

"We still don't know for sure if it was the vic's car, but put it together with the medical examiner's report, and we've got a clearer picture of what happened. It looks like the dead man was beaten up before he was run over. I wouldn't call it a fight, because they found no evidence that he did any punching. But one of those blows might have killed him or at least knocked him out. Then his assailant might have run over the body to make it look like a road accident."

"Crazy!" I remembered Rudy's nervous state when he'd come to my shop. Maybe he'd had plenty to be nervous about. But did all of this even relate to Ayesha?

Bonelli added, "Our officers checked at the roadhouse where the car was found for any reports of bar fights, even arguments that might have gone outside, and they showed the sketch of the dead man around. No one admitted to seeing him there or to hearing or seeing anything relevant. The owner couldn't even remember when he'd first noticed the old green sedan sitting abandoned in a corner of the lot." The detective sighed. "So now we're trying to find out whatever we can about this Peter Reardon from Harrisburg. You may want to concentrate your search, too, on breeders in that part of Pennsylvania."

"I sure will," I promised her. "Thanks so much for the update!"

Powering down the phone, I realized I'd let time get away from me, sitting in my car in the mall parking lot, and it was almost five o'clock. Bad enough that I'd left Sarah at the helm for most of the day, but now she'd be stuck there after quitting time! I took another minute to call her and briefly explain what had happened; as always, she was a good sport about it. Then I made my way as quickly as possible through the highway's rush-hour crawl, back to downtown Chadwick.

"Don't know if it was such a good idea for you to approach that guy with the van," Sarah said, as she rose from her stool and tucked the crutch under one arm. "If he really is up to something illegal, you don't want him to think you suspect him."

I dismissed this. "I'm sure he thinks I'm just some ditzy animal lover. He turned his back on me so fast, he probably wouldn't even remember what I looked like. And even if he watched me go to my car, which I doubt, a silver-blue CR-V does not exactly set me apart from all the others on the road."

"Maybe that's a good thing." Hooking her big purse over her shoulder, Sarah limped toward the front door. "I remember when poor Rudy came in here, how upset he acted. You and I both thought it was because his house had just burned down."

"It was a convincing story," I admitted.

"To think somebody beat him senseless and then ran him over. That person either really hated him, or is a nasty piece of work who'd be capable of anything."

As she said this, Sarah pinned me with a meaningful look, and I took it seriously. I knew she'd taught for many years in inner-city high schools and still lived in a marginal neighborhood. She didn't scare easily, but she probably also knew a badass character when she saw one.

Did the tattooed man qualify? Could I imagine

him beating up Rudy, then running him down with the old green car? So that none of his blood would be found on the tires of the black van?

Remembering the stranger's dark, angry glare, I couldn't rule him out.

"I hear you," I told Sarah as I held the door open for her. "That's one reason I don't want to leave you here alone on Chadwick Day. Anyhow, you go home now and rest that ankle!"

I fed the boarders and took note that Ayesha would need more food soon. Too bad I wasn't able to find her brand at the big-box store, but it would give me an excuse to pop over and see Dawn tomorrow.

Upstairs, I took care of my own cats and threw together a quick dinner. I phoned Nick Janos and left him a request to stop by soon and fix the door of the quarantine condo. Ayesha had been so hard on it that I worried one day soon she might actually break out. I figured that right now, while she was a little mellowed, would be a good time to reinforce it. After all, it looked as if she might be in residence for a while longer.

Then I checked e-mails, but no more breeders had replied to my original query. I already had reached out to the northeastern Bengal rescue group, which requested more details about the missing cat. Since they had a good reputation, I dared to tell them more about Ayesha, including the information that someone had dyed her coat.

I spent the rest of the evening going through the classifieds in various pet magazines for breeders in Pennsylvania who offered any type of exotics. I also searched on a couple of lost pet databases, as well as on Facebook, for anyone claiming to have lost a Bengal. Surprisingly, there were quite a few postings, though not so many in Pennsylvania or New Jersey. Several included photos, and none of those animals looked quite like Ayesha. One owner stressed in her post that although her pet had leopard spots, he was "*not* a wildcat." She sounded worried that someone might chase the animal off, or even shoot him, because of his unusual coat pattern.

Great Britain had a whole registry just for lost Bengal cats, but I doubted that "Rudy"—or Peter—had traveled that far with Ayesha!

How far afield, though, might he have gone? New England, or the Southeast? Did I need to answer ads for those regions, too?

I decided for the time being to concentrate on those close to home. I answered the ones I could by e-mail, to avoid long-distance charges. For a couple of lost cat postings in New Jersey, I phoned and left messages.

Tired out, I had finally settled down to watch a movie on cable when my phone rang. The unfamiliar number had a central Jersey area code, so I answered the call with my guard up. "Hello?"

"Hi, you called earlier? You said you found a Bengal cat? I think it's mine!" The woman sounded breathless with excitement.

"That would be great, if it is," I told her, and meant it. "Can you tell me your name and where you live?"

"Doris Meacham, and I'm in East Brunswick,

New Jersey. Where are you?" When I told her, she said, "Oh, my. I can't imagine how my Xena got all the way up there!"

"As I said in my message, someone dropped her off at my shop, so it's possible he found her and took her out of your area." I grabbed a notepad from my end table to write down the name and location. "So the cat you lost is a female? How old?"

"Hmm. She's been missing a couple of months, so she'd be around three now."

My hopes rose—that was the age Mark had guessed for Ayesha, too. "I should explain, there are a lot of people out there looking for lost cats, even for Bengals, so I have to be sure I'm returning her to the right owner. Can you describe her coat? Y'know, its color and pattern?"

"It's totally gorgeous!" Doris gushed. "Honey-gold, and she has those leopard spots all over."

"Spots or rosettes?"

The woman paused. "I dunno. What are rosettes?"

"More like open circles."

"Gee, I don't remember. . . . Yes, I think she did have some of those."

I wasn't sure whether to hold this mistake against Doris—she just might not be very observant. "Are you a breeder?"

"No, no, we just got her as a pet, when she was a kitten."

"And I guess you had her spayed." Trick question.

Another beat of silence. "Not so far. We thought she should have at least one litter first, and experience being a mother. It's only natural, right?"

Bad answer, but correct in the sense that it fit

Ayesha. Maybe before giving her back, I'd try to persuade Doris to have her fixed. "Has she got any special habits that would identify her? Things she likes to play with or things you've taught her to do?"

"Let's see . . . We have a screened porch, and she liked to sit out there for hours and watch the birds. And my husband and I would throw those catnip mice for her to chase."

Too normal, I thought. I'd try lobbing her an easy one. "Ever try to walk her on a leash?"

Doris laughed out loud. "Oh, my, no. I can't imagine she'd put up with that!"

"Or give her a bath?"

The laugh took on a panicky edge. "Are you kidding? She absolutely hates water! If I want to stop her from doing something, I just have to point the plant mister at her and she runs. Anyhow, I didn't even think you were supposed to wash cats—are you?"

I thought of how patiently Ayesha had tolerated the four baths we'd given her since she came to my shop. "Mrs. Meacham, how exactly did you lose Xena?"

"We don't usually let her out, because we did pay a lot for her. But one day the delivery man was bringing in a package, and she just darted past my legs. Probably chasing a bird. I couldn't catch her. My husband and I searched for her, asked the neighbors, and even posted signs. That's why I think somebody picked her up, maybe because she was so pretty."

I asked Mrs. Meacham if her cat ever had a microchip, and needed to explain to her what that was. She said she'd never had it done, and the breeder hadn't mentioned anything like that, either.

"We got a regular license for Xena, from the town, but even that was just to be extra safe. Like I said, we never let her outside."

Mark had seemed pretty sure that Ayesha's wound came from someone removing an implant, and if the breeders had put a chip in the kitten, wouldn't they have mentioned that to the buyer? It was just one more wrong answer that tipped the scales for me.

I told Mrs. Meacham, "You seem like a nice person who really loved her cat, and I hope you do find her. But I don't think the one in my shop is your Xena."

"Oh, but she has to be!"

"I understand you're disappointed, but—"

"This is some kind of a scam, isn't it? You're preying on people who are heartbroken, who just want their animals back—"

"Not at all, Mrs. Meacham. I just need to be sure I'm returning this cat to the right person. As you said yourself, she's probably worth a lot of money—"

"Is that it? You said in your message that you weren't asking for a reward, but I thought that was too good to be true. How much do you want for her? We probably can't afford to pay what she's really worth, but . . ."

This exchange was becoming almost as emotionally draining for me as is seemed to be for Doris Meacham. "Ma'am, I'm not holding your cat for ransom. It's just that I can tell, from the way you answered some of the questions, that this isn't Xena. This Bengal did have a microchip until recently, she's fine with being bathed, and she walks on a leash. Does that sound like your cat?"

I heard silence for a moment. Then Doris came back in a defeated tone, "No . . . I guess it doesn't."

"I'm very sorry. If, while I'm networking, I hear of anyone in New Jersey who may have found your cat, I'll be sure to let them know. In the meantime, you might try contacting this Bengal rescue group. . . ." By the time I got off the phone, I'd left the woman a bit calmer and armed with information that might help her track down Xena.

The movie I'd planned to watch was almost over, and anyhow, all I could think of was hitting the sack. But frustration over the latest phone call even dogged me in my sleep: I dreamed of a certain warrior princess, dressed in a leopard skin, war-whooping and swinging a sword as she chased me through the dark, tangled woods of Rattlesnake Ridge.

"Got just the thing for you, I think!" Nick Janos announced Thursday morning when he arrived at my back door. In one hand, he toted his enormous, battle-scarred red toolbox. In the other, he proudly brandished some tightly-rolled black mesh.

"Oh, yeah?" I asked. "Some wonder product?"

"It's fiberglass. They also use it for safety window screening. Y'know, so little kids don't fall out. Supposedly you can't bite or scratch through it."

"Maybe I can't and you can't," I warned him, "but you haven't met Ayesha."

"No, really. This stuff's guaranteed."

We made our way from the back door to the condo area. The sturdy little man with the thinning gray hair hadn't been out to do work at my shop in a while, and I asked how he'd been. "No more trouble with the ticker, I hope?"

He thumped his chest. "Keepin' good time, these days. Probably since I haven't had any more worries about my boy."

When his son Dion was accused of murder a few months ago it had stressed Nick badly. "I guess he's doing great now, huh? Since Encyte bought that cybersecurity program he invented?" A big California firm recently had paid major bucks for software that Dion had developed while working as a video game tester and freelance programmer.

Nick chuckled. "I guess so, though you'd never know it. Still sleeps in the same room he had as a kid, works in his office in the basement and sees clients there. Pays me a little rent. You'd think he'd want his own place, now that he can afford it, but I 'spose he likes having the company. Tell the truth, since my wife passed, I do, too."

"Well, that makes sense. And especially after your health scare, he probably wants to keep an eye on you."

"I just worry that he doesn't get out enough. I'd like him to meet a nice girl, have a family of his own. You can't live all the time in a make-believe world of video games. But it's his life." The handyman shrugged. "Anyway, where is this crazy cat you told me about?"

I showed him to Ayesha's condo, and after murmuring appreciation for her athletic physique and slightly muted spots, he agreed that she'd really done a number on the door of her enclosure. Still, he sounded confident that he could fix the problem. I removed Ayesha to the playroom so Nick could work his magic.

Unscrewing the door from its hinges, he asked me, "Where did you say you got this cat?"

Since it wasn't a secret anymore, I told him the whole story of how a man going by the name of Rudy Pierson had brought her to my shop, and was later found dead of an apparent hit-and-run. Nick froze with the door suspended in his hands.

"Jeez, you're kidding." He stared at me. "It had to be the same guy."

"Same as who?"

"I think *I* sent him your way. About a week ago, I stopped in the convenience store at the big Gulf station up on Carter Road. While I was waiting in line, the young guy in front of me asked the owner if she knew any place nearby that would keep a cat for him, just for a couple of days. Said he'd had a house fire and was desperate. I could tell the shop owner didn't want to be bothered. Finally she told him that an old lady up the road had a lot of animals and maybe would take another. But I knew the place she meant, and I figured that wouldn't work out, so I chimed in and told the guy about your shop."

Another mystery cleared up. I'd been wondering if Pierson/Reardon could have somehow found me online, but it had seemed unlikely. "They ran his picture in the *Courier* when he was killed, asking if anyone knew who he was. I guess you didn't see it."

Nick's mouth twisted beneath his trimmed gray mustache. "I don't always read the paper, and if I watch TV news, it's usually the national stuff. Tell you the truth, I completely forgot about meeting and talking to him until now." He went back to his work, using a hammer to pop off the staples that held the old, damaged mesh to the door frame. "I thought I was just throwing a little business your way. I sure didn't mean to get you mixed up in anything crooked. They think somebody might've killed him on purpose?"

"The cops are looking into it, anyway. And I'm trying to help, by contacting any breeders who might be missing a cat." A sudden connection occurred to me. "This old lady, the one the store owner mentioned. Do you know anything about her? Where she lives?"

Nick rolled up the ruined mesh and tossed it aside. "I used to do a little work for her, years ago, but then I started to make up excuses not to go back. Her place is a holy mess, just overrun. Cats, dogs. I think she's also got a coupla birds flying around. It's not even healthy to breathe in there."

"Sounds bad. Does she breed any cats like Ayesha? Could Rudy have gotten her from there?"

The handyman reflected for only a second before shaking his head. "I don't think so. Her cats breed, all right, but they're just mutts and strays. None of 'em look like your fancy cat. Hold this in place for me?"

I held the edge of the new screening against the inside of the door frame while he secured it with a staple gun. Between shots, I told him, "A shame, when people let a situation get out of control like that."

"Gotta feel sorry for her," Nick agreed. "She can't be right in the head. I worry sometimes about Dion being obsessed with his computers. Then I see a case like her, and tell myself, hey, it could always be worse."

Chapter 12

Nick finished the repair job in about half an hour. I returned Ayesha to her condo, and from what we could see, the new mesh did hold up much better, even when she climbed on it with her full weight.

After Nick had gone, I left Sarah comfortably settled behind the shop's counter and headed off on some more errands.

I stopped by Alpha Printing to collect my table runner, which had turned out nicely. The shop's name in a cheery purple font attracted attention, and Keith's cartoon of the long-haired cat smiled proudly beneath. Dave, the printer, had also made me a foot-tall, stand-up sign that read, HAVE A FELINE-RELATED PROBLEM? ASK THE CAT LADY!

He bagged both of these products for me. We chatted for a minute about how his store had been in town for more than twenty years. With his wife and grown daughter as helpers, he'd so far managed to survive competition from the highway office supply stores. I also told him a little more about my business. Dave wished me luck on Chadwick Day and then I hit the sidewalk again.

En route back to work, I dropped by Nature's Way and showed the runner and the sign to Dawn, who approved.

"I just hope I didn't waste my money." I explained why I might have to skip Chadwick Day. "Of course, I suppose there'll be other events where I can use these to promote my business."

Meanwhile, Rick, from the organic farm, had come in the store's rear entrance. I smiled and said hello to the guy, but he just grunted back. That surprised me, because Teri had been so friendly. Not the first time, though, that I'd come across a couple where one was pleasant and outgoing and the other standoffish or even a real jerk. At least, I assumed Rick and Teri were a couple. His trimmed beard, olive-green T-shirt, and guerrilla-style pants also made an odd contrast with what I remembered of her disheveled, farm girl style.

He hovered a few feet away from us, holding some paper that he probably needed to discuss with Dawn. Tigger made a playful attempt to climb his leg, but when Rick felt the tiny claws pierce his camo pants, he shook the kitten off.

"Well, at least your mother volunteered to help this weekend," Dawn reminded me. "I know she's not the world's greatest cat lover, but maybe that will solve your problem."

"If it doesn't, I might have to pay a professional pet sitter," I told her. "I need someone reliable.

Sarah's going to help me at my table with Harpo, and even if I close up the shop, I don't want to leave it unstaffed."

My friend stepped away then, to settle up her bill with Rick. Meanwhile, I picked up another case of Ayesha's food, which drew Rick's attention when I brought it up front. Maybe he'd noticed the price and wondered how I could afford it? I was starting to wonder that myself. Another reason why I wanted to find the Bengal's owner soon—the slim hope that I might get reimbursed for feeding Her Voracious Majesty for a whole month.

Rick had another brief conversation with Dawn and then the two of them approached me with smiles. Common for her, unexpected in his case.

"Cassie, Rick just had a suggestion that might help you out," Dawn said.

"You met my partner Teri, right?" he asked me. "She loves cats, had 'em all her life. If you really need somebody to watch your shop for you on Saturday, she'd probably be glad to do it."

It took me aback just a little to realize that the guy had been eavesdropping on us. Then again, Dawn and I hadn't made any effort to keep our voices down. His offer kind of blindsided me, too. It was nice to have another option, but I knew very little about Teri or Rick except that they ran a fairly successful organic farm. I felt I needed more credentials than that, but I had to be tactful.

"Well, thanks," I said. "Dawn may have told you that my mother has volunteered. She's coming by tonight, in fact, to learn the routine. But if you want, give me your number, and I'll keep Teri in mind."

"Here's one of their cards," Dawn said, and passed it to me. Rick shook my hand with another of what I suspected were his rare smiles.

After he went back out to his truck, I expressed my misgivings to Dawn. "I really don't know Teri well enough to leave her in charge all day. Especially with all the drama going on around Ayesha."

My friend shrugged. "I thought you might feel that way, but, hey, he offered. Guess you still haven't tracked down the real owner of your mystery cat, eh?"

"Unfortunately not. Last night, I had a caller who sounded promising at first." I sat across from Dawn, in one of the paisley-draped chairs near her dormant cast-iron stove, and explained about the woman who'd refused to believe that I *didn't* have her cat. "She was so desperate, I might even have been able to sell her Ayesha as a replacement, but I couldn't do that. Not if there's any chance the real owner is still out there looking."

Tigger, bored again, attacked Dawn's sandaled feet where they peeked out from beneath her long sundress. With a groan, she scooped the kitten into her arms. "Call that lady back and tell her she can have an eight-month-old tabby, for nothing!"

"Aw, you know you'd never give away this little guy." I scratched the top of his striped head until he slitted his eyes and purred like a miniature lawnmower.

Dawn offered me some organic iced tea, and when I accepted, she retrieved two bottles from a big, glass-fronted refrigerator at the back of her store.

"So, did you and Mark ever make up after Saturday?" she asked.

"We finally did, thank goodness. He also helped me out with an urgent problem last night." I told her about the after-hours trip to the clinic with Ayesha. "While I was there, I had a brief conversation with Jennifer. She confided in me that she's doing all she can to help the clinic run more efficiently because she finds Mark so 'inspiring.' "

Dawn's mouth dropped open. "She didn't!"

"I'm telling you, either the girl is totally clueless—which I doubt—or she's an expert at this game. Just in case, I'm keeping my eye on her."

My friend shook her head and took another swallow of her tea. "Speaking of banes of your existence, did you hear that Todd Gillis has disappeared? Keith was at the garage yesterday, getting a part for his motorbike, and old man Gillis is doing all the repairs himself. He's really upset, and asking everyone who comes in if they've seen or heard from Todd."

"I know. He even called me on Sunday." I told her, then, about my session with Bonelli and Naughton. "They were speculating that Todd might have gone out looking for the wildcat and gotten lost or hurt."

"Never thought of that. It'd be a nutty thing to do, especially by himself, but who knows?" She rolled the frosty bottle thoughtfully between her palms. "If Todd might have gone up to the ridge, I should ask Rick or Teri if they've seen him."

"Maybe Todd found their 'tomato plants,' " I

suggested, with an evil grin. "He smoked a lot of ganja and just forgot to come home."

Dawn laughed and wagged a finger at me. "Cassie, don't you say anything. . . ."

"If the cops don't ask, I won't tell. Anyway, if nothing worse than that has happened to Todd, his folks will be lucky."

Back at the shop, I parked the case of cat food on my sales counter and asked Sarah if anything had happened while I was out.

"You had a call from Madame Bonelli," she told me. "No emergency, but she's got some new information on the guy who dropped off Ayesha."

"No kidding!" Mentally, I reviewed my schedule for the afternoon. Latte's owner was picking him up at two, but that left me plenty of time to give the Abyssinian a final brushing before then. I returned the detective's call.

Bonelli told me, "The photo Motor Vehicles has on file for Peter Reardon matches our sketch of the hit-and-run victim. He was registered at a Harrisburg address and we located a sister in the same area. She was upset, of course, to hear about his death. She said her brother had been going through a rough time and working at a string of part-time jobs. The last was helping out at 'a cat place' in Grantville, which is maybe twenty miles away. Since it's a small town, we didn't have too much trouble finding out if anyone there bred cats."

"And?" I urged her.

"We came up with Brewster's Bengals, which is

probably just run out of somebody's house. I talked to a Don Brewster, who said he's all but shut the business down. His wife mostly ran it, and now she's seriously ill. Reardon was working for them until recently, but Brewster let him go, along with a couple of other staffers. He was shocked to hear that Pete might have been killed and offered to cooperate fully with our investigation."

Then Brewster probably isn't a suspect in the hit-and-run, I reflected, though you could never be sure. "That's good progress. Did you ask him about Ayesha?"

"I just told him a woman here in Chadwick might have one of his cats, brought to her by Pete, which is why we ended up looking for a breeder in Pennsylvania. I figure you'll want to take it from there, since you've got your own methods for screening out people who make false claims."

"Thanks, Angela, this is great. We finally got a real break, eh?" I remembered something else. "Did you ever get a chance to check out that guy with the van, the one I saw arguing with Todd?"

"I tried. Didn't sound familiar to Bob Gillis, but he said Todd handles some customers while he handles others. If the guy paid in cash, they might not even have his name on record." Before signing off, Bonelli assured me, "We're still looking into it."

I brushed Latte's short coat and had him ready when his rather elfin-looking male owner arrived at a little after two. Luckily, Ayesha had piped down considerably since Mark gave her the shot, and no longer wailed at a volume that reached customers all the way out by the sales counter.

After that, I put in a call to Don Brewster, but got his voice mail. Nevertheless, I felt I could see the light at the end of the tunnel. I would kind of miss Ayesha, but she was high-maintenance and took time and attention away from my paying customers' cats, not to mention my own. Returning her to her rightful master should be a win for all concerned.

Around four thirty I told Sarah, "I'm ordering a pizza, since Mom will be coming here without supper. You're welcome to join us, if you don't have plans."

She hesitated. "Well, I'm supposed to help out with a game night at my church. But that doesn't start until seven, and they only serve desserts . . . so I guess I can have a slice with you before I go."

"Please do." I pulled out my phone. "Half mushroom and half plain?"

"Okay by me."

The pizza arrived at about the same time my mother did, and Sarah let the delivery guy in the front door while I unlocked the back for Mom. She commented on this new element of caution, but I brushed it off. "Sometimes cats are loose in the playroom, so I have to make sure no one accidentally lets them out."

When Mom saw and smelled the pizza, she tried unsuccessfully to pay for it.

"Not necessary," I said. Then I surveyed her

cream tailored slacks, yellow knit shell, and linen blazer. She was dressed impeccably for a law office in early August, but not so appropriately for eating gooey cheese and tomato sauce.

"Guess I should have warned you." I got out some paper plates and napkins to mitigate the damage, and Mom hung up her blazer in a safe spot.

"I'll just use plenty of these," she said, taking a fistful of the napkins. "So Sarah, how are you doing? Cassie told me about your accident."

Sarah and Mom had met that spring, and ever since, my mother kept reminding me how lucky I'd been to find such a competent, responsible, and pleasant assistant. Little did she know that I confided far more in Sarah than I did in her about my everyday problems. That was partially because it would have been hard to hide them from Sarah and partially because she was less prone to pass judgment or have an anxiety attack.

Occasionally, she even conspired with me to spare my mother's feelings. For example, when Mom offered her sympathies now over my assistant's sprained ankle, Sarah echoed my explanation that she'd fallen in the parking lot, leaving out the detail that she'd been pushed by a would-be mugger.

Mom preferred her pizza plain, so Sarah and I started on the mushroom half. Meanwhile, I showed off my new table runner and sign, and both ladies got a kick out of them. We went on to discuss our agenda for Chadwick Day.

"You may want to wear something a little more . . . uh . . . fur-resistant on Saturday," I advised my mother.

"Well, you mainly need me to help Sarah here in front, don't you?" she asked.

"Yes, but she's going to join me outside for a couple of hours, for a grooming demonstration with Harpo. He belongs to Sarah now, y'know."

"You remember Harpo, don't you, Mrs. McGlone?" my assistant teased.

"How could I forget?" Mom laughed, with an edge that suggested she was reliving that spring's drama. "He's certainly had more than his fifteen minutes of fame."

Scoring a second slice of pizza, I stepped toward the front display window and pointed out into the deepening twilight. "I'm hoping to set up on Center Street, right near this corner. I don't want to be too far away, in case I have any problem with Harpo or you need me back here."

Sarah used a paper napkin to wipe her hands and mouth. "Well, that was a treat! But now I'd better get going."

"Your life is a whirlwind of activity," I told her, with a laugh. "Just don't overdo it with that ankle."

"Ah, it'll be fine by next week."

I held the front door open, as it was still easier for Sarah to park on the street and avoid the rear steps. As she hopped out to her car with the aid of her crutch, she called back, "Nice seeing you again, Mrs. McGlone."

When I got back to the sales counter, Mom was

closing up the pizza box with two plain slices still inside—curtailing temptation for both of us.

"How are your Pilates classes going?" I asked.

"Oh, they're all right. I don't go as regularly as I should. It's hard to make time in the morning before work, and at night I'm too tired."

I was sorry to hear that, because I'd been trying to nudge Mom into finding a hobby. Anything besides worrying about me, which she'd been doing more of since my father passed, three years ago. So far she'd tried her hand at golf, because some of her work friends played, and for a while she'd halfheartedly joined an evening book club. But nothing seemed to hold her interest for long.

"That certainly was a good pizza," she said, collecting our plates and tossing them in the trash.

"Wasn't it? Mark tipped me off about that place. He's kind of a foodie."

"Oh, really?" This caught her attention, because I guess I rarely volunteered information about my veterinarian friend.

"He made dinner for us at his place last weekend," I added. "Some kind of pasta with chicken and spinach, and a big salad. He can really cook!"

"Sounds ideal, since I know that's not one of your favorite pastimes." Mom used the side of her hand to guide a few pizza crumbs from the counter into her napkin, which she neatly balled up and threw in my trash can. "Did he ever solve those problems at his office?"

I'd forgotten I even told her about that. "He's still dealing with them. Frankly, I think one of his employees is causing most of the trouble, but I have to tread lightly. You know how it is—he can say negative things about his people, but he doesn't like to hear me do it." Time to move things along, I thought, before Mom segued into asking if Mark and I were serious, and if marriage and grandchildren might finally be on the horizon. "C'mon, let me show you around to refresh your memory."

Although Mom had visited my shop a few times before, I updated her on the latest features, including the new alarm system. She didn't question the need for that, knowing I'd had a break-in the past spring. Next, we visited the nearly full boarding quarters, where Ayesha greeted us by climbing her new screen door. I explained to Mom that she was an exotic breed called a Bengal, she'd been dropped off about two weeks ago, and would probably be picked up by her owner soon. I did add, "She's very valuable and kind of mischievous, so now and then she may need extra attention."

Mom was already giving her that, though she seemed less admiring than apprehensive.

"There are no pick-ups or drop-offs scheduled for Saturday," I went on, "and I'll clean the litter pans and feed all the boarders before I leave. Some of them will need to eat again, though, in the middle of the afternoon. Sarah can do some of the feeding, but since she's still on the crutch, she'll need your help. Why don't you give me a hand now, to get the hang of it?"

Mom did help me scoop dry food into most of the cats' bowls. But when we opened one condo, the Siamese—not happy to be confined in a strange place—snarled at us; Mom jumped back as if she'd been snakebit. A few boarders, including Ayesha, needed canned food, which took a bit more time and care to dish out. The impatient Bengal sprang forward to swat at the can, and Mom dropped it with a shriek.

This made me do a rethink. When I lived at home as a kid, we had indoor/outdoor cats. The times that Mom had visited my apartments, she tended to keep a distance from my pets, but I always assumed she just didn't want fur on her clothes.

Now I began to wonder.

"She wasn't trying to hurt you, she was just playing." I rested a hand on my mother's shoulder and noted the stoic thrust of her small, round, Irish chin. "Do you have a cat phobia?"

"I wouldn't call it a *phobia*," she insisted. "It's just that they're so fast . . . and unpredictable. And they make that nasty hissing noise."

Good Lord. No wonder she hadn't been terribly supportive about my choice of career. She'd always seemed okay with dogs, though, as long as they weren't too big or vicious-looking. Maybe there are cat lovers and dog lovers because the two species have very different body languages.

Whatever the reason, Mom might have a steep learning curve before she really felt relaxed around felines.

"The last thing you'll need to do"—and by now, I didn't have high hopes for this, either—"is let a cat out into the playroom for a while and then put it away again. We'll try that with Jimmy, since he's very sweet."

The handsome gray Chartreux had finished his

dry meal, so I opened his door and let my mother gingerly take him out. I demonstrated how she should hold a cat against her body, facing over her shoulder, so he felt secure. We took him into the playroom, and I showed Mom how to get him to chase the fishing pole toy. Jimmy played with it right away, helping to boost her confidence. Then he scampered up onto the shelves, halting on one about five feet up.

My mother looked dismayed. "Now what?"

"That's fine, they're supposed to climb on those. If you have to bring him back from a really high shelf, you can lure him with the toy or a treat. Since this isn't too far up, though, just go lift him down."

I might as well have asked her to defuse a bomb. Mom is short, so the shelf was about at her eye level, and she could not figure out how to take hold of Jimmy. Probably, she was afraid he would claw her face! She reached toward him and then backed off so many times, from different directions, that even this mellow boy laid his ears back and looked ready to scratch her.

One rule in handling most animals: Do it with conviction, or don't do it at all!

I handed Mom a cat treat, which did bring the gray cat down to a lower level. But she still was afraid to let him take it from her hand, so she just set it on the shelf. I should have insisted that she at least pick him up, but my impatience won out and I did it myself.

"I dunno, Mom," I said. "Sarah can't really carry the cats until she gets rid of her crutch, so this is something I would need you to do. And if there was any kind of emergency, like if a boarder got loose, you'd have to be the one to catch it. But if you're really afraid . . ."

"I'm sorry, Cassie." Her head of auburn waves drooped. "I didn't know you needed me to be so . . . hands-on. And I didn't think it would bother me this much."

I put Jimmy away and accompanied Mom back to the front of the shop, her cat-free comfort zone. "I probably could help you get over your fear a little at a time. I don't think we can accomplish that, though, by this Saturday."

My phone rang then. The screen showed an out-of-state number, which could have been a solicitor . . . except the caller was leaving a message.

"Aren't you going to answer it?" Mom asked.

"It can wait." I put the phone back in my pocket.

She smiled knowingly. "Mark, eh? I can take the hint. I'll leave so you can talk to him in private." She retrieved her linen jacket.

Seeing her out the back door, I gave her a goodbye hug. "Don't feel bad, Mom. You might not be much of a cat wrangler, but you're still a terrific mother and a heck of a good paralegal."

"Well, those things *are* higher on my list of priorities. But I'm sorry to leave you without anyone to watch your shop Saturday."

I shrugged. "I've got one more day. Maybe I can still find someone."

Once she had left, I double-locked the back door and set the alarm, as I always did these days. Then I played the phone message and heard a man's upbeat voice.

"Hi, this is Don Brewster. I understand one of

my former employees, Pete Reardon, brought you a cat that might be mine. Detective Angela Bonelli said, to prove I'm the real owner, I should tell you this—not sure why, but—anyway, the cat's full name is Brewster's Champion Crown Princess Ayesha."

Chapter 13

I was as excited to return Brewster's call as he was to hear from me. I told him I had been e-mailing breeders and scouring ads for any mention of a lost female Bengal.

"Wow, I'm sorry you went to all of that trouble," he said. "The truth is, I haven't been looking for her, because I didn't realize she'd been stolen."

That sounded odd. "You mean, because you have so many cats, or . . ."

"No, but I never had that much to do with the business part of the cattery until recently. It was really my wife's project, but Laura's been ill for the past few months. Very ill . . . She's had a recurrence of breast cancer. So she's been gradually getting out of the business, let most of her staff go and sold a few cats. After I started handling things, I noticed Ayesha was gone. I just assumed Laura sold her to another breeder, but you say Pete had her?"

I told him how Reardon, going by a different name, had brought the Bengal to my shop with her coat dyed brown.

"Well, that's a damned strange thing!" Brewster said. "If he wanted to sell her, why do that? It would diminish her value. Be hard even to prove she was a Bengal."

"That's what I thought," I said. "I figured there must be something underhanded about it. Maybe the sale was prearranged, but he still wanted to keep her under wraps? Didn't want to call attention to her breed before the deal went through? When he left her at my shop, he swore he'd be back for her in just a couple of days. But he also seemed scared of something."

"And then he was found dead? That's so hard to believe." Brewster grew quiet for a second. "I hope we're not to blame."

Seizing on any possible explanation, I asked, "You and your wife? Why?"

"Pete was one of the employees we let go. He was never one of our most conscientious workers—a lot of late arrivals and sick days—but I think that's because his job with us was part-time, and he had to work at others to make ends meet. He did have a way with the cats and really seemed fond of them. I suppose when we fired him, he saw a chance to make up the loss of income by stealing Ayesha."

I had once thought that Rudy might have stolen the cat to rescue her from an inhumane situation, but that didn't sound like the case with the Brewsters. Of course, I hadn't seen their facility, but

don't want to call Teri? At least she's comfortable with cats. When she comes here, she always makes a fuss over Tigger, and she's good at playing with him."

I thought this over. Maybe it could work, but . . . "I just don't know anything about her, except that she and Rick have a farm that grows great produce. With a little fancy oregano mixed in."

Dawn laughed in surprise. "Is that what you're worried about? I'm sure she won't be smoking anything while she's at your shop! Sarah, the former schoolteacher, will see to that. Besides, you have a smoke alarm." Then my friend turned more serious. "I realize your Mom would have done it for free. . . ."

"I don't mind paying—I'd have to do that with a pet sitter. The main difference is, they come with references."

"But maybe the other one will be busy, too, during August. Why don't you just give Teri a call? If she sounds like she might work out, have her drop by and test her a little, same as you did with your Mom."

While I was considering this option, I saw a middle-aged man come in the front door of my shop and speak to Sarah. My heart did a hopeful skip. I doubted that Ayesha's owner could possibly have found a way to get to Chadwick this quickly, but maybe he'd sent a friend?

"Gotta go," I said. "A guy just came in who might be"—I caught myself—"a customer."

"Is he fiftyish and balding? Wire glasses and a round, rosy face?" When I affirmed all this, Dawn told me, "It's Roger Upton, the chairman for

Chadwick Day. He's making the rounds of the businesses. But you're right, you do need to talk to him."

I hung up and introduced myself and Sarah. Upton wore a short-sleeved yellow business shirt that strained a little over his stomach. He apparently was making his rounds on foot in the day's heat, because beads of perspiration dotted his high forehead.

He had never been inside my shop before and proclaimed it "wonderful." I gave him a quick tour before bringing him back to the front sales counter, where my table runner and sign lay in plain view. Sarah helpfully pointed these out to Upton, and he agreed they should attract attention to my display.

"I'm just visiting the merchants who are signed up for Chadwick Day, to finalize all the arrangements," he said. "You understand that you supply your own table, canopy, and chairs?"

"Got all that," I told him.

He scanned some instructions on his clipboard. "Because your display will be on the sidewalk, any canopy will have to be weighted down. You can use jugs of water, or sand, or . . ."

"Cat litter." I smiled.

Upton laughed. "Of course—I imagine you have plenty of that. You wrote that you won't be using any electrical equipment. . . ."

"No. I'll be doing a cat grooming demonstration, but just with special brushes and combs."

He adjusted his glasses, his expression turning wary. "So . . . you'll be working with a real cat."

"The fake ones aren't much of a challenge." I

guessed his concerns. "I'm using Sarah's cat, and he'll be wearing a harness."

"He's very mellow," my assistant added, with her motherly smile.

"Because a lot of people bring their dogs to a street fair like this," Upton explained. "Also, the FOCA shelter will have a space not too far from yours, and they'll have a few animals for adoption. They'll be in cages or on leashes, but . . . We wouldn't want to set off a melee."

"Harpo will only be out there for about an hour. I'll keep a carrier right on hand, and at the first sign of trouble, I'll put him back into it."

"Oh . . . Harpo! He's something of a celebrity in this town, isn't he?" Upton chuckled. "Well, sounds as if you've thought of everything. And you'll also be selling merchandise?"

"I'll have some of our cat furniture and grooming tools on display, and I'll be taking special orders," I told him.

"Very good." He made another brief note, then met my gaze again with a beaming smile. "Well, Ms. McGlone, I have a few more merchants to visit, but we're delighted that you're taking part your first year here. It's new businesses like yours that are helping to revitalize Chadwick. We plan to transform it from just another tired small town to a charming destination for city folks who want to get away from the hustle and bustle, whether for a day, a weekend, or longer."

The shop phone rang, but Sarah answered it. Meanwhile, I had to admire Upton's obviously rehearsed speech, and wondered if he had any political aspirations beyond the Chamber of Commerce.

"Of course you, in particular, did our town an unusual service this spring," he added, "by helping to solve a local murder at great personal risk. I'm sure many of our residents will be excited to speak with the cat lady sleuth on Chadwick Day!"

I shook his outstretched, pink hand. "Thanks. I'm looking forward to it."

While I watched Upton head off to visit his next merchant, Sarah sent me a crooked smile. "You might've committed yourself too soon."

"What's wrong?"

"You only called two pet sitters, right? That was the second one—she's also booked solid through this month."

"Oh, Lord." Now, after all of Upton's enthusiasm, I really didn't feel I could just back out of Chadwick Day at the last minute.

Okay, I'd give Teri a try.

Chapter 14

I poured myself another cup of coffee, for energy, before I phoned Schaeffer's Organic Produce.

"Hello?" said a gruff voice.

"Hi, is this Rick?" I asked.

"Who is this?"

"Sorry, this is Cassie McGlone. We spoke at Nature's Way yesterday, about Teri maybe helping out at my shop tomorrow during Chadwick Day?"

"Oh, sure! I'm sorry, I thought you were . . . Yeah, she'd be glad to do it. She's real good with cats. Want me to put her on?" He called out to her, as if from another room. They had a brief, muffled exchange before she took the phone.

"Hi, Ms. McGlone!"

"Call me Cassie, please. How are you doing?"

"Great, just great. I hear you need somebody to watch the kitties tomorrow while you're doing the street fair."

"Yeah, I'm kind of stuck. Rick probably told you, my assistant sprained her ankle, so she can't do much except sit at the front counter. My mom turns out to be cat-phobic, and the professional pet sitters I called were tied up."

"Sure, I can do it. Rick can spare me for a few hours. He's got a couple of other guys to help out here."

"Great! I can pay you the typical sitter's fee, if that's okay." I quoted her a modest rate, and she said it would be fine.

I glanced at my watch—it was about two. "If you're not too busy, could you drop by the shop this afternoon so I can orient you? I'll be moving pretty fast tomorrow morning, to set up. It would be better if you know the routine ahead of time."

She checked with Rick and got back to me. "I can be there around three, three thirty. That okay?"

"Perfect. I'll see you then."

I hung up feeling a bit more relaxed.

"The lady from the farm is gonna do it?" Sarah asked me.

"She sounded positively eager," I said. "Who knows? Either they need the extra money, or she really loves cats."

Rick dropped Teri off at my shop right at three. As when I'd seen her before, she wore a floaty top that covered her upper arms—this time beige mesh over a white tank—with hip-hugger jeans. Her long, layered hair was parted in the middle and blonder near the ends. I introduced her to

Sarah and showed her around the boarding area. Teri commented on the different breeds of the cats, as if trying to reassure me that she did know her stuff. But at least she seemed perfectly at ease around them.

"Don't be insulted," I told her, "because I put my own mother through this same routine, but I'd like to see you feed a couple of the boarders."

"No problem," Teri said.

I figured I'd really put her to the test, asking her to deal with the two liveliest cats, Mia and Ayesha. She first removed their empty bowls, being careful not to let the animals slip out of their condos. She measured out the right amount of food into clean dishes and replaced Mia's with no fuss. When Teri stretched out her arm, the mesh sleeve fell back and I noticed four short, purplish marks on the inner flesh, just below her elbow.

Scratches, maybe, from one of her own cats? But they look too wide for that. . . .

Next, she opened Ayesha's door while holding the bowl of fresh food. Predictably, the Bengal charged forward and tried to grab the dish.

"No!" Teri scolded, and with her free hand slapped Ayesha lightly on the head. While it certainly didn't do the cat any harm, it shocked her and made her shrink back. Satisfied, Teri set the dish down and closed the condo.

She turned to me with a smile, maybe expecting praise for the way she'd handled the challenge.

"Obviously, you're not afraid of cats," I told her. "And you didn't give either of them a chance to escape, which is a good thing. But I wasn't so crazy about the hitting."

Teri looked wounded. "Gee, I didn't do it to hurt her. Just to make her back off."

"I understand, but it's not a good idea to make a cat afraid of people's hands. These aren't my personal pets, and I try not to discipline them any more than is really necessary. Okay?"

"Got it," she said, with a nod.

For her final challenge, I turned Heckle and Jeckle loose in the playroom. Teri showed real skills in getting them to chase the "bird" on the fishing pole and clamber up on the wall shelves. After a couple of minutes, I told her to catch them and put them back in their shared condo.

Heckle (I think) had made it up to the five-foot-high shelf, and even though Teri was taller than my mother, this also posed a challenge for her. She stood on her tiptoes to reach the cat, but he was enjoying his freedom and shrank away from her. As he made a move to jump down, she grabbed him by the scruff of the neck. Though he howled in protest, she carried him that way for a second before putting her other arm under his back legs to support him.

I took him from her. "Okay, not crazy about the scruffing, either."

"Oh, sorry. I do that with my own cats all the time. It's the way their mother carries them, after all."

"When they're kittens, not when they weigh ten pounds. Here, we only do that in case of a real emergency, okay?"

Teri nodded, and at my direction, she used a treat to coax the other tuxedo cat from his shelf.

After he reached the floor, she squatted to gather him up more gently. Her low-rise jeans rode down a little in back, revealing pale skin and a mottled lavender-and-yellow rainbow that arched above her waistband.

"Wow," I said, "where'd you get that nasty bruise?"

Teri straightened up with a start, clutching the cat to her chest. "Oh, that?" She made a face. "I backed into some tools in the garden shed. Too lazy to turn the light on first. Dumb, right?"

I said nothing more. Together, we put Heckle and Jeckle back into their shared condo.

My criticisms still seemed to worry Teri, and she apologized again. "I should have asked you ahead of time if you had any special rules for handling them. Really, I won't do anything you don't want me to."

"It's okay." I tried to convince myself, too. "Just keep in mind that they belong to other people. We don't want any of the owners coming back to say his cat suffered some kind of trauma while it was here. Being boarded and groomed is enough to shake up some animals, so I try to stress them out as little as possible."

"Makes sense."

We walked back out to the sales counter, where Sarah sat. She still wore the padded boot, but no longer needed to keep her foot propped up. I made an executive decision: I would let Teri help out, but only under supervision.

"If you have any questions tomorrow," I told her, "just ask Sarah. She'll be here all day, too."

My assistant looked surprised to hear this, but Teri even more so.

"Oh . . . she will?" The younger woman glanced sharply at Sarah.

Now what? Don't tell me she's a racist! I'd learned, since moving to this semirural suburb, that a few people here still were more bigoted than I'd thought possible in modern-day New Jersey.

"I mean," Teri amended, "that's great. I thought she was going to be out helping you, and I'd be on my own."

Sarah glanced at me as if she'd thought the same thing—that Teri would be alone for at least an hour or two.

"I can groom Harpo for the demo by myself. Things will probably go more smoothly if I have the two of you here. Okay?"

Both women nodded in response.

A honk outside. I saw Rick's truck pull up to the curb. This time, I finally got a good look at his dark green pickup with SCHAEFFER'S ORGANIC PRODUCE stenciled on the cab. The sides of the rear bed had been built up high, with a tarp fastened over the top, probably so they could stack the maximum amount of crates.

"I told him to come back for me around three thirty," Teri explained. "So, I've got the job? Thanks so much!"

"Be here around seven thirty tomorrow. That's when I'll start setting up."

"If I tell Rick, he'll be *sure* to get me here on time. Thanks again."

I watched her dash out the door and hop into the passenger seat of the truck's cab. I hoped she didn't oversleep, because I feared Rick might not take it well.

The marks on Teri's arm had come from fingers, rather than claws. And the big bruise on her back reminded me of one I'd gotten a couple of years ago, just below my left shoulder. But I hadn't backed into any tools.

I'd dared to argue with my boyfriend—now my ex—and he'd shoved me into a metal bookcase.

Later, on the phone, I told Dawn that I had agreed to let Teri help out the next day. I mentioned that I had a few misgivings about the way she'd handled the cats, and had decided to leave Sarah in the shop to supervise. I didn't mention, for the time being, my concerns about the marks I'd seen on Teri's body. After all, she could have been telling the truth about an accident in the tool shed.

I might just be hyper-alert to such signs because of my own experience.

After Sarah left for the day, I got a call from Mark, and also brought him up to speed.

"So, I'm gearing up for the street fair," I finished. "Too bad you can't take part. My offer still stands, to display some of the clinic's brochures at my table."

"That would be nice, if you have room." His voice sounded so weary, though, that I asked what was wrong.

"Another mess here," Mark admitted. "We were treating a cat for inflammatory bowel disease. I tried him on a grain-free diet, and he seemed to be recovering well. He was set to go home today, but overnight he had a setback, because Sam gave him regular food. Elena was supposed to transfer instructions about the cat's diet to his chart, but she never did."

Sounded like yet another screwup by staffers who were usually reliable. "So, Elena just forgot?"

"I personally added a note to the cat's chart, where she couldn't have missed it, but she swears she never saw it." He laughed, with an edge. "Reminds me of that old movie, *Gaslight*, where the husband plays tricks to drive the wife crazy. Except I don't know who's gaslighting who around here! All I know is, the animals are suffering."

I braced myself before I asked him, "Mark, what did the note look like? Was it on a bright green Post-it?"

"Yeah, it was. Why?"

"You're not going to like this. When I was over there the other night, talking to Jennifer, I saw her take a Post-it off one of the charts, read it, and then throw it away. She'd told me she was cleaning out old records, so at the time I didn't think anything of it. Then she put the file folder back in the cabinet."

The silence on the line worried me. Finally, he said, "I guess you wouldn't make this up."

"Of course not. Besides, how would I know the color of the note? Maybe you can still find it in the wastebasket behind the reception desk. Has your trash been taken out yet?"

"Sam would have emptied it last night." More silence.

"Are you angry with me?" I asked.

"No, babe, not with you. With myself, I guess."

"It's not your fault. Jennifer acts very sweet—I

can see why you wouldn't want to suspect her." I paused. "What are you going to do?"

"Ask her about it, tomorrow. And she'd better have a damned good answer."

"Sorry," I told him. "Try to get some sleep, okay?"

"I will, Cassie. You, too."

That was going to be hard, I thought as I hung up. So many questions, so many situations unresolved. But I made myself turn in early and tried to relax.

After all, I had to be on my toes tomorrow, for Chadwick Day.

Chapter 15

I didn't get as much rest as I'd hoped to, because my mind kept scrolling through all the things I needed to have ready for the big day. When I finally gave up at five thirty a.m., got out of bed, and fed my own three cats, I already could hear muffled sounds of activity starting up toward Center Street.

I ate a quick breakfast, showered, and dressed to prowl in a peach T-shirt, Laurel Burch cloisonné cat earrings (a birthday gift from Dawn), khaki Bermuda shorts, and cat paw print ankle socks. I chose my footwear with special care. Having taken part in a few daylong outdoor events, over the years, I wore sneakers that would be comfortable not only for lots of walking but for many hours of standing.

Rick dropped off Teri at seven thirty as promised, pulling up to the curb just long enough for her to hop out. When I met her at the door, he acknowledged me only with a combination wave and jaunty salute before he drove away.

"He doesn't like to leave the farm for too long," Teri explained. I thought of the bruise I'd seen on her lower back the day before, then wondered again if I might be jumping to conclusions.

At the sales counter, she held out a ceramic platter covered in clear plastic wrap.

"What's that?"

"Tarts, for Sarah and me," Teri said. "I thought, since we'll be here all day, we'd need something to snack on."

"Beautiful! You made 'em?"

She nodded. "With our own fresh blueberries."

I leaned over for a better look at the four tarts, each topped with a dab of whipped cream and a mint leaf. They looked delicious, and professional enough to have come from a bakery. Teri certainly did have her talents.

She set the platter on the coffee stand in back of the front counter and told me, "I didn't know if you had anything else planned for lunch. . . ."

"Oh, I wouldn't let the two of you starve. There are cold cuts, iced tea, and lemonade in there." I pointed to a mini refrigerator next to the coffee stand.

Teri and I set to work, then, tending to the boarders. Soon afterward, Sarah showed up, still on her one crutch, with her son Jay toting Harpo in a carrier. This was the second time I'd met Jay, a tall, good-looking guy in his mid-thirties with a fade haircut. He'd inherited his mother's easygoing disposition and was even following in her career footsteps as a high school math teacher.

After I introduced Jay to Teri, she helped me transfer Harpo from his carrier to my only available condo, meanwhile stroking his long, glamorous coat in awe. The beautiful, cream-colored Persian did look wonderful. I hadn't seen him since I'd officially turned him over to Sarah, but she obviously was taking good care of him. He rubbed against my hand and purred as if he remembered me.

Sarah oohed over the tarts Teri had brought and hinted that she might not wait until lunchtime to sample one. Then she explained, "I'm volunteering Jay to help you out today, Cassie. Otherwise, I figure you're going to be tied to that table all day with nobody to relieve you. Besides, somebody's got to bring Harpo to you for your demonstration, and Teri might get busy here."

Once more, I thought Teri looked startled by this suggestion, though again she quickly covered it. "Oh . . . good idea."

"I can't impose like that," I told Jay. "It'll take up your whole Saturday."

He turned up his palms in submission. "My wife, Ginny, works Saturdays at Bed Bath & Beyond up at the mall, so I'm at loose ends anyway. And this Chadwick Day thing could be fun. You should see the main street! They've got streamers on the lampposts and red, white, and blue flowers all around the park gazebo. There's a big banner across the street that says they're going to have live music later on and a classic car parade. I wouldn't mind catching some of those things."

"Well, if you really don't mind, I probably *can* use the help." I glanced at my watch. "Yikes, it's almost eight. I'd better get up to the corner and stake out my spot."

Teri squared her shoulders, ready for action, and Jay asked, "What can I do?"

"Help with the canopy, for starters. It's tricky to put up—I may need both of you."

"You got it." Jay spotted the long, zippered case leaning against the sales counter. He picked it up by the loop with one hand, far more easily than I could have.

Cars already had filled up all the legal spaces along the curb, so there was hardly any point in loading stuff into my CR-V. In the same amount of time, the three of us could carry everything up to Center Street ourselves. I hauled my six-foot folding table and let Teri bring my two pink nylon camp chairs. The trek up was only a couple of long blocks, but slightly uphill, so it gave us a mild workout.

When we reached my allotted patch of sidewalk, ten feet square, the three of us managed to raise the canopy on its telescoping pipe legs. Jay was especially helpful in securing the upper braces. Then, as per the chairman's regulations, we traipsed back to my shop to get four heavy plastic jugs of cat litter. We secured one to each canopy leg with nine-inch bungee cords. Even in a hurricane, which didn't seem likely, that baby wasn't going anywhere.

I set up the table, draped it with my new runner, propped up the new Cat Lady sign, and filled a clear plastic, vertical holder with my brochures. Finally, we brought up some samples of merchandise from my shop, ranging from cat treats, toys, and collars to a few carpeted tunnels and towers.

Teri returned to the shop then, to help Sarah staff the counter. Jay and I opened the camp chairs and set them behind the table. I donned my dark green grooming apron with the shop's name printed on the front, so I'd be a walking advertisement wherever I might roam.

The cops had closed the street to anyone not involved in setup. By eight thirty, tables and displays lined the main drag of town as far as the eye could see. The heat and humidity already foretold a scorcher, and I was glad that, now that she'd moved to an apartment, Mom had given me the family's old party canopy for occasions like this.

"As long as you're here," I told Jay, "I'm going to stroll around and check out the other displays, before the crowds start swarming."

"Sure, have fun." He folded his tall frame comically, but comfortably, into one of the pink chairs. "Just be warned, though—if anyone asks me advice about their cat, I don't know a scratching post from a lamppost."

I laughed. "I'll be back by nine, I promise."

Wandering down Center Street, I noted that these days my town certainly boasted a good assortment of merchants, businesses, and nonprofit groups. Cottone's Bakery, Chadwick Books, Towne Antiques, and the jewelry boutique Jaded all had sidewalk displays, with merchandise at special Chadwick Day prices. Beneath a canopy that read MAKING MEMORIES, a wedding and portrait photographer fussed with an arrangement of his images, blown up large.

Eye of the Beholder was even offering the silk screen of the woman and the leopard for sale at a discount. My stomach dropped. Though it was still more than I could comfortably afford, I hated to think of someone else snapping it up.

I checked in with Dawn, who already was blending chilled smoothies in front of Nature's Way. Keith lounged nearby in a director's chair, sporting his trademark black artist's beret and waiting for customers to caricature.

The bank, the medical center, a lawyer, a Realtor, and an insurance company had put together less elaborate displays, mainly their business cards and brochures. The town emergency squad, the scouts, and the historical society all had taken spaces. As Upton had warned me, the Friends of Chadwick Animals, or FOCA, was set up about half a block from me. I didn't anticipate any problem, though. Their caged dogs were far enough away not to bother Harpo. He was pretty unflappable and, at any rate, I planned to keep a tight hold on him. On the plus side, I might get some spillover from FOCA's audience of animal lovers.

As I strolled back to my table, Mark showed up to intercept me. He smiled and held up a fistful of brochures from his clinic.

"You kindly offered to display these," he said.

"Glad to." I introduced him to Jay, whom he hadn't met before. They chatted while I arranged the clinic's brochures next to my own flyers in the plastic stand, to keep them safe from stray breezes.

"Poor you," I told Mark. "On a day like this, having to work."

"Only until two, so I should be able to drop by again later." He paused and added, "Providing there's not too much drama today."

His serious tone made me study his face. "Expecting more problems?"

Mark took a step away from where Jay sat and lowered his voice. "I'm going to speak to Jennifer around closing time. I have no idea how that will go down, and in case it's messy, I don't want our clients to overhear."

I nodded. "Good thinking. Well, who knows? Maybe she really will have some explanation. Maybe her throwing out the note was an honest mistake."

"Always a chance, right? Except, coming on top of so many other things . . ." Mark frowned. "I'm not good at disciplining people, I guess. But it has to be done."

As he turned to go back toward his clinic, I gave his arm a squeeze. "Good luck."

"Thanks, I may need it."

The increase in foot traffic now told me, even before I checked my watch, that it was past nine and Chadwick Day had opened to the public.

I told Jay, "Feel free to roam for a while, if you want. I'll mostly need you to bring Harpo up from the shop at about one for our demo. Until then, I should be fine on my own."

He stood up. "For starters, I'll get us both some cold water."

"Excellent idea. It's getting steamy out here already."

Down toward Riverside Park, a country-western band started to play the rousing Bon Jovi song, "Who Says You Can't Go Home?" A good choice, I thought, to set the right nostalgic tone for the summer day.

As strollers began to fill the street, the interest

in my display surprised me. Over the next couple of hours, quite a few visitors stopped by. Some asked the usual questions: "Don't cats groom themselves?" and "Why do they need their own boarding kennel?" I told them that longhairs and some other breeds developed matted coats and skin issues if they weren't groomed properly, and that because cats could be so temperamental, many pet groomers would not even deal with them. I also explained that some cats fared badly in boarding facilities where they could smell dogs nearby and hear constant barking.

Whether or not those folks ever became customers of mine, at least they left with a greater understanding of why there was a need for my services.

Among the cat owners, a few told me they'd gotten long-haired cats, sometimes as rescues, without realizing their coats would need so much care. I explained how to deal with a few common problems and showed them the tools I used, without aggressively pushing them to buy anything. I also encouraged them to come back at one, when I'd be doing the demonstration with Harpo.

Many commented on the brochure that showed my shop's condo system and playroom. A number of passersby also took up my invitation to "Ask the Cat Lady" about behavioral problems.

"I have two rescues that fight constantly, and it's terrible. One keeps attacking the other. Now I have to keep one in the garage all the time, and it doesn't seem fair."

I asked this lady a few questions about how her house was set up. Then I told her to start switching the cats' rooms sometimes—putting Cat No. 1 in the garage while Cat No. 2 had the run of the place—so they would smell each other in both spaces. I also told her to play with the bully cat more, to drain off some of his hunting aggression.

"Then try feeding them a few feet apart with a sturdy, see-through barrier in between," I suggested. "Keep doing that until they'll both eat quietly that way." Finally, I advised her to put up some shelves within easy access of the floor, so the meeker cat could climb to escape the bully.

Taking my tips seriously, she actually made notes on the back of a flyer. I invited her to call and let me know how things worked out.

Someone else said his eighteen-year-old cat was starting to use the upstairs bedroom closet as a litter box, something she'd never done when she was younger. The vet had found no medical issues except some arthritis.

"Where are your actual litter boxes?" I asked her owner, a well-groomed older man wearing a T-shirt from a charity marathon.

"We've just got one," he said. "It's in the downstairs mud room."

Not hard to diagnose the problem here. "You need a second box. With the arthritis, it might be hard for her to climb up and down stairs. She gets the urge, but the first-floor mud room is too far away, so she goes wherever she is. Try adding one in the upstairs hall or bathroom."

The guy wrinkled his nose. "My wife isn't going to like that."

Suck it up, guys! But I wanted to work with him—I knew litter box issues were the top reason why many healthy cats went to shelters or even were euthanized. "Wouldn't it be better than having her mess in your bedroom closet?"

He acknowledged this, thanked me, and took a brochure.

Jay returned in time to hear some of the last exchange. He waited until the fastidious guy had left, then joked, "You should probably charge for your advice, too."

Not such an outlandish idea, I supposed. I did have credentials, after all, as an animal behaviorist. The other tips, I'd picked up just by talking with vets, reading articles by experts, and working with so many cats.

"I never thought of it," I said, "because to me, the solutions are mostly common sense. A problem cat usually needs more of something. More, or more comfortable, litter boxes. More play time with his owner. More positive associations with some other animal or person in the house. And more levels to climb, explore, and feel safe."

"To you, it's common sense," Jay pointed out, "but not to the average person. I'm just saying, you could charge for consultations."

As noon approached, he went to get us some lunch, happy to stretch his legs again. Meanwhile, I saw the green Schaeffer's truck cruise slowly by in the distance, just beyond the police sawhorses. If Rick needed to make a delivery somewhere in town, he must have been having a hard time working around the barricades.

The street was really filling up now. I knew Chadwick had a population of about eight thousand, and it felt like at least half were on the street today. Whole families browsed together, a few including babies in strollers. Now and then, someone who wasn't up to walking—usually elderly, but not always—cruised by on a medical scooter.

Jay came back with a couple of gyros from Chad's wrapped in tinfoil. A smart guy, he'd also brought a wad of paper napkins, because this specialty of the diner's could also be sloppy.

As we sat behind the display table trying to eat our lunches discreetly, muffled voices echoed from the direction of the park gazebo. I knew the mayor, the head of the chamber, and other local dignitaries were speaking, and I heard the name of General Grayson Chadwick—a minor player in the Revolutionary War, and the town's founder—invoked more than once. I'm sure the rest of the speeches sounded pretty much like the one Upton had given in my shop, about how Chadwick was transforming itself from just another shabby small town off the beaten path into a picturesque getaway with a tree-lined main street, neighborhoods of well-kept old houses, artsy shops, top restaurants, and even specialty services. I supposed my business fell into the last category.

Finished with his gyro, Jay folded his tinfoil tightly to catch any last drips of cucumber-yogurt sauce. "Probably time for me to go get our star attraction."

"It is, thanks. Let your mom get him into the grooming harness, then just snap on the leash before you put him in the carrier. If you have any questions, ask her." As Jay stood to go, I added quietly, "And let me know how she's getting along with Teri, okay?"

He grinned. "You bet."

In the meantime, I cleared as much stuff as I could off my table, thinking I should have brought a second one just for grooming. I spread a towel on top to catch any fur, and hoped that Harpo wouldn't get scared and relieve himself on my new banner. The FOCA dogs did sound off occasionally, and, as Upton had warned, many fairgoers had brought along their own pooches.

Once the Persian arrived, he did attract quite a bit of attention. Although his backward-curling tail had disqualified him from being a top show cat, he still sported a spectacular, full coat, which Sarah had kept in fine shape. She claimed she'd purposely neglected it this week so I'd have some mats to work with, but they were very few. Jay held the leash and even played carnival huckster—"Step right up, folks. Learn to groom your cat right, without a cat fight!"

As soon as the first couple stopped by to watch, more folks kept coming. I demonstrated how to use a shedding rake to thin out Harpo's dense undercoat and a wide-toothed comb to loosen the knots in his fur. I explained that if you ever had to cut any out, you needed to be very careful not to nick the cat's very thin skin.

Now that my display featured a live animal, more kids drifted over from the FOCA table to marvel at the Persian. Harpo remained a very good sport as they asked to stroke his fur and marveled at how light and fluffy it was. He did shrink back once, when someone's Doberman sniffed the edge of my table, but he didn't panic. The owner quickly tugged the dog away.

Fortunately, only one or two of the adults asked me questions about the cat's innocent connection to that local murder a few months back. I tried to answer in a way that wouldn't provoke too many questions from the children.

I was able to keep this up for more than the hour I'd planned before I finally sensed Harpo was starting to mind the crowds and the heat. "He's had enough," I told Jay as I guided the cat back into his carrier. "He did good, though. And thanks so much for the assist."

"Glad to help." Jay carried the Persian back to my shop.

While he was away, another of the day's attractions began—the parade of classic cars. They'd been scheduled to rally in the municipal parking lot at the northern end of town, near the old train station, and now they cruised slowly through the crowd. The oldest vehicles, such as a 1920s Ford and a 1940s Nash, led the way. From there, they gradually became more modern. Two bicolored models from the '50s with huge rear fins, and a '60s Volkswagen bus painted with psychedelic flowers, drew especially loud cheers from the crowd.

Suddenly, an argument broke out toward the end of the parade. At least two men were yelling, one sounding really hysterical, and the onlookers seemed to be holding him back. A young, freckled cop who'd been chilling near my street corner snapped to attention and strode off in the direction of the noise.

I stepped away from my table for a better look. The back end of the parade had come to a halt, unable to proceed because of the fracas. The car holding things up appeared to be a red Camaro driven by a dark-haired young man. A couple of folks restrained an older guy who screamed and cursed at the driver.

"You thief! That's my son's car—I'd know it anywhere. How the hell did *you* get ahold of it?"

Chapter 16

Jay came back around the corner just then. I asked him to watch my table and sprinted toward the knot of people near the Camaro.

The freckled cop beat me there and took charge of the paunchy man with the mussed gray hair. "Sir, what seems to be the problem?"

"That car belongs to my son, Todd," declared the older guy, who had to be Bob Gillis. "He drove off in it a week ago, and no one's seen him since. I wanna know how this kid ended up with Todd's car, and what the hell happened to my son!"

By that time, the cop must have recognized the garage owner. "Mr. Gillis, I understand why you're upset, but how can you be sure this is the same car?"

Bob stabbed a finger toward the top of the Camaro. "See that gap between the roof panels? We tried everything to fix that, but never could. And those 2002 OEM wheel covers, with the black trim, were special order. Too big a coincidence that this kid has the exact same ones!"

Considering this testimony, the cop turned his attention to the driver. By now, the dark-haired young man had removed his cool, wrap-around sunglasses, revealing wide, terrified eyes.

"You pull over to the curb," the officer told him. "No sense holding up the rest of the parade."

The driver steered his car out of line, and the last few vehicles proceeded along the route. The cop, whose nametag read C. WALLER, tried to disperse all of us rubberneckers and eavesdroppers. I told him I'd been a friend of Todd's (slight exaggeration) and had been working with Detective Bonelli to solve his disappearance (pretty much true). So Waller let me stand on the fringes.

He asked the young driver for his license and registration. The dark-haired man produced the first from his wallet, and it passed muster. Then he handed Waller a folded yellow paper from the glove compartment. "Didn't get to Motor Vehicles yet, to register," he explained, "but here's the title."

Waller unfolded the paper, studied it with a poker face, and did not give it back. "So, Mr. Lorenzo, you heard what this man said. Where did you get this car?"

"I . . . I answered an ad online," Lorenzo stammered. "Met somebody at a parking lot out on the highway, behind that Frosty Freeze that's been closed for years, and paid cash. It looked in good shape, and they were selling it really cheap, so I didn't ask a lot of questions."

"When was this?"

"Coupla days ago . . . W-Wednesday morning."

His wide-eyed stare swung toward Bob Gillis. "Sorry about your son, man, but I got no idea where he is."

"Maybe he sold you the car?" Waller suggested.

"Could be, but I wouldn't know him to see. I talked to a guy on the phone, but a chick met me in the parking lot and gave me the keys."

Hearing this, Gillis protested. "That's a load of bull—"

"Does sound funny," Waller agreed. "If you met out by the old Frosty Freeze on the highway, how was this 'chick' going to get home?"

Lorenzo's features twisted. "I kinda wondered about that, too. It was a big lot, though. Her boyfriend coulda been parked somewhere out of sight, behind the building."

Gillis, red-faced, began to storm again. "You're making all this up!"

Waller pulled out his radio and called for backup. Then he announced, "We'll sort all this out at the station. Mr. Lorenzo, Mr. Gillis, you'll ride with me. Another officer will bring the Camaro."

A moment later they had gone, and I started back to my table, my brain reeling with questions. It sounded as if someone had sold Todd's Camaro under sketchy circumstances reminiscent of a drug deal. They hadn't charged very much, as if they were simply trying to unload it. Ominous, I thought. Still, it was the business of the Chadwick PD to get to the bottom of it, not mine.

I passed by the FOCA booth, staffed by four members of the animal rescue group, and did a double-take. The scary tattooed man had stopped at their table.

They all chatted in an amiable way, sometimes laughing quietly and shaking their heads. I tried to slip by unnoticed, but the long-haired guy must have spotted me anyway. By the time I returned to my table, he was staring hard in my direction. He turned back to the FOCA crowd, as if maybe to ask about me, and I wanted to hide beneath the overhang of my new table runner. Instead, I turned to Jay and filled him in on the controversy over the Camaro, hoping his presence might offer some protection.

"'Scuse me," said a deep voice, and I knew there would be no escape. "You Cassie McGlone? You got the cat place around the corner?"

I made myself face the tattooed man with a smile. "That's right." Up close, there was definitely something Charlie Mansonish about his piercing, dark gaze, though offset by a glint of humor. Today, with his black jeans, he wore a faded Alice Cooper concert T-shirt, less garish than the tattoos it partially covered.

"Arnie Lang. We ran into each other a coupla days ago up at PetMart." I shook his big hand, with its ropey veins and scaled-down but still lurid illustrations, and introduced him to Jay.

"I'm afraid I was kind of rude to you that day," Lang added.

A polite apology was probably the last thing I'd expected to hear from him. "Oh no . . . don't be silly. I interrupted you. I should have seen you were busy."

"Mmm. Busy and in a real pisser of a mood, but that's no excuse."

I wondered why he was going to the trouble now

to set things straight. "You know the FOCA people?"

"Yeah, they've been helping me out." Lang hooked his thumbs in the waist of his jeans and sighed deeply. "I've been trying to talk my Aunt Gail into getting rid of some of her animals. She lives here in Chadwick. I visited her last month, for the first time since my uncle died, and her house was overrun with cats and dogs. 'Course, she didn't want to give up any of them."

The situation began to sound familiar. Then I realized this could be the same house Nick had mentioned to me, where he used to make repairs for the owner.

"That's a shame," Jay commented. "We had somebody like that on our block, a hoarder. When he died, they had to condemn the place."

"Luckily, with Aunt Gail it wasn't that bad yet. Anyhow, somebody told me about FOCA, and they've been terrific, talking sense to her and offering to rehome her animals."

In spite of the day's heat, cool relief swept over me. "So, the day you were stockpiling all of those carriers . . ."

"I was taking them to her place. I knew she was gonna be upset, and I've been trying to keep it quiet what a mess she's made of her house. It's embarrassing for her, y'know? So I guess I didn't want a stranger prying into our business. But now I see it's kind of your business, too."

This story put a new slant on Lang's sinister one-sided phone conversation at the diner. He'd been trying to keep the police from finding out about all the "damned animals" his aunt had been hoarding in her house.

"Well," I told him, "even though I don't do rescue work, I have to admit I was curious. It looked like you were loading up Noah's Ark!"

"Yeah, I guess you're not the only one who noticed. A cop even stopped by to ask what I was up to."

Probably in response to my call. I cringed. "Oh, gee. I'm sorry to hear that."

Lang shrugged. "I'm used to it. The way I look, people tend to think the worst, especially in a quiet area like this. When I'm on the job, though, all this ink is good for business."

"What is your business?" Jay asked.

"I just opened a new hard rock club about half a mile off the highway. I've got one in the city that's doing pretty well, and this'll be my second. Didn't know how it would fly in this area, but so far, so good." In a well-practiced move, Lang reached into his back jeans pocket and pulled out two purple business cards, with the club's name in agitated-looking white letters: NOYZ2.

And that explained the van's license plate.

"Welcome to Chadwick, then," I told him. "Are all your aunt's animals taken care of now?"

"FOCA let her keep a couple of her dogs, and a cleaning service is going to get her house back in shape and help it stay that way. At least now I'll be coming around more often, too, and can keep an eye on her."

Jay grinned. "You're a good nephew."

He was, I thought as Lang sauntered off. *And not*

likely to be a secret breeder of vicious wildcats. Or the kind of guy who'd run somebody over and leave him to die on the road.

I felt only a twinge of disappointment. *Just when I thought I might have solved the case!*

While gazing off into the distance, I spotted the Schaeffer produce truck again, this time cruising just a block away. It turned off Center Street into a residential area behind my shop.

Not time yet for him to pick up Teri, is it?

I checked my watch—almost three. Still a couple more hours before the business vendors would pack up, though the food services and the live music would probably go into the evening. Things had grown a little quieter for the moment, though, at our end of the street. Feeling the strain of being on all day, I had just sunk into one of my pink chairs when I thought I heard someone down the block scream my name.

"That's Mom!" said Jay.

Forgetting about my table, I ran back to the corner, where I could see my shop. In spite of trees and bushes in the way, I could make out Teri in her light-colored net top walking briskly across the small parking lot. Sarah leaned out of the shop's rear doorway, on her crutch. When she sighted me, she yelled again.

"Stop her, Cassie! She's got Ayesha!"

Both Jay and I dashed down the street, while Sarah gamely hobbled outside and tried to intercept Teri. I could see the younger woman had gotten Ayesha into her mesh harness and was walking her toward the far corner of the lot. Through the trees that edged my property, I glimpsed a patch of darker green. Rick had parked his truck there to meet them.

In only a few more yards, Teri would reach the truck. Jay and I might not make it in time to stop the cat-napping.

But Ayesha balked now, and Teri had to stop to pick her up. Meanwhile, Sarah closed in. Ever resourceful, my assistant swung her crutch and smacked the younger woman in the butt. Teri fell forward, and Ayesha, startled, tore the leash from her hands.

Rick saw this, jumped from his truck . . . and stopped. He watched Ayesha streak off toward Center Street, then his eyes flicked back to me and Jay bearing down on him. Not one to gallantly come to his partner's defense, he sprang back behind the wheel and sped off.

Now our familiar friend Officer Jacoby, wearing his official police cap and dark sunglasses, came jogging up behind us. "What's going on here?"

Before I could explain, we heard furious barking out toward Center Street. I saw that Jay held onto Teri, so she wasn't going anywhere. Out of breath, I asked Sarah, "Can you talk to the officer? I've got to catch Ayesha!"

I sprinted back to the main drag, then paused to figure out where the Bengal might have gone. Since the FOCA dogs were all stirred up, she must have passed thataway. But with many blocks of canopies, tables, and crates of merchandise—not to mention strolling human bodies—she could be hiding anywhere.

In theory, there are bush cats and tree cats, ones that like to hide low and others that prefer the high road. Any animal scared and desperate enough can break from its usual pattern, but still . . .

My eyes scanned some of the tall maples that lined Center Street beyond the sidewalk. About eight people had clustered around one of them.

An older woman in the group saw me staring and called out, "He's up here."

I joined the group and peered straight up. Holy cow, Ayesha had outdone herself this time—she must have climbed at least fifteen feet. I could just glimpse her spots and her dangling blue leash.

"Is he yours?" the woman asked with admiration.

"She. Not exactly, but she's boarding at my shop. Someone accidentally let her go."

A man in back of us yelled to his friends, "Hey, come see this! It's the wildcat that attacked the kid!"

My heart froze. "No, no," I told the group loudly. "This is a tame cat, a show cat! She's even wearing a harness and a leash. My . . . helper was walking her, and she got away."

Jay showed up at my side. "Find her, Cassie?"

I pointed up. He squinted to see through the leaves, then whistled. "There's a fire truck doing a demo about four blocks away," he said. "Maybe they can get her for you."

I worried about how the Bengal would react to something as huge as a fire bucket coming toward her. This tree was tall enough that she could still climb a lot higher! "Maybe if we just had a good, long ladder. The hardware store . . . ?"

"That's a thought. I'll go ask."

As Jay disappeared to my right, someone clutched my left arm. I jumped.

"Easy," said Mark. "What the heck happened?"

I told him as briefly as I could. He gazed up at Ayesha with the same look Jay had worn, mixed bewilderment and amusement.

"It's the killer cat!" someone else announced to the swelling crowd. "They've got it cornered."

"Oh crap, Mark," I breathed. "These people are just going to make things worse."

He faced the group with an air of professional authority. "Folks, folks, this is *not* a dangerous cat. In fact, she's a valuable cat, which is why we need to get her down without stressing her out. So please, give us some room."

Minutes later, Jay and a brawny guy from the downtown hardware store showed up with an extension ladder. Dawn, who by now had heard about our crisis, brought me a feathery wand from my sales table and a package of cat treats.

"I asked one of the FOCA kids to watch your table," she told me.

"Good work," I said. "Thanks."

The guys extended the aluminum ladder to its full sixteen feet and leaned it against the tree trunk. As it brushed noisily against the small inner branches, I saw Ayesha scramble a little higher. But so far, the top of the ladder still came pretty close to where she had perched.

The hardware store guy put a foot on the first rung, but Mark stopped him. "I'm a vet, I'll be able to handle her better."

I stepped in. "Thanks, Mark, but she's used to me."

"No, Cassie. It could be dangerous."

"Please. I climbed shakier ladders than this when I was painting the ceilings in my apartment."

He frowned. "The ceilings in your apartment aren't *that* high."

Great. Now the whole town would know Mark had spent time in my apartment. "If I blow it, you'll have your chance. Meanwhile, you guys please just hold the ladder steady." I lowered my voice. "And try to keep the spectators quiet."

Mark took a firm grip on the right rail. "You be careful."

With one more look up—way up—I drew a deep breath. What I didn't confess to Mark was that I've always had a touch of acrophobia, or fear of heights. It had bothered me a little when I was painting my ceilings, and this climb would take me a lot higher. But if a total stranger or even Mark reached for Ayesha, she might get scared and retreat farther. I just hoped she'd trust me enough to let me carry her down, without clawing me to ribbons.

I opened the package of cat treats, shook a few into my hand, and stuffed them into the front pocket of my shorts. I also stuck the wand toy through my belt. Then I started up.

Chapter 17

At this late stage of summer, the maple tree's hand-sized leaves were very full, and they brushed my head and shoulders as I climbed. This actually gave me more of a sense of being safe and enclosed, though, than if the branches had been bare.

A woman's voice floated up from below. "Why can't the cat get down by herself? She ran up there okay."

I hoped Mark might explain that, the way a domestic cat's claws curved backward, they gripped really well for climbing up but not for coming down, especially not head first. Of course, Mark probably would just ignore the woman because he was worried about me. Well, if he'd gone up, I would have had to worry about him. And Ayesha *was* my responsibility.

When I reached about twelve feet, my calves began to feel the strain. A wide limb of the maple stretched almost horizontally at that point, and I thought I'd try my luck. I reached into my pocket for a few cat treats and held them up where I hoped the Bengal could see and smell them.

I called to her in a high, soft voice. "Ayesha, see what I got here? Bet you're hungry, huh? Come and get it!"

She did peer down, pupils wide. But she couldn't make a clear leap to the lower limb, and when she tried her grip on the tree bark, she drew back, not trusting it.

I took stock. If I could lead her over to a narrower branch at the left, she probably could jump to the wide one from there. Stowing the treats for a moment, I pulled out the wand. I flitted the feathers through the air and made them land on the lower branch. That was still kind of a tricky jump, but Ayesha was a special cat.

"Oooh, look, bird! Get the bird!"

She crouched, the feathers even more tempting to her than the food had been. She vaulted across and landed neatly where I wanted her, her claws digging into the rough bark like grappling hooks.

"Good *girl!* Now over this way . . . You can do it."

More confident now, she sprang onto the wide limb. I petted her, put away the wand, and fed her some treats. She seemed less frightened, which was a good thing, because now I was the one who had to trust her.

I gathered up her leash and tucked the treats and toy away. Then with my free arm, I caught the cat tightly against my chest. I let her face backward over my right shoulder as I began to carry her down.

A few people below started to clap and cheer, but I heard Mark silence them. I descended slowly, rung by rung, hoping my luck would hold out. Though very sleek and fit, Ayesha still must have weighed about fifteen pounds, enough to unbalance me if she made the wrong move.

Fortunately, she reverted now to her more civilized nature. She seemed to realize she needed my help and shouldn't shake things up. She rode on my shoulder as easily as a trained monkey.

As we neared the ground, I could hear people snapping cell phone pictures.

Once on terra firma, I petted Ayesha, told her again what a good girl she was, and popped her into a carrier that Jay had waiting. Mark hugged me—not concerned about the onlookers—and whispered, "Great job."

Hugs from Dawn and Sarah followed.

"You walked all the way up here on the crutch?" I asked my assistant.

"I know, right?" Jay grumbled. "I could have driven her, but by the time I turned around, she was behind me."

"Couldn't miss seeing the daring rescue," his mother insisted. "Don't worry, I locked up the shop."

"What happened with Teri?" I asked her.

"Cops took her to the station. Her boyfriend got away, though."

I thanked Mr. Reynolds of the hardware store for the loan of his ladder. A little woman with wiry gray hair and a sharp nose, who said she was from the *Courier,* tried to interview me about the cat rescue.

"She escaped from a handler who removed her from my shop without permission," I said. "There may be more to the story, but right now that's all I can tell you."

At this point, I and my Chadwick Day display had begun to attract way too much attention—the street fair crowd suddenly had lots of questions to "Ask the Cat Lady." Mark and Jay helped me fend them off. Since it was almost four thirty, we hastily packed up my stuff, took down the canopy, and carted everything back to my shop. I'd sold a few pieces of the cat furniture, so at least our load was a bit lighter for the return trip.

Jay brought up the rear to keep in step with his mother. I noticed then that Sarah wobbled a little, even with her crutch. Maybe the two-block trek uphill had been too much for her.

"Are you okay?" I asked her.

"Just a little groggy," my assistant said.

"Thanks to Teri," her son added with a scowl.

"Y'know those tarts she brought us?" Sarah went on. "There must've been something in them. I ate about half of one, but it didn't taste right to me, so when she wasn't looking, I threw it out. A few minutes later, I dozed off at the counter. Just for a second, but Teri must have thought I'd be out longer. That's when she made her move."

Mark stopped in his tracks to gape at this. "Unbelievable!"

"God, Sarah." I hugged her. "I'm so sorry."

"Good thing I've heard of kids pulling pranks like that on teachers over the years." She sniffed. "Otherwise, she and her boyfriend might have gotten away with it, and Ayesha would be long gone.

When I saw what she was up to, I guess I could've hit the alarm, but I was afraid she'd get away, so I just went after her as fast as I could. My adrenaline kicked in."

"It sure did." I laughed. "You clobbered her pretty good for someone who was still woozy."

As we all resumed walking, Mark and I ahead, I remembered his own challenges of that afternoon. "Say, speaking of sneaky females, how did things go with Jennifer?"

His lips tightened before he answered. "She's history."

"No kidding? Because of the note?"

Mark shook his head sadly. "You were right about everything, Cassie. Not that she admitted it, but her excuses were ridiculous. I started with the note—she told me she thought Elena had already entered the information in the computer, so we didn't need it anymore. I mean, come on! Then I asked her if she'd handled that dog last week, whose neck cone got loose. Jennifer said she didn't even stay late that night, when I know she did. After a few more questions, she got flustered and said she couldn't believe I was cross-examining her like this, when all she wanted to do was *help*. Didn't I appreciate her loyalty?"

"Oh, man." I could imagine how uncomfortable the scene must have been for Mark, who hated any kind of drama.

"At that point, she turned on the waterworks." He mimed sniffing and dabbing at his eyes. "You'd have been proud—I just ignored the whole performance. I said I need a cooperative team, not one member sabotaging things and blaming the others. I told her she was out, effective immediately, and I'd put her last paycheck in the mail."

I was truly impressed. "Bravo! I'm not happy to have been right, because I'm sure it was painful for you. But at least now you know the rest of your staff is still reliable."

"I owe a few of them apologies, too. I can't believe I let the girl play me like that!"

"Hey, she was pretty clever. Maybe this will teach her to use her powers for good instead of evil."

The two of us stepped into the shop's welcome air-conditioning and laid our burdens down. When Jay and his mother followed, they'd obviously been talking also, and wore grave faces.

Jay said, "Mom just told me something else, Cassie, that you should hear."

I gave Sarah my full attention. "What's that?"

My assistant sat on one of the counter stools and began slowly, choosing her words. "This whole thing today had to be planned for a while. I spent a fair amount of time with Teri this afternoon, and something about her made me uneasy, but I couldn't pinpoint it. Not until I saw her walking off with the cat, in a hurry, across the parking lot. Cassie, I think *she's* the person who bumped into me and knocked me down."

Just one more rude shock in a day full of them. I sank onto the other stool, opposite her. "Really? But you kept saying 'he' . . ."

"I just assumed it was a small man or a teenaged boy with a slim build. But if Teri had on boyish, baggy clothes . . . and the hoodie pulled up in a peak, to make her look taller . . . I swear, I recognized that fast walk. Even the sound of it over the gravel was the same."

I glanced toward the coffee stand, where two blueberry tarts still remained on a paper plate. Got up and crossed to the back for a better look at them. "Did Teri eat one of these?" I asked Sarah.

"She did. That's one reason I never imagined anything was wrong with them."

"They have two different kinds of leaves on top." The difference was very slight, but I guessed one might be peppermint and the other something like spearmint.

Sarah huffed in annoyance. "Probably two of them were regular and two were doctored. Dumb of me not to notice that!"

"Unless you already had some reason to be suspicious, though, you wouldn't."

Not knowing which of the remaining tarts might be the bad one, I covered them both tightly in the plastic wrap again, as evidence.

At least Sarah seemed fine now, but it still horrified me to think that Teri had tried to drug her. Back in front, I slumped in my pink chair again, feeling suddenly exhausted.

"Boy, I made a great choice of somebody to watch the shop, eh?" With a bitter chuckle, I told Mark, "Guess I've got nothing on you when it comes to judging character."

"Well, Teri offered, didn't she?" Sarah reminded me. "Maybe she and Rick saw an opportunity and grabbed it. Very strange, though . . . I hope someday we find out the whole story."

Jay, who leaned against the counter, silently

clenched and unclenched a fist at his side. As if he wished he could belt the person who had so callously hurt his mother.

My phone rang, and I checked the ID. "Hmm. Wonder if this might bring some answers."

Detective Bonelli's richly sardonic tones filled my ear. "Cassie McGlone, did I ever tell you that I started out as a beat cop on the mean streets of Paterson? Just out of the police academy, I had to face down drug dealers, gangbangers, pimps, and all kinds of lowlifes. Not to mention the hassling I got from some guys on the force. But I worked my way up, over many years, and took special training. When I made detective and got assigned to Chadwick, I thought I'd struck gold. Out here, my family and I could finally relax a little. Enjoy the beauties of nature, take things slower."

I wondered where all this was leading, but she was on a roll, and I knew better than to interrupt her.

"Take today. I thought I could go to my son's baseball game and actually get to stay for the whole thing. I mean, what could go wrong at a nice, nostalgic street fair, with everyone just out to have a good time? But no. A guy in the classic car parade turns out to be driving a vehicle that belonged to a missing person. And if that weren't enough, a woman tries to make off with a valuable cat that also might be evidence in a murder. Seems like these two incidents have no connection, except for . . . you."

Though I picked up on her teasing tone, I went on the defense. "As far as Todd's car goes, you can't blame me for anything except suggesting that you search for it. And in terms of the cat-napping, since my business was robbed, I was the victim. I even had to climb a tree to get Ayesha down after she escaped from Teri."

"Yes, I heard about that. Guess I have to give you credit, at least, for not tying up the resources of the Chadwick Fire Department."

"See? I'm sure the hardware store got great publicity out of it, too."

"I suppose so." She sounded disappointed that she couldn't lay the blame for the day's chaotic events on me. "And actually, having all these incidents happen at once, and all the people involved down at the station at the same time, turned out to be a stroke of luck for us."

"How so?" I asked.

"Well, we had Danny Lorenzo and Bob Gillis both on the bench in the waiting area, since neither of them is under arrest as yet. Officer Waller sat in between, to keep Gillis from harassing the kid. Meanwhile, in walks Jacoby with this Teri Marshall in cuffs. When Lorenzo sees her, he yells to Gillis, 'That's her—the chick who sold me the Camaro!' "

"You're kidding." Connections started forming in my brain, swiftly but still just below the surface. "Did you get a chance to ask her about it yet?"

"I tried. She wants a lawyer. She was allowed one call and she made it, but whoever she tried to reach, I don't think he picked up."

I remembered how quickly the green truck had pulled away when it became clear we were going to catch up with Teri. *That slime.* "I can tell you who she was trying to reach. Her business partner, Rick Schaeffer. I can give you a lot of dope, so to speak, on those two."

"Well, if you do have a free moment, Ms. McGlone, want to join us down here at the station?" Bonelli suggested. "The more, the merrier!"

Chapter 18

In Bonelli's office, still wearing my cutesy cat earrings and socks, I told her that Teri might have been the one who'd knocked Sarah down in my parking lot, and that Schaeffer's Organic Produce included more than just fruits and vegetables. I also handed over the tarts for testing, and relayed my assistant's theory that Teri had attempted to drug her.

"Personally, I think Rick masterminded all this and Teri was just carrying out his orders," I said. "I suspect that he knocks her around. She's got a big bruise on her lower back and pressure marks from fingers on her arm."

Angela met my eyes and then nodded slowly. She knew about my history with my ex-boyfriend. "So, you think she's scared of him."

"She might have good reason." I remembered the photos of Pete Reardon's battered face after he'd been run down on Morton Road. "Rick was the one who suggested that Teri help out today at my shop. It had to be a setup, so she'd get a chance to steal Ayesha."

"For money? Is the cat valuable enough for them to go to so much trouble?"

"A few thousand, at least. But you're right, I think there's something more going on."

Bonelli ran a hand through her blunt, dark bangs, the gray roots still needing a touch-up. "I'd love to grill this chick on the Todd Gillis disappearance, but I can't do that if she lawyers up. Unless she and Schaeffer have deep pockets, all she's going to get is a public defender, anyway. She'll probably do better if she cuts a deal to give evidence against him."

"Maybe I can talk to her?" I suggested.

"That's what I was hoping. As far as you know, you hired her to watch the shop and something went wrong. Start with that, then gradually try to get her to open up about the rest."

"Might work," I agreed. "After all, Teri and I both love cats . . . and we have a couple of other things in common, too."

A few minutes later, I was back in the all-white interrogation room, seated across the metal table from Teri Marshall. Bonelli could hear and see us through a two-way wall mirror, but Teri might not know that.

The young woman slouched in her chair, arms wrapped tightly around herself, as if the station's very moderate air-conditioning felt arctic to her. Even her center-parted hair and her gauzy top seemed to have gone limp with defeat. She eyed me defensively and said, "What are you doing here? You're not a cop."

"I asked Detective Bonelli if I could talk to you first, as a friend, and find out what happened today." When she said nothing, I began, "Sarah dozed off, and you decided to walk Ayesha in the parking lot. How come?"

"She was acting restless, and I was bored, too. Dawn told me she could be walked on a leash." More likely, Pete Reardon had told them that, I thought. Teri added, "She wouldn't have gotten away if Sarah hadn't come after me and knocked me down."

"She thought you were trying to steal the cat. And I saw Rick's green truck pull up at the curb, like he was waiting for you. Was that the plan?"

Teri's gaze slid sideways to avoid mine, and I figured this would be the hard part for her—betraying Rick.

"I think I know where you're coming from," I told her. "I had a boyfriend who hit and bullied me, too." Her eyes came back, finally connecting with mine. "One of the reasons I moved to Chadwick was to get away from him. He stalked me for a while, but when I threatened to tell the cops, he finally backed off. Unfortunately, I think you're in a worse situation, but this could be your way out."

"No, you're wrong," she argued, but without conviction. "Rick just loses his temper sometimes, but he wouldn't . . ."

"I think at heart you're a good person, Teri. You help grow all that wonderful produce and you handle cats well, too. You're good at nurturing things, and you shouldn't let someone like Rick drag you down."

Flatly, she demanded, "Am I under arrest?"

I dodged that question, because I knew Bonelli didn't want Teri to clam up and demand a lawyer. "Right now you're suspected of assault and attempted robbery. At least you didn't use a weapon to attack Sarah. Although . . . did you put something in those blueberry tarts to make her fall asleep?"

She let a second pass before admitting, "Nothing terrible. Just some of that nighttime cold medicine. It's fruit-flavored, so I figured she wouldn't notice."

"Unfortunately for you, she did," I said. "So, you were going to give the cat to Rick, and then what? Tell us Ayesha just got loose and ran away?"

A sullen shrug. She was closing down again.

I pushed harder. "Like I said, Teri, so far you're only in medium-sized trouble. But if Rick has committed worse crimes and you cover up for him, you'll be charged as an accessory, which is much more serious." Once again, I tried to get her to meet my eyes. "Rick doesn't care about you. He ditched you pretty fast when you lost the cat, and now he's not even taking your phone calls. You need to protect yourself. If you do, the cops can protect you from him. Don't you see that?"

A tear rolled down her thin cheek, and I detected a trace of a nod.

I saw my chance to get some real information. "Okay, let's talk about something else. What was the deal with the Camaro? Danny Lorenzo said you sold him that car. Did it belong to Todd Gillis?"

"I really don't know. Gillis answered one of our ads and came up to the farm. He was kind of a jerk from the start. We didn't have exactly what he wanted, and he asked to see what else we had for sale. But Rick doesn't let just anybody go prowling around."

"I don't imagine he does. You guys grow some marijuana with the vegetables, don't you?" When Teri stared as if I must be psychic, I explained about the leaf I'd found among the tomatoes. "Is that what Rick didn't want Todd to see?"

"Th-that's part of it, anyway. Rick's pretty paranoid, and he started thinking the guy might be a narc. On top of that, Gillis asks him if we're married or just business partners. Like he's trying to hit on me!"

"So what did Rick do?"

"I don't know, honest. Rick wanted him off the property and offered to walk him back to his car. Like, to make sure he really left. Gillis said he parked a ways off down the road and walked up to our farm. They left together, and about ten minutes later, Rick came back alone. If they got in a fight or something in the meantime, he didn't say anything to me about it."

Not likely he would, if he'd done something to Todd. "And the Camaro?"

"If Gillis was driving it that day, I never saw it. I just know it showed up at our farm a couple of days later, when I came back from working in the garden. Rick said some guy had ditched it out on the highway, and we should take an ad to sell it. I did ask if it belonged to Gillis, but he said no and just got angry, so I let it drop. Anyway, that guy Lorenzo answered the ad, and we sold it to him."

Something occurred to me. "Rick wasn't worried that someone might recognize Todd's car?"

Teri frowned. "Lorenzo lives a couple of towns away, so I guess Rick figured it was safe. Who the hell would expect the guy to show up in the Chadwick Day parade?"

Unlikely, yes, but the classic car parade had been open to the public. "So, that's your side business? Is that what Todd wanted to buy from Rick, another car?"

Once more, Teri looked surprised. "Oh . . . no. He wanted a cat."

Of course—I was a slow study today. "A special kind of cat? A hybrid?"

"Rick got the idea about a year ago. We get all kinds of feral cats living in the woods, and one night he trapped a bobcat. Rick grew up on a farm, so he knows about breeding animals. He wanted to mate the bobcat with one of the ferals, and it worked—she had a litter of kittens with traits from both. So Rick and a couple of his buddies got the idea that they could charge big bucks for cats like that, and started selling them on the down-low."

I leaned back in my chair, dazed. "That's why you wanted Ayesha, to improve the stock and get nicer-looking kittens?"

She nodded. "Rick wanted a queen—that's what they called a breeding female—with top bloodlines. He advertised, and this guy from Pennsylvania said he could deliver one. When he showed up with her, we couldn't believe how beautiful she was."

"Wait a second," I said. "You saw her natural coat?"

"Sure." Teri's tone saddened. "This guy Pete was ready to sell her to us, but he wanted to see the cattery first. Rick took him through, and meanwhile explained that he'd be mating Ayesha to bobcats and other hybrids, to get spotted kittens with a really wild look. Pete left his cat up at the house, and Rick told me to show him around the pens. While I did, I could see he was starting to change his mind. We stopped by one of the cages, and one of our big, hybrid bobs snarled at us. Especially after that, Pete got quiet for a while.

"Once we got back to the house, Rick met Pete outside and tried to hand him cash for Ayesha. But Pete said he wanted to think it over. He went inside, where he'd left the cat in the carrier on our kitchen island. She was still there, but she was making this horrible moaning sound, like she was in pain. When Pete opened the top of the carrier, she hissed at him, and he asked why there was a bandage on the back of her neck. Rick said he'd felt a microchip there, and he couldn't buy her that way, so he'd cut it out."

I remembered discovering the old wound above Ayesha's shoulder blades and wondering who would slice into a cat that way. Now I had my answer.

"Pete looked furious, ready to slug him," Teri went on, "but Rick still had the knife he'd used on the cat. It was a just little hunting knife, about six inches long, but enough to make Pete back off. He closed the carrier, though, and said he'd have to treat the wound and make sure it didn't get infected. Rick asked, 'You're gonna bring her back, right?' He still had the knife, so Pete said sure. But I could see by the look on his face that he was done with us."

"I'm sure Rick could, too."

Teri's mouth twisted, and her hands knotted more tightly. "He'd screwed it up, but of course, I couldn't tell him that. After Pete left, Rick worried that he might rat us out. Also, I knew he felt cheated and really wanted that cat."

"Meanwhile," I finished, "Pete treated her wound, dyed her coat, and put her in hiding at my shop."

I didn't bother to draw Teri out on the rest of the sordid story. A day or so later, Rick probably had caught up with Pete somewhere and demanded to know where he'd stashed the cat. Or maybe he thought Pete had seen too much at the farm and would tell the SPCA about the operation. In the process of roughing him up, Rick either killed Pete or thought he did. He tried to make it look like a road accident by running the guy over . . . but with Pete's own car, so there would be nothing to lead the police back to Schaeffer or his farm.

"Thanks for telling me all this, Teri," I said. "Would you be willing to write out a formal statement for Detective Bonelli?"

She balled her fists on the tabletop and nodded. "Just talking about it all again made me see . . . Rick shouldn't get away with this."

I glanced toward the big mirror on my left, and Angela Bonelli stepped into the room.

When I finally got back to my shop, I found Mark, Dawn, and Keith all hanging out. They were gulping cold bottled water and eating chocolate chip cookies. A Cottone's Bakery box stood open on the sales counter.

Dawn, perched on one of the high stools, pushed the box toward me. "Guaranteed undoctored."

"In that case . . ." I grabbed one hungrily.

From the other stool, Mark reached out to hand me a water. "Poor baby, you look like you need something stronger than this."

"Jay took Sarah home because she was still really tired," said Keith, who had balanced his slim frame on a three-foot-high upholstered cat tower.

"We had to stick around, though," said Dawn, "to hear what happened with Teri."

They all offered me their seats, but I just opened one of my pink camp chairs and dropped into it; there was even a convenient pocket for my water bottle. I bit into the just-crisp-enough cookie, let the chocolate chips melt in my mouth, chewed, and swallowed. Thus fortified, I brought my friends up to date on what I had learned from Bonelli and Teri.

"She'll get a lawyer and probably try to cut a deal," I added. "In the meantime, she gave the cops directions to the farm, so I guess they're headed out there tonight. With any luck, they'll be in time to catch Rick."

"He's got to be on the run by now," said Mark.

Keith snorted. "In that green truck with his company name on the cab? Not the best way to avoid attention."

"That sign could be removable," Mark pointed out. "Take it off, and he'll be driving just an unmarked truck."

"Yeah, I get the feeling Rick is pretty sneaky and thinks ahead," I said. "He might have an escape plan all worked out."

Dawn had been quiet for a while and now looked close to tears. "Cassie, I am *so* sorry I talked you into using Teri to mind your shop. Talk about putting a fox in the henhouse! I had no idea about any of this."

"Of course you didn't," I told her. "I know you thought she was a decent person. Even when I had some misgivings about her, I never imagined anything this bad."

Mark's wide shoulders slumped, too. "You ladies aren't the only ones who've had some rude shocks today about people you thought you could trust."

Keith slapped his knees and stood up. "Well, enough gloom and doom. I think we all deserve some fun, and Chadwick Day isn't over yet. Let's go grab dinner."

"Have something in mind?" Dawn asked him.

"I do. The Thai place has tables on the sidewalk, and it's close enough to the park for us to hear the music. The bands tonight will be more professional, and my friend Vince plays guitar in one of them, the True Blues."

Everyone seemed to like this suggestion. At the moment, I could have fallen asleep right in my hammocky chair, but an evening of good food and live music was enough to rally me, also. "You're right, that sounds like exactly what we need. Just let me settle up my accounts first."

Before I had a chance to forget, I deposited my take for the day in the cash register and made note of the products I'd sold and items people had ordered. Dawn and Keith probably had done those things for themselves while I'd been at the police station, and they gabbed with Mark until I was ready to join them all for dinner.

Outside, the sky had clouded over a little and a breeze had kicked up. Though this probably meant rain overnight, for the moment, it simply cooled things off nicely. We all ambled up the street, which was less crowded but still busy, to the restaurant, Kim Khao.

Passing the art gallery, which had closed for the evening, I planted my heels. The leopard lady print was now in the window. It hadn't sold and was still marked down.

"Something wrong?" Dawn asked me.

"No, I just like that piece a lot." I told them about my visit to the gallery a few days earlier.

"And that picture spoke to you?" Mark smiled teasingly. "Gee, I wonder why."

I swatted his arm. "It's still more than I can afford. Let's get going, so I won't obsess over it."

Kim Khao had set up about eight tables in front, draped in their trademark red cloths. We arrived just in time to grab a vacant one.

It was my first chance to appreciate the red, white, and blue plantings around the park gazebo. What I presumed to be Chadwick's town flag flew from a nearby mast, its design a montage of images such as a mill, a mine, and a railroad train. Next to the gazebo, a shaded temporary stage held speakers, microphones, a drum kit, and a piano, not in use at the moment.

We were given menus, and I opted for my usual, the not-too-spicy pad thai.

The rest of our group made slightly more adventurous choices. After the waitress had taken our orders and left, I bragged to Dawn and Keith about Mark's cooking prowess.

"If it weren't for you and him," I told Dawn, "I'd probably be malnourished. Or at least bored to death with my own subsistence-level cooking."

"I'll teach you how, anytime," Mark offered.

"You can try, but it may not stick. The way my mother doesn't do cats, I'm afraid I don't do fancy cuisine." As our waiter placed my Thai meal in front of me, I amended, "Except for eating it."

The others fell to talking about dishes they had attempted to make over the years, successfully or not. I ate, sipped my white wine, and actually relaxed for the first time all day. Only then did I appreciate the stress I'd been under and how much I owed to Sarah, Jay, and Mark for helping me keep Ayesha safe.

Tonight, all I want to do is enjoy this moment, eating a good meal with my friends outdoors on a summer evening. Listening to music, helping to celebrate the history of my adopted town. And remembering that, scary as some of today's events were, they probably created a ton of publicity for my shop, which has to be good for business!

I tried to focus on these positive things, but as

the sky darkened overhead, I couldn't suppress a shiver. A woman I'd liked and trusted had deliberately injured Sarah—probably just to make my shop less secure—and had attempted to steal Ayesha. Her partner, a man I'd seen and talked to personally, was suspected of murdering Pete Reardon/Rudy Pierson. Todd Gillis, who'd recently visited their farm, had yet to be accounted for. Meanwhile, Teri, at Rick's direction, had actually sold off the treasured red Camaro. Since this didn't sound like something Todd would ever condone, it didn't bode well.

The True Blues took the stage and played a fine opening set, sweet and sultry to go with the sunset mood. Keith applauded for his friend's band and glanced toward Dawn, expecting her to do the same. But it took her a second, I noticed, to give the performance her full attention.

Was she asking herself the same questions I was? *How could I not have suspected something? How could I have trusted these people?*

During a break, she told me, "I can't get over the idea that Teri and Rick have been breeding those hybrid cats out on their farm. You don't think they could have been responsible for the one that's been attacking pets and people, do you?"

"Scott Naughton, the SPCA guy, thinks it's possible. Bonelli told me that's one reason why he's so intent on finding out what they're up to." I remembered something then and checked my watch. Bonelli had said the cops were going to Schaeffer's farm tonight. I wondered what they'd found. With any luck, they had Rick in custody by now.

Mark must have noticed me shivering, because he rubbed my upper arm. "Are you cold? Too bad you didn't bring a sweater."

"It was so hot all day, I didn't expect to need one." Leaning against him, I reminded myself that at least one thing had turned out well today. He'd learned the truth about Jennifer and followed through by firing her. At least there should be no more dirty tricks after hours at the veterinary clinic.

We enjoyed the True Blues' set and hung out to listen to one more band. Then all four of us started to flag, having been up early that morning. We walked back to Nature's Way, where Mark and I said good night to Dawn and Keith, and I thanked them again for their help during and after my cat crisis. When we reached my shop, Mark and I checked to make sure the alarm was still turned on and there was no sign of tampering.

"After all," I reminded him, "as far as we know, Rick Schaeffer is still at large. And if he's really nuts, he might still be trying to get his hands on Ayesha."

"That *would* be pretty nuts, now that his girlfriend's already in custody," Mark said. "He has to know she's spilling her guts to the cops."

"Speaking of cops . . ." I checked the shop's answering machine and saw a message from Bonelli. She'd left it just after eight o'clock; it was nearly ten now.

"Thought you'd want an update," the recording said. "We found the farm and checked it over. No sign of Schaeffer or his truck, and it looks like he burned some of his sales records in a fire pit. They have quite an operation here—large plots of vegetables, berry bushes. Even some herbs they might have a harder time selling on the open market." Bonelli took a breath. "But that's not all. Back in the woods, they've got the cats. The SPCA guys are pretty sure this is the source of our infamous killer bobcat, and they set a trap for it. They're going back tomorrow, and Naughton said he'd like your help. Call me if you're interested." She left a cell phone number.

I gave Mark the basic synopsis, then returned the detective's call. "Sorry to get back to you so late," I told her.

"Not at all," said Bonelli. "I apologize for disturbing *you,* after you had such a long and crazy day. Anyway, here's the deal. There are a lot of cats at the farm, most with issues, and one not-so-friendly dog. The SPCA has a warrant to seize the animals, but they cover the whole county, so they're short-staffed. They're even bringing in some of the FOCA people to help. Cassie, they could use your extra hands and your expertise. I want to reach out to Dr. Coccia, too, but I only have his office number."

"He's right here," I admitted. As if Bonelli hadn't already figured out that Mark and I were an item. She is a detective, after all.

I put the shop phone on speaker so she could brief Mark, too. "If you're free," Bonelli told him, "we can use a vet on the scene. Sorry to spring this on you with so little warning. Naughton said they should go early tomorrow because the animals are suffering."

"We'll be there," Mark said.

"Do I need to bring anything?" I asked the detective.

"As many carriers as you can spare, and maybe gloves and whatever else you'd use to handle a nasty cat." Dark humor tinged Bonelli's voice. "I don't think you'll have to climb trees this time, Cassie, but be ready for just about anything else. From what Naughton told me, it's not going to be pretty."

Chapter 19

Ever since hearing Teri's explanation of the scheme to steal Ayesha, I'd been wondering how she and Rick expected to get away with it. Even if we believed that the Bengal simply escaped, surely we'd spread the word about the missing cat and post her picture far and wide. Wouldn't somebody see her at Schaeffer's farm and rat them out, sooner or later?

Sunday morning, though, I began to understand why they imagined their plan might work.

Just after dawn, in a heavy mist, I followed Mark's RAV4 along the highway spur that ascended Rattlesnake Ridge. He, in turn, followed a big black-and-white SPCA van with Naughton behind the wheel. We had been asked to bring as many vehicles as we could to today's raid on the farm.

I wound around the forested mountain, glimpsing vistas that I'm sure would have been dramatic on a clear day but became haunting when veiled by the morning mist. In the silvery, filtered light, the mountainside on my left streamed by in vivid green interrupted now and then by an outcropping of ancient rock. To my right, just beyond the guardrail, a low cloud seemed to fill the valley, blurring the details of the landscape that stretched far below. It reminded me of travel photos I'd seen of the Blue Ridge Mountains in Virginia.

I asked myself why I had never yet explored this area, just a few miles outside of Chadwick. Of course, I'd been busy with the shop during my first year, and also would have thought twice about wandering in a wild, strange place alone. But maybe next time Dawn and Keith went hiking up here, Mark and I could go along. Might do the two of us good to get out of our suburban comfort zones.

As long as we wore boots. We'd been given that advice today, and you can bet I had mine on, with my jeans tucked into the tops. Even though it was August, and the arrangement would probably have me sweltering in a few hours, it would give me the best protection against deer ticks and, especially in this area, timber rattlesnakes.

As volunteers, Mark, the FOCA members, and I also had signed legal waivers holding the SPCA and the Chadwick police harmless for any injuries we might incur while carrying out our duties today. In other words, we got fair warning that we were entering a danger zone.

The night before, I'd found an e-mail from Mom on my phone. Apparently, some brief footage of me rescuing Ayesha from the tree during Chadwick Day had made the local news. Fortunately, the newscaster simply repeated what I'd told the

Courier reporter, that the cat had gotten away from its handler and had run up a tree. I'm sure it just made an amusing story to anyone except Mom, who felt responsible for not having been able to mind the shop for me.

With so much still unsettled, I definitely had not wanted to phone my mother last night and tell her about the escapade Mark and I would be taking part in today. I had just e-mailed her back that none of my Chadwick Day problems had been her fault—I'd just trusted an inexperienced person, but no real harm had been done. I'd added that I was dead tired and needed to be up early in the morning, but I'd fill her in as soon as I could.

Which might be, oh, November, depending on how things went today. To be on the safe side, I'd turned off the ringer on my phone before heading out to Rattlesnake Ridge.

Now the SPCA van made a sharp left into what appeared to be the midst of the trees. Then Mark did, too. Once I reached the spot, I realized it was actually a dirt road, with a faded wooden marker I couldn't read. The cops had gone ahead of us and would be at Schaeffer's property by now; they'd matched up Teri's directions with the crude, hand-drawn map found in Pete Reardon's motel room. Naughton, up ahead, also had that information, so I assumed he must know where he was going.

From that point on, the trip devolved from a scenic adventure into more of a wilderness trek. The mist lay heavy between the trees here, and the narrow road became an obstacle course of stones and ruts. Even though I drove as slowly as I could while still keeping Mark in view, my trusty Honda suffered some cruel jounces. It reminded me of an eerie sequence from a horror movie—I saw few signs of human habitation. Once in a while, a mailbox or a dilapidated shack materialized for just a second before disappearing back into the haze. If an actual person had stepped into my path, I probably would have screamed and driven into a tree.

What would possess someone to move out here, even start a business out here? A bargain price on the property, no doubt. An urge to bond with nature. But maybe also a desire for isolation? The need to hide what he or she was really up to?

After about ten minutes that seemed more like hours, we made another turn and pulled into a small, gravel parking lot. It already held a black-and-white patrol car with two cops beside it, a second SPCA vehicle that looked more like a van, and a few people I'd seen at the FOCA table the day before. The rest of us pulled up near them and parked.

Just as I stepped out of my car, I heard someone in the distance shout, "We got him! Damn, I think we finally got him!"

I fell in step with Mark, and we traded curious glances. "Think he means Schaeffer?" I asked.

But two young guys in black SPCA polo shirts emerged from the woods carrying a cage-like trap about four feet long. Barely contained inside was an enormous tan, spotted cat. It snarled at its captors in sharp, explosive bursts, almost like barks, and tore at the wire mesh of the cage with hawk-like talons. The animal must have been fairly heavy, because the two men balanced the trap between them. As they drew closer, I could see the beast had a neck ruff and tufted ears like a bobcat, but lashed a full-length tail more like a domestic cat's.

Yeah, that definitely could have killed a small dog. In fact, the little boy from the second attack had been darned lucky to get away with just some deep scratches.

The two SPCA investigators set the trap down in the middle of the parking lot, where Naughton met them wearing his regular black uniform, plus short boots and a visored cap.

Even when set down on the gravel, their captive continued to growl and spit. Mark bent as close as he dared. "Is that the demon cat we've all heard so much about?"

"Fits the description," said Naughton, gazing down at the cage. "I don't know about the 'demon' part, but he's a nasty one. I've seen bobcats caught in this kind of trap before, and usually they're pretty intimidated. They tend to quiet down, waiting to see if you're going to hurt them. But this guy's full of fight."

With perfect timing, the cat let out another mini roar, flashing long fangs I could easily see even from a safe distance. The FOCA and SPCA people clustered around, and one young woman snapped cell phone pictures to document the capture.

"What happens to him now?" I asked. After all, I thought, if this creature had been purposely bred by man, he couldn't help his unnatural behavior. He posed a greater danger than a normal wildcat precisely because he lacked any fear of humans.

"That's a tough call," Naughton said. "Except for the aggressiveness, he doesn't show any obvious signs of rabies. Unfortunately, the only sure way to make that diagnosis is after an animal has been euthanized." He turned to one of his assistants, a lanky, acne-scarred fellow. "For now, put this guy in the back of our van, shake some dry food into the cage, and, if you can, slip him a pan of water. We've still got a lot more work to do here."

Naughton led the rest of us up a rise, where we came upon a weathered, dark brown farmhouse, a few decades old but in reasonably good shape. Free-range chickens prattled nearby. As we passed the rear of the house, a Rottweiler-type guard dog sprang from beneath the porch and charged to the end of his chain, barking furiously. The thickness of the chain reassured us all that we could ignore him for the time being.

Raised beds near the house held flourishing herbs of all kinds—no doubt peppermint and spearmint among them. Farther on, we passed rows of larger garden beds, some shaded with fabric stretched over wire arches, others left open to the sun. I glimpsed brilliant heads of lettuce, kale, broccoli, and other leafy greens. Another section combined bush beans low to the ground with pole beans on tall wire supports. Toward the edge of the woods, we passed clusters of berry bushes, one group covered loosely with protective netting—those would probably be the blueberries.

Knowing what I did now about Rick, I suspected Teri deserved the credit for most of this meticulous work, which paid off in the high quality of the farm's produce. Ironic that even this had been twisted for use in their scheme to acquire Ayesha for their breeding business.

It didn't surprise me to find a couple of Chadwick PD officers closely inspecting the battalions of healthy tomato plants. They snapped photos and plucked and bagged samples, though seemingly not of any actual tomatoes.

Still, I began to wonder why we'd been summoned here in such numbers and told to bring all the pet carriers we could pack into our vehicles. So far, Schaeffer's Organic Farm appeared to be—if you overlooked the marijuana—a fairly legitimate business.

Except for one odd thing. Besides the absence of Rick and Teri, I saw no workers anywhere. Surely they employed a few extra people to help them tend and harvest all of these crops.

Mark must have formed the same impression, and called out to Naughton, "Looks deserted. Where is everybody?"

The tall, blond SPCA chief shrugged. "The cops already searched the house. No sign of Schaeffer, so they put out an APB on him. If he had workers, he probably warned them to make themselves scarce."

"You think he's responsible for breeding that cat you caught?" I asked.

Naughton nodded. "You'll see why in a minute. The worst is back here, behind this patch of woods."

I smelled it before I saw it—the pungent reek of

cat urine. It's particularly strong with unneutered males, and there must have been quite a few up ahead.

Past the trees, we came upon a home-built arrangement of stacked wooden cages. Some were dual-level, kind of an outdoor, Appalachian version of my cat condos. All housed what seemed to be the more rough-and-ready breeding stock: a couple of genuine bobcats, a long-legged exotic that could have been a Savannah, and some burly domestics that might have been feral. A few paced and cried out when we approached, while others cringed in their corners, growling or panting.

The trees provided some shade from the day's increasing heat, but even so, these natural hunters could not happily sit in their cages around the clock. With Teri arrested and Rick in the wind, these cats had run out of food and water, and their crude litter pans had reached critical mass.

One hungry bobcat rallied enough to snarl at me as I passed. Suddenly, I understood Pete Reardon's reaction when he learned that Ayesha would be bred to one of these animals. Let's face it, cat sex is a little rough to begin with. Faced with a male half again as big as she was, with fangs and claws designed to bring down serious prey, the beautiful Bengal would have been lucky to survive uninjured. At the very least, she'd have been badly traumatized, her friendly, confident personality destroyed forever.

I sent a silent message into the ether: *Good call, Pete. In the end, you redeemed yourself by sparing her this.*

The FOCA volunteers muttered their disgust

over the conditions of the cages, and Mark asked Naughton, "What's in store for these guys?"

"I've been in touch with a sanctuary in upstate New York," the investigator said. "They take ferals and hybrids that haven't been socialized. Give them something close to a natural environment and treat them like the wild animals they are."

Near the outdoor cages, we found a type of cat run, also hand-built of wood and chicken wire. It measured about six feet wide and high, and ten feet long. It enclosed a small, box-like shelter, some shelves, and a long tree limb for the animals to climb. None were turned loose in there now, though, and I wondered how often they got even that much exercise.

Finally we reached a small barn, its wood faded over the decades to dull gray. Its door stood ajar, the padlock cut and hanging.

"We broke in here yesterday," Naughton said. "Good thing we did, 'cause some of these cats are in a bad way. Plus, it needed airing out overnight."

The outbuilding held stacks of standard wire cages, lined at the bottom with plastic pans. The smell here probably had dissipated a little, or maybe I'd adjusted by now. Our companions from FOCA also soldiered on bravely—probably, doing rescue work, they'd seen worse conditions.

Schaeffer's breeding operation appeared successful in that the barn housed a fair number of young cats, as well as one new mother nursing five kittens. But Rick and Teri had fallen short in their goals to produce saleable pets, because at least a third of the younger cats appeared to have health problems.

Mark pointed these out to me as we looked over the cages. "Digestive trouble . . . that's common with hybrids. This one's got a limp . . . too young for arthritis, so it might be a bone deformity. And see the skin irritation on this female? Probably a flea allergy."

The mention of fleas made me squirm, and I hoped my pants-tucked-into-boots would give me some protection from those, too. "What about the bald patch on this kitten's leg?" I asked.

He squatted for a closer look. "Could just be overgrooming from stress. Animals can't stand being shut up for days on end like this. They get neurotic, just like we would."

The barn upset me even more than the outdoor cages, maybe because these cats seemed tamer and some were less than a year old. Nothing like a sick kitten meowing at you, and pleading with its eyes for help, to break your heart.

With tears coming on, I muttered, "I need to get out of here."

"Yeah, the smell is really . . ." Mark saw my face, put his arm around me, and took me outside. "I know, it's bad."

I realized that, since he'd volunteered to help, he would probably end up dealing with most of these casualties at his clinic.

At that point, Naughton called us together in an open area. "Okay, folks, you've seen the situation. My guys will take on the wildcats, since we've had the most experience. Becky and Allen, your FOCA team can load up the tamer animals and the kittens. Cassie will give you a hand and provide some more carriers. Dr. Coccia, let us know if you see any animals in immediate distress or that might need to be quarantined for any reason." He glanced back over his shoulder. "Meanwhile, Officer Baylock will keep an eye out, just in case any of Schaeffer's pals come back—"

A shrill police whistle sounded from the high ground to the west of the house. Officer Baylock raised a finger, signaling us to wait, then dashed off in response.

Naughton also hesitated, no doubt wondering, like the rest of us, what was up.

I really must have been turning into a part-time detective, because I couldn't resist trailing after Baylock. My curiosity must have been catching, because Mark also came along. By the time we reached that stretch of woods, the officer came trudging back toward us, talking on his radio. We both heard him say something about a "body of a male Caucasian" and a "mine shaft." I remembered Dawn saying the area was dotted with entrances to old iron mines.

After Baylock hung up, I asked, "It is Schaeffer?"

"There's no ID," he answered shortly. When a second officer emerged from the dense greenery, Baylock told him in an authoritative tone, "We need to secure this scene. Detective Bonelli is on her way with the medical examiner."

I rejoined Mark, who wondered under his breath, "Not another murder?"

By now, the whole animal rescue crowd had gotten sidetracked from its duties and had gathered at the edge of the woods, but Baylock warned us all back.

"The rest of you, go about your business," he said. "The department is sending out more manpower to search these woods, so it will help if you can relocate the cats ASAP. Meanwhile, keep your eyes open and be careful."

We didn't need much more encouragement. It was late morning by now, the mist had burned off as the day heated up, and especially in the shade near the woods, the mosquitoes were starting to bite. We doused ourselves liberally with bug repellent and went to work in the barn.

First, we settled the mother cat and her kittens all in one roomy carrier. Mom looked like a regular domestic with flashy tiger stripes, but the big paws on the kittens suggested they had some wilder genes. At this age, anyhow, they were friendly and cooperative. Maybe if someone hand-raised them carefully, they might make decent pets.

Meanwhile, of course, I continued to burn with curiosity. Who was the dead man? Could it be Rick? Even without ID, Baylock ought to have a photo to work from. Maybe he had been told by Bonelli to keep the details quiet. He might not even know the cause of death yet. Anyway, he hadn't commented on that, either, except for the reference to a mine shaft.

The cops seemed to be treating the wooded area as a crime scene, but that could be just a formality. *Be ironic if it were an accident. If Schaeffer went on the run, fell into an old shaft, and broke his neck.*

Most of the tamer cats from the barn came along without much of a fight, though once in a while we had to wrap one in a bath towel just to make the transfer to the carrier. In cases where two buddies had been caged together, we put them in the same carrier.

The four of us were working as quickly as possible, shuttling to and from our vehicles, so we left the barn door open. When I reached into the cage for the year-old kitten with the twisted leg, he turned out to be surprisingly agile. He shot right through my hands, dodged around everyone else, and made it out the door.

"Oops, lost one!" said blond, ponytailed Becky from FOCA.

"I'll catch him," I promised. "With that bad leg, he shouldn't get too far."

Of course, the silver-gray tabby had done a pretty good sprint out of the barn, so I might have been too optimistic.

He bounded off toward the woods, and I saw the white tip of his raised tail disappear into the underbrush. Still toting a small carrier, I dashed after him. Meanwhile, I fished in my pocked to see if I had any cat treats left. Still one almost-full packet.

I heard voices calling after me, but I didn't want to give up on this little guy. At worst, maybe his leg could be surgically removed and he still could live a fairly normal life. At best, the deformity wasn't serious and he'd never be any more handicapped than he was now. All he'd need would be someone kind enough to adopt him. He deserved a better life than he'd had so far.

I tried to make as little noise as possible as I crept through the prickly bushes and entangling vines, and kept an eye out for poison ivy as well as for the lost kitten. *This is probably nuts—I'll never be able to spot him in here.* On the off chance that I could lure him to me, I made whispering noises and opened the package of treats. If he wasn't afraid of people and had been hand-fed before, that might draw him out.

To my delight, the little white-masked face reappeared from under a big bush. At least I assumed it was a bush, though the shape seemed oddly squared-off. Holding out the treats to the kitten, I stole closer. I put some food on the ground and, after he emerged to gobble it, I scooped him up and stashed him in the carrier. Only then did I really focus on the object that had sheltered him and brush away some of the leaves that covered it.

It was an ATV, the kind a farmer or rancher might use to get around his property. This one was a little different, though, than any I'd seen before. It had a pipe framework on top—probably a roll cage—and the exterior sported a camouflage pattern, handy for hunting, I guess. Along with the partial covering of real leaves, this had made it nearly invisible, at least from a distance.

I heard a stealthy step behind me. Before I could turn, cold steel pressed against the back of my head.

A low voice rasped, "Okay, Cassie McGlone. You got me into this mess, so you're going to get me out of it. Or else."

Chapter 20

Rick Schaeffer and I had never shared a long conversation, but we'd spoken often enough that I recognized his voice. His breathing sounded labored now, though. And although he kept what I presumed was a gun to my head, he didn't try to hold onto me otherwise.

Breathing hard now myself, I wished I'd followed Naughton's advice to keep my eyes open. "W-what do you want?"

"First, put that cat down." When I balked, he shouted in my ear, "*Now.*"

I stooped to set down the carrier, wishing I knew some clever martial arts move to disarm Rick from that position. But I didn't have the nerve to elbow him in the groin, and he kept the gun pointed at me. I figured even if I made a run for it, he'd just shoot me.

"Now we'll go around to the back of this vehicle and you'll open the cargo compartment."

I obeyed, but wondered why he couldn't do this himself. I lifted the lid of the oblong, metal compartment and choked off a shriek.

Inside lay a thick-bodied snake, probably four feet long, doubled back on itself. The rough scales were tan with brown, chevron-like bands. I'd seen this kind often enough in movies and on TV shows to have a gut reaction—I jumped back even before I noticed the segmented rattle at the end of its tail.

But it didn't move. I realized its triangular head had been nearly blown off, the blood congealing beneath.

"Dead," Rick confirmed, in a strained voice. "Shot it right after it bit me. See that yellow box underneath? You hafta get that."

Being an animal person, I'd never had the irrational fear that some folks do of all snakes. In my vet tech training, I'd learned to handle harmless ones. Still, my every instinct rebelled against touching this large, poisonous serpent, though I knew it couldn't do me any harm. I glimpsed enough of the printing on the yellow box to understand why Rick demanded I retrieve it. So I gritted my teeth, lifted the reptile's back end, and pulled out the snakebite kit.

"I can't do this for myself," he said, between breaths. "You have to."

I started to read the instructions on the back of the box. "But I've never used—"

"I have, and you're gonna do it." Still with the gun trained on me, he sank down in the ATV's passenger seat, and I finally saw what handicapped him. His right hand was puffed up to half again its normal size, with two dark puncture wounds on the back ringed by a reddish bruise. The fingers were stiff as sausages, useless to hold anything.

"Hurry!" Rick barked. "Clean the bite with alcohol. In the packets."

I opened the kit, found some small, square envelopes, tore one open, and used the pad inside to do this. Meanwhile, I noticed the kit also included a compact, folding type of straight razor, probably to shave hair from the affected area. Rick didn't have much hair on the back of his hand, though.

"Now, see those clear cups? Get one big enough to cover the whole bite—the middle one should do. And take out that yellow pump."

The pump, or extractor, was about the size and shape of a toilet paper tube. He directed me to fit it snugly over the cup, and I prayed he wouldn't make me suck out the venom. But no, I just had to push a plunger at the top, which drew the skin of his hand and some dark blood into the cup. Rick told me to hold it that way for thirty seconds.

I counted, meanwhile thinking I would have preferred to do CPR on the rattlesnake than to help Schaeffer. Only the gun motivated me. This guy probably had killed at least one person already, maybe two, so I was sure he wouldn't hesitate to add me to the list. If he thought I could help him survive, on the other hand, that gave me better odds.

When the waiting time was up, I removed the cup and checked the back of the box again. "Rick, it says to do this within the first five minutes after you've been bitten. How long ago did the snake—?"

"Never mind. Clean that damned thing off and use it again."

Still at gunpoint, I complied. My captor was starting to flag, though, and his eyelids drooped.

"Little bitch," he spat. "Had to be her. . . . Tried to kill me. Snake didn't get in there by itself."

I used the extractor again to pull out a little more poisoned blood, but I doubted it would do much good. "Look, this isn't helping. You need to go to a hospital."

"No way. They'll be looking for me." He muttered curses. "Jim was supposed to come back for me. . . . Took off in my truck!"

"Rick, you need a doctor to give you antivenom. Otherwise you're going to—"

Voices floated toward us through the trees not far off. Two people coming.

"Cassie?"

"Hey, Cassie, where are you?"

The gun's muzzle shifted to my left temple. "Don't answer."

Crap, one of those voices was Mark's. If he found us first, Rick might shoot him!

I groped backward with my right hand, as if to brace myself. Made contact with the open snakebite kit. Rick still couldn't restrain me with *his* right hand, and I began to suspect that was his good one. He might not be so adept at firing a gun with his left. As long as he had it against my head, of course, he didn't really need to aim. But if I could twist away somehow . . .

The voices again, closer. Two silhouettes pushed their way through the bushes.

"What the—?" Mark said.

"Oh my God!" said Becky.

Rick stiffened, focusing for a second on them, not me. I grasped my secret weapon by the stiff handle and worked it open. Mentally picked my spot, just beneath the sleeve of his T-shirt, on his uninjured arm.

"Stay back," he told them, "or I'll—"

"Watch out!" I screamed, and slashed upward.

At the sudden pain, Rick jerked his arm away and fired a wild shot into the trees. I scrambled in the other direction, where Mark and Becky caught and shielded me.

In a bad way by now, Rick tottered on his feet. He gaped in confusion at the blood dripping from his left bicep. Lucky for me, I'd given him a pretty good cut with the razor.

Meanwhile, Mark took a step forward, as if looking for a way to jump in and grab the gun.

Rick's shot finally brought Baylock running, along with another cop. They must have recognized the man they'd been hunting, because Baylock turned his gun on him and quickly relieved Rick of his weapon.

I gave the officers the shortest explanation that I could. Nodding toward Rick, I said, "A rattlesnake bit him, at least fifteen minutes ago. He made me use a kit on him, but it didn't do much good."

While the other officer radioed for an ambulance, Baylock sat his prisoner on the passenger side of the ATV and handcuffed Rick by his good arm to the steel roll cage. Then the cop slid into the driver's seat.

By now, Rick's head was lolling. Thickly, he asked Baylock, "M'I gonna die?"

"Probably no such luck." In a cheery tone, the cop added, "Might lose that arm, though."

Jouncing over the rough terrain, he drove off in the direction of the farm.

I felt unsteady on my feet, too, and was grateful to lean on Mark. Becky and the other officer, meanwhile, had found the body of the snake in the open cargo compartment.

The cop whistled. "Big mother. What the heck was he doing, carrying it around in this box?"

"He seemed to think his girlfriend planted it there," I said. "Probably hoping something like this would happen."

"Huh," said Becky. "She must be a piece of work, too."

"He had it coming," I said.

I felt Mark's rib cage twitch as he held back a laugh. "Can't argue with that." He turned to peer closely at me. "Are you okay?"

"Not really, but I will be."

Becky also eyed me with sympathy. "If you need to go home, Cassie, I'm sure Scott will understand. You didn't sign up for . . . *this.*"

I smiled. "I kind of did, when I signed that waiver. Anyway, you still need all the help you can get. C'mon, let's finish getting these cats out of here."

Mark held my hand as we walked back, which bolstered my courage. I realized that, in all the excitement, I'd forgotten about the kitten with the crooked leg. Did we leave him in the woods?

I asked Mark if he had seen the small carrier on the ground, but he didn't remember.

"Could be that Becky picked him up," he said. "Check with FOCA."

Sure enough, when we got back to the farm and I passed the dozen carriers already stacked by the rescue group, I recognized a familiar, white-masked face. I poked a finger through the grill to tickle his nose. "You naughty thing—you almost got me killed!"

It took us another hour to finish the feline roundup, and at the end, we'd rescued more than forty cats. That including a few pets the SPCA found in the house, in better condition than the breeding stock. So many of those in that second group had health problems that a veterinary van filled up, and I had to take about half a dozen patients in my small SUV. The guard dog got a cage of his own in the front of the SPCA van, coming along meekly enough once he was freed from his chain.

A couple of times during the process, I felt my phone vibrate. When I paused to check it, I confirmed that Mom was trying to reach me. No, I'd need some time before I even tried to describe to her what I'd been up to today. Somehow, I'd have to gloss over the part about being held at gunpoint by a murderer while trying to save his life with a snakebite kit. I didn't think Mom's nerves were up to knowing about that. Mine just barely were.

Our furry caravan was ready to depart when Scott Naughton came up and personally thanked me and Mark for all our help.

"Detective Bonelli did us a solid when she suggested we work with you," he told me. "Not every animal lover is cut out for this kind of work. Some just can't take it, emotionally or physically. You not only handled the rescue well, but from what I hear, you brought the killer to heel rather nicely, too."

I shrugged. "The rattlesnake did most of the damage to Rick. By the time he threatened me, he was so far gone that it wasn't hard to outwit him."

"Still, it took a cool head. Thanks for being on our team."

He clapped me on the shoulder, and I'm sure I blushed. After all, it wasn't every day that I heard such high praise from a six-foot-plus New Jersey version of Crocodile Dundee . . . in an SPCA uniform.

I wasn't the only one who noticed the faint spark between us. As Naughton left for his vehicle, I caught Mark watching from the corner of his eye.

He and I should have been eager to get going, too, but curiosity made us hang back in the parking lot. Rick had gone off to the hospital, but one mystery remained to be solved. From the gravel lot, we could just see the fringe of woods that now had been taken over by the Chadwick PD, crime scene tape stretched across the outermost trees and an ambulance parked on the grass nearby. Cops continued to search, I guess in case Rick had any helpers still lurking or any more bodies turned up.

"The dead guy in the mine shaft could just be coincidental," Mark speculated. "That might not even be on Schaeffer's property. I heard somebody say most of those mine entrances are covered over with brush. You might not even see one until you're right on top of it."

I went along with his theory. "So someone could have just fallen in, gotten hurt, and not been able to climb out. Maybe a hunter, someone out looking for the killer bobcat."

I was on the verge of saying what we both were thinking, though, when Bonelli emerged from the woods, talking on her cell phone. She was followed by a rawboned, older man in a white polo shirt and jeans and two EMTs who carried an orange plastic stretcher that held a black body bag. The medical examiner and forensic team must have finished examining the site, and the body was being released to the morgue. On such a hot day, I'm sure they didn't want to postpone that any longer than necessary.

With no more worries about contaminating the crime scene, I jogged out to meet Bonelli. As she got off the phone, I asked, "Who is it? Anyone we know?"

She answered with a guarded look. "Not sure yet. We have a photo, but it's a few years old. We're waiting for a family member to come and make an ID."

Was there a reason why she didn't want to share any of her theories with me?

Suddenly, I felt as if I'd swallowed a block of ice. "Maybe I can help."

"You sure, Cassie?" she asked. "You've already been through a lot today."

Mark had come up behind me, and I felt his hand on my shoulder.

I nodded.

One of the EMTs unzipped the top of the body bag. Gray and slack-jawed, the victim's face no longer wore the taunting smirk I remembered. Dirt had caked in the hair that still rose in a flame-like peak above the young man's forehead.

"You said he was down a mine shaft. Did he die from the fall?"

The older man in the white shirt shook his head. "Shot at close range."

"A hunting accident . . . ?"

"In the back, probably with a Glock."

I swallowed hard. No doubt the same weapon I'd felt pressed against my temple just over an hour ago. Time seemed to stretch out, voices faded into the distance, and I realized I was starting to pass out. Mark grabbed me around the waist and held me until my head cleared.

With the dead man officially identified, the EMT zipped up the body bag again. I silently forgave Todd all of his boorish blunders, now that I knew he'd never again speed along the ridge, always pushing the limits, in his vintage red Camaro.

Chapter 21

In the dusk, I followed Mark's RAV4 back to his clinic. We all wound over the narrow, rutted roads, finally picking up more speed on the highway spur. The trip felt shorter now that the sun was high, the mist had burned off, and we knew where we were headed.

I finally had the time to wonder how things were going back at my shop. Since it was Sunday, when I usually cared for all of the boarders myself, I'd asked Dawn to look in on them and give the high-maintenance cats a noon feeding.

I'd learned my lesson about trusting just anyone to pinch-hit for me. And Dawn was only too glad to help, since she still felt guilty about having pushed Teri on me.

The drive also gave me time to brood about Todd's murder. Besides thinking that I could have suffered the same fate, I hated to imagine how the news would affect his poor parents.

By about seven p.m., Mark, the FOCA volunteers, and I reached his clinic with all the cats that urgently needed to be examined and treated. Dr. Margaret Reed and a couple of the vet techs came in to help. They would deal with the most desperate cases first and then stabilize the animals with more chronic complaints.

As they all set to work at peak efficiency, I sensed I'd just be in the way. "I'd better get back to my place," I told Mark.

"Oh . . . sure." About to open the carrier with the mother tabby and her kittens, he paused and pulled me aside for a kiss. "You were amazing today, dealing with Schaeffer. I couldn't believe how you kept your cool."

I smiled. "I figured he wasn't going to shoot me as long as he needed me to help him with the snakebite kit. After that, I couldn't be so sure."

Mark's arms tightened around me, and I knew he was reliving that terrifying scene. "I was damned scared for a moment that I might lose you. I just wish I could have gotten there sooner, to help."

"You did help. You showed up at the right time to distract him so I could use the razor. I'm just glad he didn't turn the gun on you!"

He relaxed his embrace a bit. "Guess we all had luck on our side. I have to say one thing for Teri—if she did plant that snake in his vehicle, she at least gave the cops a chance to overpower him." One of the techs called out to Mark then for help. Before responding, he told me, "I'll drop by your place later, okay?"

"Please do. I'm sure it will take you awhile, though, to deal with all of these unexpected patients."

He just shook his head, but I know both of us were glad he had a chance to make a difference.

Dawn sat behind my sales counter and buried both hands in her long, wavy hair. "I can't believe it. Rick Schaeffer murdered two people in cold blood? He was beating up on Teri, and she tried to kill him with a live rattlesnake? I thought these two were nice, peaceful organic farmers! How did I not sense . . . something?"

"You judged Teri by the fruits of her labor. Which were all pretty good, from what I saw—the crops looked in great shape. The hybrid cats, not so much."

"And *they* bred the vicious cat that went on the rampage?"

"Seems likely. We did find one big cage, among the wild male cats, where the wire mesh had been chewed or torn through. Guess it wasn't strong enough to hold their Frankenstein monster." I glanced around my own shop, which felt like a haven of tranquility after Schaeffer's farm. "So, nothing new around here, I guess?"

"Oh!" Dawn grabbed a piece of lined notepaper from the counter. "I hate to even show you this after all you've been through today. I found it in under the front door this morning."

The paper had been folded in half and one corner had ripped a bit, maybe from being forced under the door. In a loose, loopy script, it said:

I know what you did. You'll be sorry!

All of the fleas I'd been exposed to that day seemed to march in a column down my backbone, and I shuddered. Just when I'd thought I'd left the dangers of Schaeffer's farm behind me!

I wanted to scream, *Enough.* Dawn was right—in my current state, I didn't feel up to dealing with yet another threat.

"Who could have written that?" she worried aloud. "Teri's in jail, right? Could Schaeffer have done it? Maybe last night, before the raid?"

"Possibly." I calmed a little. If he blamed me for Teri's arrest, he might have left me this threat in the middle of the night. Seemed kind of subtle for a guy like him, though—I'd expect him to come pounding on the door. Of course, he knew by now that my shop was alarmed.

What if it was written more recently than that? Who might still be at large? Teri said that Rick was into the breeding operation with a couple of buddies. Maybe one of them heard about my role in the bust and is out for revenge.

I didn't share that scary thought with Dawn, though. Refolding the note, I told her, "I'll show this to Bonelli, just to be safe."

"You had a phone call, too," she told me. "Don Brewster thinks he can come pick up Ayesha at the end of this week."

"Fantastic! About time we had some good news." Impulsively, I hugged Dawn. "Thank you so much for watching my place today. I'm sure you're eager to get back to your apartment and relax, and I really need a shower. It may be just my imagination, but I feel like I'm crawling with all kinds of vermin."

"At least you're not crawling with snakes." Dawn shimmied her shoulders in revulsion. On her way out, she added, "Listen, dinner's on me tonight."

"Okay . . ." I paused. "Mark said he might be coming over."

"That's fine. I'll make enough for both of you, drop it off here about six, and scram." When I started to protest, she insisted, "It's the least I can do after hooking you up with the Bonnie and Clyde of Rattlesnake Ridge."

After my shower, I phoned Mark and told him our dinner would be provided courtesy of Nature's Way. It was just past four, but he already sounded beat after hours of performing triage on the rescued cats. He vowed to also clean up, though, and maybe take a short nap before coming over.

I left a message for Bonelli about the threatening note, just in case. I didn't intend to tell Mark, but that was one more reason why I was glad he would be spending the night. If the threat came from Rick, I had nothing to worry about. If it came from someone else, though . . . I might not be up to fending off any more bad guys on my own.

Dawn returned promptly at six to drop off a microwaveable pot of vegetarian stew, then vanished again, a bohemian version of the Good Fairy. Mark arrived about half an hour later, and we embraced like survivors of the same battlefield. It might have been only the aroma of the simmering food and our hunger pangs that kept our behavior PG-rated, for the moment. Over dinner, he related all the frantic activity at the clinic, with doctors and staffers reporting for work on what should have been their only full day off.

"In the end, I think we did the best we could." He helped himself to another serving of Dawn's stew. "A few of the cats almost certainly will have to be euthanized—they're too far gone. Most can recover, though, if they get the right treatment. The SPCA has offered to foot the bill for that, though I'm sure they aren't rolling in cash, either."

"They've got a tough job." I refilled our wineglasses. "Imagine walking in on situations like that all the time. I don't think I could take it."

Later on, the two of us were chilling out watching a sitcom—neither being in the mood for any crime shows—when my phone rang. I saw the ID and let it go to voice mail.

Mark glanced at me in curiosity. "Solicitor?"

"Bonelli. I just don't feel like any more cop talk right now." But since I knew she must be responding to my call, at the next commercial I listened to her message. It didn't tell me anything I hadn't already considered. The handwritten note might have been from Rick, and if so, he was securely in custody. In case it was left by one of his employees, though, I should keep my eyes open. She wanted to see the original tomorrow.

When I put down the phone, Mark had muted the TV and wore a concerned look. "What did she want?"

Okay, he'd gone through the whole ordeal with me today, and if somebody did plan to cause trouble at my place overnight, Mark deserved some warning. I explained about the note, got it from my purse, and showed it to him.

As he read it, his face darkened.

"If Rick or Teri wrote it, I probably don't have anything to worry about," I pointed out. "I'm just wondering if it could have been one of Rick's partners. They must still be out there somewhere."

Mark laid a reassuring hand on my shoulder. "I don't think you have to be concerned about that, either. Let me get something from my car."

Without further explanation, he went down the stairs and out to my parking lot. I followed and met him as he came back in. Mark doesn't completely trust electronic records, and likes to carry an old-school planner that includes a calendar, an address book, and compartments for business cards and notes. From one of these slots, he pulled a similar piece of lined paper. He unfolded it and cursed under his breath.

"You got one, too?"

He showed me his note. Dated a few days earlier, it read: *I'll be delayed just a little tomorrow because I have an 8:30 dentist appointment. Will stay late to make up. Sorry for any inconvenience!—Jennifer.*

I almost laughed. "You can't be serious."

Mark whipped out his own phone and began punching numbers.

I touched his arm. "Now, now. Take a deep breath. You don't want dear Jennifer to be able to twist things around and claim you threatened *her.*"

"You're right." With a frown, he pondered his options for a minute. Only then did he redial.

He got voice mail, which probably was a blessing. "Jennifer Hood, this is Dr. Mark Coccia. I've just become aware that Cassie McGlone, of Cassie's Comfy Cats, received an unsigned note making a vague accusation and threat against her. She showed it to me, and I recognized your handwriting. You should know that she is turning it over to the police, and I am also going to tell them about the stunts you pulled while working at my clinic, for which I dismissed you. They all have been documented and confirmed by my colleague Dr. Reed and the rest of the staff. If you harass us or Cassie McGlone in any way, I will take legal action. And if this is typical of the way you go after your goals, Ms. Hood, I suggest you get some professional help before you end up in even bigger trouble."

With no goodbye, he hung up.

"Nice going." I applauded him. "I'd say you've officially overcome your reluctance to kick butt."

Mark tucked the phone back into his jeans with a restrained smile. "I figure we might as well make your friendship with Bonelli work in our favor. If that doesn't scare Jennifer off, she's tougher than I think."

"It ought to do the trick."

"Took a lot out of me, though." As we headed back upstairs, he asked, "Got any beer in the fridge?"

"Absolutely," I told him, "although this occasion almost calls for champagne."

I slept extremely well that night. For one thing, the last mysterious threat to my home security had been identified and neutralized. For another, hearing your boyfriend take your side against a sexy, younger rival, in polite but blistering terms, is a heck of an aphrodisiac.

The next morning, Mark took off early for work, and Sarah arrived at nine, minus her crutch. She'd been cleared to walk carefully on her injured leg with the soft boot and seemed to be faring well. She was able to help me more than before with feeding and watering the cats, though litter duty still involved carrying a bit too much weight. Our chores went fast as I regaled her with the adventures of the previous day. As she listened to my tale about the murder and mayhem up on the ridge, Sarah's eyes grew wider by the minute.

"That's crazy," she said. "I felt there was something a little off about that girl, but I never would've thought she'd be involved with not just one, but two murders."

"Well, how involved she was remains to be seen. Teri told me she had no idea Rick had killed anyone, but she must have suspected something. Just goes to show, Sarah—anyone mean enough to hurt someone as nice as you, on purpose, is capable of anything!"

Once she had settled in at the sales counter, I retreated to the playroom for privacy and finally responded to the three phone messages my mother had left the day before. She'd heard on the news and read in the paper about the raid on the backwoods cattery, the discovery of a body in a nearby mine shaft, and the probable connection to another man murdered a couple of weeks back. My name and Mark's were mentioned as participants in the raid. Fortunately, the police seemed to have omitted the detail about my being held at gunpoint.

I didn't tell Mom about that part, either, and I minimized the drama of Rick's capture. "While the cops were searching for him, he'd been bitten by a rattlesnake and was pretty sick," I explained. "So they were able to take him into custody without too much trouble."

"That's incredible!" Mom said, and for a second I thought my sanitized version hadn't convinced her. "And they said on the news that this girl Teri was working with him."

"She was trying to steal Ayesha for their breeding operation," I admitted. "The whole thing was a scam from the beginning. She injured Sarah so that I would need another assistant. Then she arranged to offer her services in a way that wouldn't make me suspicious."

"Now I feel even guiltier," my mother moaned on the phone. "If I'd been able to help out, she wouldn't have gotten that chance."

"She and Rick probably would have found some other way, and maybe they would even have hurt you. Don't give it another thought, Mom. Everything turned out for the best, and now they're both in custody."

I could tell from her shaky tone that she wasn't going to calm down from this one for a while, but at least she found a way to comfort herself. "I guess it's a good thing you've made friends with the local cops, isn't it?"

"Yes and no. Bonelli was the one who asked me

and Mark to help out with the raid. But I'm glad she did—the SPCA needed the extra hands, and we got most of those cats into either the clinic or the local animal shelter."

The phone went silent for a minute, so that I thought we'd lost our connection. "Mom?"

"I'm still here," she said quietly. "You've really found your calling, haven't you, Cassie?"

The question startled me, but I understood what she meant. Not just operating the shop, grooming and boarding the cats. But advocating for them and protecting them from people who would neglect or harm them.

I chuckled to lighten the mood and admitted, "Yeah, I guess I have. Too bad it involves animals you aren't too fond of."

"Well, for your sake," she promised, "I'll try to get over it."

We clicked off soon after that, without Mom finding out that I'd been held at gunpoint by a double-murderer. With any luck, she never would.

There were no special appointments scheduled that morning, so I left Sarah in charge while I walked to the police station. I popped into Bonelli's office and gave her my note from Jennifer Hood. She already had heard from Mark and said it was smart of him to cover his tracks with the former receptionist.

"If the girl's that bent, she might try to accuse him of sexual harassment and claim he fired her because she wouldn't cooperate," said Bonelli, sitting across her desk from me. "It sounds, though, as if just about everyone at his clinic can testify that this Jennifer was the troublemaker."

"That's probably lucky for him," I agreed. "Could be worse—when I first opened that note, I thought maybe it had been left by Rick, or one of his partners. Teri did say he was working with a couple of other guys, and I figure they're still on the loose."

"Oh, we got one of them last night," Bonelli told me, with a grim smile. "We had an APB out for a green truck with Rick's plates. State troopers pulled it over in the next county, with a Jim Duprey behind the wheel. Guess he was smart enough to ditch Schaeffer and take the company signage off the truck, but didn't have a chance to change the plates."

I shook my head. "Sounds like you've nailed most of the culprits, then."

"I'd say so. If there was anybody else involved with the operation, they're on the run by now."

"Which leaves Teri. What's happening with her?"

"She's got a lawyer, and she might get off a bit easier than her boyfriend. Of course, that stunt with the rattlesnake will count against her. She told me she found it in the garden shed, curled up in an empty burlap sack. She was carrying it into the woods to turn it loose when she spotted Rick's ATV. She knew he always stashed energy bars in that cargo box for long drives around the property, and she'd often seen him reach in for one without even looking. She said it was no problem to just let the snake crawl out of the bag into the box and close the lid."

"Lucky for all of us that she did, really," I admitted. "I guess Teri got desperate. She was isolated out there with Rick, she suspected he'd killed at least one person, he was beating her up, and he had a gun. To poison him in some sneaky way must have seemed like the only escape."

"Well, she's spilling the beans to us in exchange for a lighter sentence. The fact that she's claiming abuse will help, and she has the bruises to prove it. Plus, Schaeffer's got a couple of priors for assault—one road-rage incident and one bar fight."

Sounded like a guy with a world-class temper. Still, I had to ask, "How's he doing? Baylock said he might lose the arm."

"Don't think it will be that bad, but he's got nerve damage and will need skin grafts. He'll be fit enough to stand trial."

Good, I thought. Let everybody hear what he'd been up to. He'd be tried for the murders, of course, but in the process, there should also be multiple charges of animal abuse for the horrendous conditions at his farm.

I glanced up from my musings to find Bonelli staring at me. Her heavy-lidded, evaluating look always made me straighten up in my seat.

"You're really earning your stripes these days as a detective, aren't you?" she commented.

"My tabby stripes?" I joked, to deflect the scrutiny. "I do seem to specialize in cat-related crimes."

"At the start, yeah. But we got to the bottom of two murders with the help of your tips. If you hadn't been concerned about Pete Reardon, or whatever name he gave you, we'd have found his body but probably never connected him with Schaeffer. And unless we had reason to raid the farm because of Teri's information, who knows how long it would have taken to find Todd?"

I leaned back in my hard metal chair and sighed. "His poor parents. Do you have any idea how they're taking all this?"

"When I talked to them, they were pretty devastated. Even though, after a week, they had to be expecting the worst."

"Are they having a funeral?"

"Friday, family only. But there's a viewing the night before, five to seven, at Dewey's."

A few minutes later, walking back to my shop, I reflected that two very smart women had just proposed different suggestions for my life's calling. Should I keep working with cats or go into law enforcement?

Much as I respected Detective Bonelli's opinion, it was no contest. Mom might struggle to get over the idea of me devoting my time to a species of animal that gave her the willies. Her blood pressure would probably shoot sky-high, though, if I actually chased down criminals for a living.

Plus, what on earth would I be able to tell her then, when she asked about my day at work?

Chapter 22

The Dewey Funeral Home was right in Chadwick, and sadly, this was not the first time I had attended a viewing there. I brought Dawn along for moral support, because I didn't expect to know anyone.

In fact, I only recognized Bob Gillis because I'd seen him flip out on Chadwick Day when he saw someone else driving Todd's car. He resembled Todd if you overlooked his glasses, his trim beard and mustache, and his more conventionally barbershop-styled gray hair. His dark suit looked as if he might have purchased it years ago when he had a trimmer waist. His slim wife, Julia, had let her short hair go naturally silver—it was becoming, I thought, and refreshing, when most women would have dyed it. She wore a very plain, three-quarter-sleeved black dress that looked as if she might have purchased it just for funerals. Or maybe just for this one.

I'd heard that the loss of a child is the hardest kind to bear, and that seemed true for the Gillises. They both wore haunted, hollowed-out expressions. To my surprise, though, they brightened when I introduced myself and Dawn.

Julia took one of my hands in both of hers and squeezed it. "Cassie, my dear, how can we ever thank you?"

I thought she meant for coming to the viewing. "I just wanted to pay my respects, because I know all of this must have been terrible for the two of you."

"We heard, though, how much you did to solve Todd's murder," Bob explained. "Detective Bonelli said you helped catch that girl who sold the car to Danny Lorenzo. If it wasn't for that, the cops might never have connected Todd's . . . murder . . . to that cat business out in the woods."

"And if they never went looking out there, Cassie, who knows how much longer it might've taken to find out what happened toTodd? Or if we ever would have?" Julia Gillis dabbed at her nose with a tissue. "Awful as the truth was, at least now Bob and I have some . . . what d'you call it? Closure."

I hadn't really thought of it like that before. "I only wish I'd been able to help sooner."

Dawn explained that she had been doing business with Teri and Rick, though just for a couple of months. "Cassie and I both met them and never suspected they were violent people."

"Unfortunately, it took a while to pick up on the signs," I admitted.

We made conversation for a minute longer, Julia noting that they'd decided on a closed coffin. "Todd was so young. . . . We want people to remember him as we will—full of life, always joking and flirting."

"He did like the girls." Bob smiled with a wag of his head. "I could tell he had a crush on you, Cassie, from the way he talked. I remember him telling me that you said your dream car would be a van you could take around to groom people's cats. He thought it was too practical, but I told him it sounded sensible and that you probably had a good head for business."

Strange to imagine Todd discussing me with his parents. "Just a fantasy, I'm afraid. I've priced the kind of van I'd need, and even used, it would be way beyond my budget."

"Well, now, you never know. People sometimes bring me vehicles like that—old campers or food trucks or even ambulances. If the repairs are too high for them, they might say, 'Forget it, I'll just get a new one.' Then I usually pass the van on to a used-car dealer. But if you're really interested, I could keep an eye out for you."

Sounded like a long shot, but he was kind to offer. "That's very nice of you, Mr. Gillis. I'd appreciate it."

A few minutes later, the four of us were joined by a buxom but conservatively dressed blond named Tammy, whom they introduced as their daughter. Married and with a couple of kids, she had driven up from Delaware. It made me feel better to know that Todd's parents had another grown child, even though she lived at a distance.

Soon after, Dawn and I discreetly made our exit. Outside, I whispered to her, "Funny, isn't it? Todd was so annoying that he provoked Rick Schaeffer into shooting him, but his folks are such nice people."

"Sounds like they saw him through rose-colored glasses, too," Dawn said. "I guess romantic love isn't the only kind that can be blind."

I proposed hitting Chad's for dinner, but she reminded me that I ought to feed my boarders first. When I pulled into the small lot behind my shop, I was taken aback to see the blue RAV4 parked there. "That's odd."

"You weren't expecting Mark?" Dawn asked.

"Not tonight. And he didn't leave me any phone messages. Hope nothing's wrong."

I unlocked the back door and went to turn off my alarm, but it already had been disarmed. That was strange, too. Dawn was the only one who knew the code . . . unless at some point Mark had looked over my shoulder while I was punching it into the keypad.

No lights on anywhere. No sounds except hungry cats crying for their dinner.

I stole cautiously into the playroom. "Mark? You here?"

No answer. But in the center of the playroom, propped against a cat tower, I spotted a tall, flat package tightly wrapped in brown paper. A fat, red ribbon stretched around it vertically. A big bow near the top was secured in the middle by an oversized, advertising-style button with something printed on it.

Still alert to some kind of ambush, I ventured near enough to read the words: WORLD'S MOST AWESOME CAT LADY!

I heard Dawn, behind me, try to muffle a giggle. By now, the button, combined with the dimensions of the package, had tipped me off.

"You didn't!" I accused her.

Mark emerged from the boarders' hallway. "*We* did, actually. We went halves."

He helped me undo the ribbon, but after that I had no problem clawing off the brown paper, which had been meticulously folded and taped in the manner of a professional gallery. Dawn turned on the shop lights so I could fully appreciate the framed silk screen of the lady-leopard, now incredibly mine.

The imagery seemed even more haunting and the colors even richer than I'd remembered. Also, the dimensions of the piece even larger.

"It's wonderful!" I murmured, half to myself. Then I envisioned my small apartment, the walls already covered with bookcases, cat shelves, and lesser-quality artworks. "But where on earth will I have room to hang it?"

"Oh, well." Mark pulled the print away from me and pretended to rewrap it. "If you really don't have room . . ."

I grabbed it back. "I'll *make* room." More seriously, I told him and Dawn, "Really, thank you both, very much."

"We thought it was the least we could do," she said, "after we both talked you into trusting shady people who made trouble for you."

"Also, I thought you deserved some reward for outsmarting Schaeffer even when he held a gun to your head," added Mark. "The Chadwick PD didn't come through with a medal, so . . ."

Privately, I reflected that no one I'd ever dated before would have been perceptive enough to surprise me with something like an artwork I'd admired . . . even if Mark might have gotten a little encouragement from Dawn. And after the support he'd given me throughout the challenges of the past weekend, I was definitely starting to see him as a keeper.

I hugged both of them in thanks, lingering awhile in Mark's arms.

"Besides," Dawn went on to explain, "pretty soon you won't have Ayesha around anymore. I thought you needed something to remind you of the excitement she brought into your life."

The prospect did give me a pang of regret. "Yeah, it's going to feel awfully quiet around here without her. Dyed or not, she certainly was a cat of a different color."

Toward the end of that week, Don Brewster finally came to reclaim his Bengal queen. A slender man of medium height with thinning hair, he arrived dressed in jeans and a pressed chambray shirt with the sleeves rolled back. He wore no glasses, and a slight droop at the corners gave his eyes a sad but kind expression. His wife, Laura, did not make the trip, but he said she was doing well since her latest round of chemo, and her doctor was optimistic.

"Just like I figured, she had no idea that Ayesha was gone, and was terribly shocked to hear about Pete," Brewster said. "It's just lucky that I could tell her you had the cat and we could get her back."

Sarah, her ankle good as new, brought the Bengal out on her leash and harness and let her jump onto the front counter to greet her real owner. Ayesha definitely seemed to recognize Brewster and rubbed against him assertively with her face and hip, as if she didn't want to lose track of him again. Laughing, he pressed his cheek against her head in response.

"She looks beautiful," he said. "You've certainly taken excellent care of her."

"You should have seen her when she came to us," I told him. "I thought she was a Havana Brown."

"It took us five baths to get all the dye out of her coat," Sarah added.

Knowing the older man had driven a long way, I offered him coffee and some fancy doughnuts from Cottone's. While he relaxed, Sarah exercised Ayesha in the playroom to tire her out for the return trip. Brewster laughed out loud at some of her leaps and other antics.

"I'd almost forgotten how much personality she has," he said. "You folks have an even better play area here than we do at home."

"Ayesha certainly made the most of it," I told him. "Even before we figured out about the dye job, we could see she was more athletic than our usual boarders."

Though I wasn't trying to make him feel guilty, Brewster picked up on my subtext. "I hope she wasn't any trouble. These cats can be a little strong-willed, and they're very vocal."

"We had some adventures, but they weren't really Ayesha's fault." Easing him into the story, I told him first about the night she went into heat, because I figured he should know that Mark gave her a shot. When that didn't upset him, I recapped our hair-raising experiences on Chadwick Day.

This was obviously more than he'd expected. "My goodness, the people who killed Pete were still after Ayesha? And you had to go up a tree to catch her?"

"I saved you the article from our local paper." I fished it from beneath the front counter and handed it to him. "Your wife might enjoy reading it."

He scanned enough of the story to see I hadn't exaggerated. "Ms. McGlone, I don't know what to say. You've gone to so much trouble. . . ."

"Well, I knew Ayesha was valuable, but I would have done it for any cat that was left in my care. It actually was a little easier with this lady, because she's pretty well trained."

Brewster frowned thoughtfully. "I want to reimburse you. She's taken up space at your shop, you've fed her, exercised her, bathed her . . . and rescued her from what could have been a terrible situation. I almost don't know how to compensate you for all that."

I couldn't take advantage of the man, knowing

he must have medical bills to pay for his wife's care. "How about this? Just pay me one week's board, if you're able. Her food didn't amount to that much"—I lied—"and everything else was my pleasure. Frankly, the whole escapade brought my shop a lot of publicity, especially the spectacle on Chadwick Day."

At Brewster's insistence, I quoted him the boarding fee, and he wrote out a check. I accepted it and added, "I just have one more request. You said that you and Laura aren't planning to breed any more cats?"

He nodded. "She hasn't got the energy, and we can certainly live on my income. I think we'll just keep the few Bengals we have left, including Ayesha, as pets."

"Then all I ask, in case there was any question, is that you have her spayed. I'm afraid my experiences at that breeding farm have really soured me on the idea of bringing any more hard-to-place cats into the world."

With a warm smile, Brewster shook my hand. "We would have done that anyway, but you have my word."

He coaxed his Bengal princess into her original black carrier—with a waterproof pad on the bottom for the long drive home—and they departed. Sarah and I admitted to each other that we would sort of miss having Ayesha around to keep us on our toes.

I was turning one of our other boarders out into the playroom when the shop phone rang. Sarah answered it, then put the caller on hold. "For you, Cassie. Arnie Lang? Isn't he the guy you told me about, with all the tattoos?"

I nodded, crossing to the front counter. The rock club manager whose aunt had a pet hoarding problem? What could he want with me? A little worried that he might want me to take some cats from his aunt's house, I picked up the phone.

"Hi, Cassie? Don't know if you remember me. We talked a bit on Chadwick Day."

Like I meet so many men covered in scary ink and with salt-and-pepper hair hanging down their backs. "Sure, I remember. What can I do for you?"

"Actually, I might be able to do something for you. I was just up at Gillis's Garage, for about the third time since I've been in town. He says my heap needs a new transmission and maybe a new suspension system. I'm gonna bite the bullet and fix those things, but I've already put so much dough into it. . . . Now that NOYZ2 is doing well, I think I'm gonna treat myself to a new set of wheels. Anyhow, Bob thought I should give you a call."

I felt like I was missing something here, since I knew no more than the next person about car repair or car buying. "Me?"

"He said you might be in the market for a used van," Arnie clarified. "You've seen mine, not that it's much to look at now. It came with a dry cleaner's name on it, so I just painted it all black. Got a lot of cargo space, though."

He quoted me a price that I had to admit sounded like a bargain. Still, if his "heap" was always breaking down on him, how could I be sure it wouldn't do the same with me?

"Thanks," I said. "That is tempting. But actually, I need something I can use for my cat grooming business. It would have to have a power source in the cargo bay, and maybe water, too. . . ."

"Yeah, I figured that. But y'know, those guys at FOCA have converted a couple of old vans for their rescues. I talked to Becky about that once, and she said it doesn't have to cost much. They probably could put you in touch with whoever they use."

I wondered about this. Business had been good lately, and I'd been able to put some money aside. I wasn't sure, though, that I wanted to blow it all on rehabbing a vehicle that had seen better days. It would have to cost me, with the conversion, significantly less than a new van.

"Maybe I should talk to them about it, then," I told Arnie. "Can I have a couple of days to think it over?"

"Abso-tively. Go over to Gillis's, if you want, and check it out. My old wheels ain't going anywhere." He laughed loudly. "S'why I want to sell 'em!"

I thanked him again, hung up in a bit of a daze, and related the conversation to Sarah. After all, she is a former math teacher and pretty savvy about budgets and finances.

"What d'you think I should do?" I asked.

My assistant shot me a wary glance. "Oh, gee, Cassie, I don't know. That could be a *really* bad idea."

"Huh? How come?"

"Well, just look at all the excitement that keeps comin' our way, minding our own business and running this little shop here in Chadwick." She struggled to maintain her expression of mock alarm. "Think how much more trouble we could get ourselves into if we go mobile!"

Please turn the page for an exciting sneak peek of
Eileen Watkins's next Cat Groomer mystery

FERAL ATTRACTION

on sale wherever print and e-books are sold.

Chapter 1

"They're taking over our community! They're vicious, and who knows what diseases they're carrying?"

"They do all kinds of disgusting things right outside my front door. My grandkids visit me, and I don't want them exposed to that."

"Our walking group used to love strolling down the trails with our binoculars, looking for new birds. Now we keep coming across dead bodies."

"This is a nice, upscale neighborhood. They don't belong here."

I squirmed in my stiff metal chair. When I'd agreed to accompany my friend Dawn to this condo meeting tonight, I hadn't expected a melee. Especially given the age and conservative bent of the residents. Although The Reserve at Chadwick wasn't technically an active-adult community, most of the forty or so people jammed into the meeting room looked past middle age. Dawn and I probably stood out, not only because we weren't residents but because we were actually under thirty.

It was a prosperous, sedate crowd dressed in comfy corduroy and practical pullovers; I even spotted one turtleneck patterned with tiny autumn leaves. Still, something had set them on fire with rebellion tonight.

I asked Dawn in a whisper, "Are these meetings always so . . . lively?"

She shook her head. "According to Mom, most of the time very few people attend, and the agenda is pretty boring. But like I warned you, this issue has everyone riled up."

The four condo board members, seated behind a long table at the front of the room, also looked unnerved by the strident complaints. They included Lauren Kamper, the board president; Sam Nolan, property manager and vice president; Joan Pennisi, secretary; and Dan Greenburg, treasurer.

Lauren now leaned into her microphone and tried to regain control of the gathering. "Folks, we can't have everyone speaking at once. The chair recognizes Ted Remy."

A strongly built, balding man stood up at his seat. "Some group came here a coupla months ago to fix this problem. They were supposed to catch all these stray cats and take 'em away. What happened with that?"

A woman a few seats to his left, with short gray hair and a shrill voice, replied, "They only caught a few, and a week later they brought them all back! What the heck good does that do?"

Sam Nolan, tall and lean with salt-and-pepper hair, thumbed through some paperwork on the table in front of him. "That group"—he found the information he was looking for—"Fine Feral Friends, reported that they were able to capture, neuter, and vaccinate ten of the cats."

"And they did it for free," noted Dan, the nearly chinless treasurer.

Joan, the motherly looking secretary, suggested, "We can call them to come again. . . ."

"Forget that!" shouted a pudgy man in a rust-colored sweater. "Ten cats? There's at least two dozen, and they're breedin' all the time. We need to get rid of 'em, permanently." He swept his finger across his throat.

Dawn shot me a pleading look. "Cassie, can you explain to them? About Trap-Neuter-Return?"

At this point, I would sooner have stuck my head into a hornet's nest than provoke this crowd. But to speak up for the animals was, after all, the reason I'd offered to come along this evening. Gathering my courage, I raised my hand until Lauren pointed at me.

"And you are?" she asked, sounding wary.

I stood up. "Cassie McGlone. I own Cassie's Comfy Cats, a grooming and boarding business in downtown Chadwick. I'm here tonight at the request of my friend Dawn Tischler"—I glanced down at her—"whose mother is a resident here at The Reserve. She's off on the senior Caribbean cruise right now."

Joan bent her head to take notes on my credentials.

Lauren wore her highlighted blond hair skinned back in a low ponytail, which at least emphasized her good cheekbones. She seemed impatient now with my recital of my bona fides. "And your interest in this matter, Ms. McGlone?"

"I'm also a certified animal behaviorist, and Dawn asked me to explain the reasons behind the Trap, Neuter, and Return approach. See, if you just remove the wild cats, others will come to take their place. It's best to neuter and vaccinate the members of the existing colony so they can't reproduce and can't spread any diseases to pets or people. They also won't get into as many noisy fights with one another, so they'll cause less disturbance."

"Trouble is," Ted interrupted, "people keep feeding them. It says in our bylaws that you're not supposed to feed wildlife. And that's what these cats are!"

"Even that doesn't stop them from killing the birds," complained the lady from the trail-walking group.

From the back of the room, a woman's strong contralto rang out. "May I say something about that?"

Sam responded with a tight smile. "Might as well, Ms. Ward. After all, you're a big reason why our community's in this situation."

When I saw who had spoken, I yielded the floor and took my seat. I had not met Sabrina Ward yet, but Dawn admired her tremendously and had told me much about her. The woman had a long history of feminist and animal activism. Now Sabrina lived at The Reserve and was the staunchest champion of the feral cat colony.

About seventy years old, she rose to her full, diminutive height with the help of a cane. A dark knit cap barely tamed her long, wavy hair—dyed a burgundy shade and threaded with gray. She wore a purple paisley shawl as a muffler and a faded denim jacket over a loose, flowered thrift-shop dress. As if she needed glasses, Sabrina squinted in the direction of the board members' table. Even so, she somehow radiated steely will and determination.

"It's true what you say, Ted. Residents who feed the cats close to their homes aren't helping the problem. That's why the FFF people and I have set up feeding stations farther out in the woods. Once the ferals get used to eating there, and nowhere else, they'll be less likely to hang around the town houses."

"Those feeding stations are dangerous, too," a rosy-faced man with a blond comb-over protested.

"Chair recognizes Bert Chamberlain," said Lauren.

Bert stood. "They're too near the community trails. I was walking my dog Jojo the other day and he got into some of the cat food that was left out. I stopped him before he ate very much, but an hour later he was so sick I had to rush him to the vet. He was even having convulsions." With a catch in his voice, the man added, "They've still got him there, trying to figure out how to treat him."

"She probably put a hex on him!" The lady with the short gray hair stabbed a finger in Sabrina's direction. "She's a witch."

Dawn shifted irritably in the seat next to me. "Oh God, some of these people! How does Mom stand to live around them, day in and day out?"

A better question, I thought, might be how Sabrina fit into this community. Not only would her appearance and attitudes make her conspicuous, but if she dressed from thrift shops and couldn't afford eyeglasses, how was she even able to live here?

Meanwhile, Sabrina ignored the accusation and regarded Bert gravely. "Mr. Chamberlain, I'm very sorry about your dog. But I doubt it was just the stale cat food that made him so sick. More likely, someone in this community poisoned the food in hopes of harming the cats, and Jojo was an accidental victim."

This caused a stir through the gathering, and I heard mutters of, "Now she thinks we're poisoners!" and "Getting paranoid . . ."

Lauren commanded the microphone again and ordered the group to settle down. "Ms. Ward, I doubt anyone would do a thing like that. But even if someone did, it just goes to show that matters have escalated to a dangerous level. Ted is right, our bylaws do prohibit feeding wild animals. We've made an exception in this case, because you and the FFF convinced us that you had a plan to reduce the colony. But as Martin said, so far it hasn't been very successful."

I couldn't resist jumping into the fray again. "It takes time to get a whole colony under control. After a few cats get caught, the rest catch on and avoid the traps. You have to keep trying until you get them all."

A pretty woman with gray curls batted a hand at this idea. "This is a nice community. We have beautiful buildings and landscaping, and we all pay plenty to live here. I don't see why we should have to put up with cat traps cluttering the grounds."

Sabrina's jutting jaw made her look fierce as an Easter Island statue, and her rich voice rang out in anger. "You can't put up with a little temporary inconvenience to save twenty lives? Because that's what we're talking about. These are innocent creatures that aren't doing us any real harm. They may not be pets, but they're living the way nature intended. We need to find a way to coexist with them, not haul them off to be euthanized, just because they interfere with our scenic views."

Next to me, Dawn burst into applause. I joined in with more restraint, and so did a few other residents. The board members remained impassive, though, as did most of the folks seated in the rows of metal chairs.

"Thank you, Ms. Ward," Lauren said, evenly. "You concerns will be taken into consideration."

Off to my left, the man in the rust-brown pullover shook his head. " 'Not doing any real harm,' aren't they?" he muttered. "Crazy old bat. Somebody oughta euthanize *her.*"

* * *